Protected
from
Obscurity

EVERGREEN SERIES III

Joann Herley

ACKNOWLEDGEMENTS

Cover Illustration by: © Romikmk | Dreamstime.com

Edited by: EBH and P. Maier

Formatted by: P. Maier

DEDICATION

Mom and Daddy

You taught me to LOVE books!

SPECIAL THANKS

To Pam Maier, you have been my rock through this whole process. You have taken precious time out of your personal life to read my work, listen to a million crazy ideas, and give me great comments. Your encouragement has kept me writing, but most of all, your friendship has been a wonderful blessing.

To my husband, for giving me the precious gift of time, space to write, and his LOVE!

HISTORY OF THE ISLAND OF ALLTREE

Long ago, strong ships carrying brave explorers discovered its lush forests, fertile earth and crystal clear rivers. Hearing of the beauty of the land, Lord Evergreen boarded a ship and sailed to Alltree to see the land for himself. Captured by its beauty, he returned home to tell everyone of the faraway island and his plans to build Evergreen Castle. Returning to Alltree with skilled craftsmen, he proceeded to build a castle on the west side of the island that overlooked the sea. After a decade, his castle was finally complete, and he brought his family to the island.

One by one, Lords Cumberland, Fallon, Draglaw, and Heinrich made their journey to Alltree and began building castles of their own. They were all peace loving men, and the five lords pledged to refrain from war and live in peace.

It wasn't long before immortals heard of the island and began to sneak aboard ships to make their way to Alltree. Once they arrived, they changed everything.

Prologue

Gusty had watched Jario's men succumb to the strength and numbers of the Evergreen Army. Within moments of their arrival, he had realized that the war was lost. He had watched in horror as, one by one, his command was systematically slaughtered. Their plan of attack had been rushed by Jario's ego. Most of the men had never faced a battle against man, much less, a battle waged against aged immortals. Even though they had been able to strike a few blows, they were completely unprepared to face the skillfully executed defense that the Evergreen Army hurled at them. This was all Jario's fault. Jario's impatience had caused the loss of many brave men to a brutal death, capture, and imprisonment.

Suffering a strike to the shoulder that nearly removed his arm, Gusty continued to swing his blade at the enemy. A longsword in one hand and a dagger in the other, he moved about swiftly trying to protect his command. Hearing the sound of heavy boots behind him, he turned to suffer two well-placed strikes that severed his left leg below the knee. Attempting to swing his sword at the neck of his attacker, he lost his balance and fell to the ground. He saw the blade just moments before a well-placed strike hit him right between the eyes, offering him blindness from his own blood and then the gift of unconsciousness.

Waking to nothing but quiet, he turned his head to see bodies littering the ground. The fighting was over, and the Evergreen Army was gathering the dead and loading them onto a wagon piled high with bodies. He knew it would be carrying them off to the pyre.

Pretending to be dead would send him to the fire. If he appeared to be wounded, it would afford him the dungeon or his final death.

Carefully dragging his body into a thick patch of tall grass, he pulled what remained of his legs and his wounded arm against his torso. He needed to find a secure place to hide. His wounds had stopped bleeding, and he could feel his limbs slowly beginning to heal. Continuing to drag his body across the rough ground, the strong scent of blood surrounded him. Ignoring the beckoning scent upon his senses, he struggled to keep from growling and drawing attention to himself. Spotting a large hollowed out tree, he forced himself forward. Clenching his teeth to keep from screaming from the pain, he crammed his body into the small hollowed out space. Trying to hide himself, he began gathering the pine needles that covered the base of the tree. Spreading them over his legs to shield them from view, he leaned back into the shelter of the cool cavity. There, he gave into the darkness.

Several days had passed since dragging his body into his hiding place. He slowly pulled his body from the debris covering his legs, weak from healing. The forest had provided him a place to hide from the end of Jario's ill-fated war. He had lost all track of time and measured it only by the moments he had been awake. By that account, it had only been three days. By the amount of healing that had taken place, he was sure it had been much longer. His leg had regrown, but it was swollen and discolored. He had been lucky to have escaped the wrath of the Evergreen Army and even luckier to have escaped his final death.

Reeling from the lack of blood, the madness strengthened its hold on him. Running his hand over his face and through his tangled hair stiff from dried blood, he tried to focus on moving his body. His mind was filled with blurry visions of fighting. If he had any chance of beating the madness, he needed to find blood. Forcing his body from the base of the tree, he sat leaning his good shoulder against its rough bark. Hearing the rustle of leaves beneath soft leather boots, he turned to see a young woman with a basket over her arm picking berries.

"Can you help me?" Gusty gasped, reaching his hand toward the woman and pleading with his eyes. "I have been injured and need your help."

The young woman quickly approached Gusty and knelt beside him placing her basket of berries on the ground. Running her hand over his wounded shoulder, she felt him pull back and his body quiver from the pain.

As she looked into his dark eyes, he heard her softly gasp before he pulled his compulsion and calmly said, "You will not utter a sound. You will obey my request. Give me your wrist. You will not feel any pain."

Taking her offered wrist, Gusty let his fangs descend, and he bit into her creamy flesh. Her blood swirled within his mouth and down his parched throat. His eyes closed as he reveled in its sweetness. It wasn't long before he could feel his wounds begin to close. Pulling her wrist from his mouth, he had been careful not to drain her. Licking the punctures with his tongue, he watched them quickly heal leaving no trace.

"You will not remember our encounter or ever seeing me," he whispered. "Pick up your basket and continue to pick your berries. When you have filled your basket, you will be released from my compulsion and return home happy from your walk in the cool forest."

Gusty stood and looked down at the young woman. He felt the need for more blood to help him heal, but he turned from her and sped away into the forest, thankful for the sweet morsel she had provided.

Chapter 1

Lara felt the warmth of the morning sunlight coming through the window above her bed. Running her hand over her belly, she felt the physical changes that had taken place while she slept during the passing of six moons. Holding out her arms, she could see a warm color had replaced the once pale tone of her skin. The witch, Velsa, had made her a human and kept her promise to keep her safe. It wouldn't be long before she would be holding her daughter in her arms.

Sitting on the edge of the bed, Lara looked around the tiny bedchamber. It was sparsely furnished, but it was clean. A single candle within a pewter candlestick sat upon the small bedside table. The scent of cedar drew her eyes to a tall handmade cabinet tucked into the corner at the foot of the bed. She noticed a woolen blanket resting upon a wooden bench next to a small bundle. Lara immediately reached for the bundle and held it tightly against her chest. She had carried it to the witch's cottage, and it was all she had to remind her of Thomas and Evergreen.

Pulling the cord that bound the bundle, she unwrapped a large piece of linen cloth and spread the items it contained upon the bed. Kneeling down, her fingers touched the ring Thomas had given her when he proposed, and the blue cord that bound their wrists upon their eternity ceremony. A beam of sunlight reflected on the golden locket once belonging to Thomas' mother. It rested upon the sleeping tunic Thomas had worn their first night together. Holding the tunic to her face, she inhaled his scent and felt her eyes fill with tears.

Placing it back on the bed, she examined the remaining items, one by one. Picking up a comb, she rubbed her hand over the carved edge before she placed it on the bedside table. Looking down at four candles, a sewing needle with a spool of thread, and a small pouch of seeds she had taken from Evergreen's garden shed were not much to start a new life, but it would have to do.

Feeling a slight flutter within her swollen belly, Lara untied the tight laces from the bodice of her dress. Letting it slide off her shoulders, she took a deep breath as it draped over her belly for a moment before the weight of it caused it to drop to the floor.

Stepping from the puddle of fabric, Lara untied an under-slip and then two more before letting them fall around her feet. She had made plans for the extra fabric and would use it to make clothing for her baby. Stepping from her soft leather slippers, she bent down to roll her heavy stockings down over her knees. First one pair and then another. Leaving one pair upon her feet, she dropped the extra stockings into the growing pile.

Standing in nothing but her sleeping gown and stockings, she unfolded a woolen skirt and linen blouse she had taken from Flora's bedchamber. After dressing herself, she folded her discarded clothing and placed them on the foot of her bed. Sitting down on the bench, she tugged on a pair of boots that Elda had given her to wear one night when they had walked along a muddy road to the village. Tying the laces securely about her ankles, she stood and rubbed her hands against the rough woolen fabric of her skirt. She wondered if she was brave enough to do this on her own. Feeling tears begin to fill her eyes, Lara suddenly straightened her shoulders and pursed her lips with determination.

"I was the Mistress of Evergreen Castle," she snapped, as she looked about the bedchamber for someone to listen. "My father trained me to use a sword and a dagger. After all, I once had control of an army of humans and vampires. I am very strong and extremely stubborn. I can surely raise a child on my own. I know I will be alone and never see Thomas again, but my child will be protected."

Wiping tears from her cheeks, Lara pulled back the coarse fabric that covered the doorway from her bedchamber ready to explore her surroundings. Stepping forward, she was able to quickly take in the small space with the turn of her head. Two wooden cabinets flanked a stone hearth that held a large cooking pot, and she spied a sturdy wooden table with a bench tucked underneath that sat against one wall.

A smile graced Lara's face as she saw the large window that filled the room with sunlight and overlooked a lovely flower garden. Moving toward the window, she was glad to see two small wooden chairs and a milking stool that would allow her to enjoy the glorious view.

Looking up at the wooden beams of the ceiling, she noticed a loft. Walking toward the only door leading to the outside, she saw a small alcove to the left of the door. Tucked in the small space was a wooden bathing tub. A luxury she had not expected, but she would thoroughly enjoy. Leaning against the wall next to the tub, a ladder made from tree branches led to the loft. Carefully taking the rungs one at a time, she peered into the loft to find a cot, a small cabinet, and a woven basket. The basket was just the right size to provide a bed for her baby.

Descending the ladder, Lara decided to take stock of what she had and what she needed. Opening the door of the cabinet, two rickety shelves held several items that were covered with cobwebs. Tearing them away, she removed the items and sat them on the table. Returning to the cabinet, she noticed a wooden chest covered in a thick layer of dust tucked behind a well-used broom. Moving the broom out of the way to get a better look, she wiped the dust from its lid with her hand. It revealed beautiful hand painted flowers that had faded over time.

Pulling the chest out of the cabinet by the worn leather handle, she maneuvered it to the pool of sunlight that spilled in through the garden window. Sitting cross-legged in front of the chest, she opened the lid. A smooth leather bound journal sat upon a folded piece of lace. Opening the journal, she found the pages of parchment were blank and waiting for someone to fill them. Placing it on the floor, she removed the cream colored lace and ran her fingers over the intricate stitches. It was a beautiful piece, and she would save it for something special. Placing it in her lap, she peered into the chest to see what other treasures it held. She pulled out a small dagger in a handmade leather sheath, a small empty pouch with thin leather ties, and a woolen blanket with hand sewn flowers decorating the edges.

Placing the items back into the chest, she made her way to the other cabinet. The door opened easily to display items covered in more cobwebs. Swiping them away with her hand, she collected the dusty items and carried them to the table. Taking a step back, she viewed her collection of goods: a large cooking pot, two pails, three wooden bowls, one dented pewter pitcher, a box of flint, a broom, two candlesticks, an apron, and a knife.

Rubbing her hands together to remove the dirt and cobwebs, she felt much too warm and in need of some air. Opening the cottage door and breathing in the fresh air, she noticed a stone path that led her eyes to the corner of the cottage. Curious, she followed the path that took her to an area behind the cottage. She could see a small shed, an animal pen, and an area large enough for a vegetable garden. Tugging on the shed door several times until it finally opened, she could easily see an axe and two more buckets. Ducking her head, she took a step inside and found one length of sturdy rope hanging on a peg, three small animal traps leaning in the corner, and a woven basket that contained a nest of some kind.

I need to find food, she thought, as she looked at the items in the shed and noticed the sunlight was starting to disappear behind the clouds.

Grabbing the traps and emptying the basket, Lara made her way into the woods behind her cottage. Woodward had shown her how to set traps to catch small animals, and she easily had them set in no time at all. Remembering Flora's teachings about poisonous mushrooms and berries, Lara began to search the forest for anything eatable. If the forest participated, she would be comforted by a warm evening meal.

*** * ****

The sun was beginning to set and offer a warm glow in the sky of bright pinks and oranges. Stepping outside into Lara's private courtyard, Thomas felt the cool breeze against his face. Closing his eyes, he pretended it was the sweet caress of Lara's fingertips against his skin. Keeping his eyes closed, he tried once more to find her using his gift of vision. Again, it failed him.

Lara, my love, where are you? I am lost without you. Please come home to me.

Opening his eyes, he walked toward the fountain and sat down upon its rough stone edge. Dipping his fingers into the water, he remembered the time they had placed flowers upon its surface like small ships at sea and watched them float. Smiling, he reached for the nearest bloom and set it gently upon the water. As the water rippled beneath the bloom, he thought of the first evening they had spent together under the stars. It was the night he had felt the beginning of his love for her.

Pulled from his thoughts of Lara, he heard her footsteps before she stepped through the doorway. Thomas stood as Charlotte made her way toward him carrying a single pewter goblet. Taking the goblet from her outstretched hand, he nodded his thanks and watched her turn and quietly leave. He had made a practice of sitting in the courtyard at sunset to watch the light come to life in the tallest tower. She had made a practice of bringing him a goblet, when he did.

He no longer had to climb the tower steps to light the lantern. He had personally made sure the lantern was lit every night after Lara vanished. Since the passing of the sixth moon, it had ignited into flame on its own. He was sure this display of magic meant that she was alive. Looking up, he saw the tower window fill with light and the stars start to shimmer in the sky. Putting the rim of the goblet to his mouth, he let the blood rush over his tongue and down his throat. Now empty, he hurled the goblet across the courtyard in anger. Clenching his fists, he stormed from the courtyard in search of his brother, Tate. Tonight they would start to search the forest around Cumberland Castle. He feared it would be like every other night, a night alone without Lara in his arms.

* * *

After months of isolation after the war, Gusty felt strong enough to confront Jario. He cautiously made his way to the gates that surrounded the castle. Fearful of the current condition of Jario's mind, he slowly approached the large wooden doors and entered the castle. Standing in the entry hall of Black Thistle Castle, Gusty could hear the sound of paws padding against the stone floor. Seeing the white wolf standing in the doorway to the Great Hall, he noticed the tips of her ears flick as she sensed the sound of Gautier's boots coming toward them. Waiting for him to make his way across the polished floor, Gusty stepped back putting more distance between himself and the wolf. Looking up from her ice blue eyes, he saw Gautier leaning against the doorway.

"I am here to see Jario. Do you know where I might find him?" Gusty asked, keeping his eyes on the wolf and fearing an attack if he dared to move his boots toward the warlock.

"He is no longer here," Gautier bitterly replied, crossing his arms across his chest and glaring back at Gusty. "I have banished him from this castle. If he ever steps foot in this castle again, I will conjure a spell that will bind him for all eternity."

"I came to tell him that his army was obliterated," Gusty stated, as he shook his head while looking at the stone floor. "Evergreen's army was prepared for us and too strong for his inexperienced men. Jario's ego sent weak men against the strength of their army. I, myself, suffered injuries that put me close to my final death."

"So, you understand his banishment," Gautier smirked. "He has taken over the abandoned Crimson Claw Castle once owned by Lord Draglaw. I smell the involvement of the old witch, Velsa. Now that Magna is gone, he would need the help of the old witch."

"Where is Magna?" Gusty asked.

"Oh, you have been away and not heard of her demise," Gautier began to laugh as a nasty grin appeared upon his face. "Yes, Magna has received her final death."

Gusty gasped, "How?"

"Magna was able to flash Lord Thomas away from Evergreen Castle before the war started. She locked him in a cell within her beloved dungeon," Gautier replied. "Lady Lara and a few members of her army tried to rescue him. Magna caught them and took her sister with a blade to her neck. Trying to flash away, she tripped, and the blade penetrated Lady Lara's neck. To save her, my little wolf attacked Magna and tore her head from her shoulders. Elda took her remains outside, and the sunlight turned her to ash."

Gusty stood shocked with his eyes closed and both hands holding his face. He couldn't believe that Magna was gone. She had always been trouble as long as he had known her, but he would truly miss her.

Sensing Gusty's sadness, Gautier tilted his head and asked, "You cared for her? You actually cared for that vampire?"

"I was fond of her, but not her wicked ways. She was troubled with madness from the very start," Gusty responded. "Lady Lara tried to help her sister, long ago. Unfortunately, Magna was beyond her help."

"My wolf and I will not miss the vampire," Gautier offered. "It has been very quiet without her present to disturb us." Gautier knelt and ran his hands over the wolf's soft fur. "Would you like to stay here at the castle? I could use a vampire of your talents to protect this castle and help build a proper army."

"I appreciate your offer and will give it my consideration. However, I could still use rest to further my healing," Gusty replied. "Once I am strong enough, I will need to make my way to see Jario. I owe him nothing more than my insults for his actions, but I want him to know about the death that he caused. I need to do this to bring myself some peace of mind."

"My wolf will take you to a bedchamber you may use until you are ready to leave us," Gautier said, as he looked down at his wolf and smiled. "If you need my assistance in your healing, you need only ask."

Remembering what Gautier had done to Jario, he was too nervous to accept his offer and slowly shook his head to decline his assistance.

"Thank you for your hospitality. If blood is available, I should heal easily," Gusty said.

Stepping forward, he reached out to shake Gautier's hand.

"I will send blood to your chamber," Gautier said, as he grasped Gusty's hand tightly. "Kayleigh, once you have taken Gusty to his chamber, I would like you to join me in the courtyard."

Seeing the acknowledgement of the flick of her tail, Gautier watched Gusty follow his wolf through the Great Hall and on through the open wooden doors to the hallway.

* * *

Jario stood leaning against the open doorway to his balcony. It had quickly become his favorite place in the castle. He had chosen the enormous bedchamber for the spectacular view of the forest. The tops of the trees were completely visible through a large window that allowed him to sit away from the sunlight and see the sky above the trees. Stepping out onto the balcony, Jario watched as the sun was beginning to slip away. He spent every evening looking out over the river that reflected the colors of the setting sun. The river seemed to draw the red from the sunset causing the water to appear darker and deeper in the evening.

He had heard many different tales, over the years, about a red dragon belonging to a young woman that lived in Draglaw Castle. She had worn a red dragon claw about her neck to protect her from an evil witch. The dragon had offered his own claw to be used in the spell of protection. It was unknown what really happened to the young woman and the dragon. Some people said the river around the castle was created from the dragon's tears of joy when the young woman professed her love for him. Others told a tale about the death of the young woman and the dragon's tears of heartache after he fled to the mountain in anguish.

Time had enhanced the tales of the young woman and her dragon. Many men had found the water that ran from a crevice in the mountain and searched for the dragon's remains, to no avail. Long after Draglaw Castle had been abandoned, the villagers started to refer to the castle as the Crimson Claw Castle. The fierce sounding name had conjured romantic tales in most villagers' minds, and it wasn't long before the prior name, Draglaw Castle, was a thing of the past and forgotten.

Jario felt that Crimson Claw suited him. His plan was to dispel the romantic tales of his new castle and establish his own tales of blood, revenge and death. He had the beginnings of a vampire army and would continue to increase its numbers. After the disastrous end to the Black Thistle Army, he knew that an army of humans could never be strong enough to wage war against Evergreen Castle. His dungeon was full of men he had turned, and he had planned to train them to obey his every command.

After exploring the area around his castle, he had found Potter Post, a small village that offered plenty of ale and willing women. During one of his trips to its tavern, he learned that Lady Lara was missing, and the Evergreen Army had been searching for her. Remembering his failed attempts to secure Lady Lara as his mate, he knew he would not stop trying until he succeeded. He would devise a new plan and search for her himself. It would be well thought out and every detail planned perfectly. Another failure was not an option.

He decided he needed more information and would make a visit to see the old witch, Velsa, to find out what she knew of the missing vampire. The payments he owed Velsa were increasing in number, and he would have to make good on them, sooner or later. Surely, he could persuade her to disclose where Lady Lara had gone without finding himself turned into a lizard or a snake.

Chapter 2

The dirt path into the small village of Primrose Pond was long, but it was an enjoyable one. The path was well worn and lined with bright yellow Primrose. In the shade, the moss covered the roots of the trees, as well as, the large pond that was just over halfway from her cottage to the little village and the town square. Sheltered from the sun by the large overlapping branches of the pine trees, Lara was grateful for the cool shade. She was heavy with child, and the heat seemed to make her even more uncomfortable. Lara carried a basket over her arm filled with wild mushrooms she hoped to trade for some much needed soap. She had found the market keeper willing to trade for many of her forest finds. He had always gotten the better side of the bargain, but it kept him eager to accept her goods the next time she filled her basket. However, today would be her last trip to the village until after the birth of her daughter. She had been able to bargain for enough flour, root vegetables, and salt to keep her from making a trip back to the market keeper until her daughter was born.

Finally reaching the edge of the village, she saw the new wooden sign for the market. She was happy to see that he had replaced the weather worn sign that had fallen from one metal hinge. Lara carefully made her way across the wooden porch and into the shop. Ian stood behind a tall wooden counter offering her a broad smile of more gums than teeth. His gray hair was tied at the nape of his neck with a bit of leather. Brown age spots of all sizes covered his hands and his face, and Lara guessed his age to be in his sixtieth year. He and his wife, Hazel, ran the small shop. They were a happy couple and were always friendly to their customers.

"Good day to you, Madame Thomas," he said, as the words whistled through the spaces between his teeth. "What have you brought me today?"

"Good day, sir," Lara replied, trying to get use to the sound of the new name she had taken. "I have brought you some lovely wild mushrooms and hope to trade you for a bit of soap. Do you have any soap today?"

Before he could answer, a woman entered the shop followed by two very young girls clutching to the safety of their mother's skirt. Placing a basket of candles and eggs on the counter, she stepped back to allow Ian to complete his business.

"Madame McCash," Ian addressed the woman, as he watched the girls hide behind their mother. "I will be with you after I am finished serving Madame Thomas."

She smiled and nodded at Ian. Nodding at Lara, she gave her a smile and saw Lara smile in return.

"Now, Madame Thomas," Ian responded. "Let me see your basket."

Lara moved forward and placed her basket on the counter. She watched Ian empty the basket into a wooden bowl and meticulously examine each and every mushroom. He mumbled to himself as he looked from the mushrooms to Lara's protruding stomach. Smiling, he turned to remove a metal box from the shelf. Placing it on the counter, he opened its lid and removed a block of soap that had been wrapped in a small piece of waxed parchment.

"I find your mushrooms worth a very large block of soap," Ian said, as he looked at Lara for acknowledgement. "Is this acceptable?"

"I was hoping for two blocks of soap," Lara responded. "My baby comes soon, and I will be unable to come back any time soon." She moved her hand over her belly to reinforce her pending issue and looked at the mushrooms. "As you can see, they are very lovely mushrooms. I believe the best I have brought you, lately."

"You drive a hard bargain, Madame Thomas," Ian replied. "Two blocks of soap is a fair trade for these lovely mushrooms."

Ian put the soap into her basket and handed it back to Lara. Placing the basket over her arm, Lara stepped back and thanked Ian.

Before she could leave the shop, the sound of a woman's voice came from a room behind the counter.

"Madame Thomas, Madame Thomas," Hazel shouted, as she hurried to Lara's side. "I had this tucked away for safekeeping and find I have no use for it. I would like you to have it." She handed Lara a small woolen blanket. "My chance to use it never came, and I would like it very much if you would accept it."

"Oh, it is very beautiful," Lara replied. "I will be able to put this to good use. Thank you for your kindness."

Hazel gave Lara a hug and then stepped back to stand beside her husband. Lara could see Hazel's eyes start to water and wished she could take her sadness away. Moving toward the door, Lara turned and waved to the couple before she headed for home.

She had finally passed the pond and felt the need to rest. Finding a smooth rock beside the path, she sat down and closed her eyes. She lifted her long braid from her neck to let the breeze blow against her moist skin. Hearing the sound of wooden wheels upon the path, she looked up to see a woman pushing a small cart. As the woman approached, Lara could see the cart contained a goat.

"Good day," the woman offered. "Are you ill?"

"Good day," Lara replied. "No, I was tired and stopped to rest."

"I see you are with child and it comes soon," the woman responded. "My name is Aslev. I live in a cottage beyond the pond and west of the large broken tree. You would not notice it from the path. It is well hidden by the trees."

"My name is Lara Thomas," she responded. "Where are you taking your goat?"

"She is a wicked little goat," Aslev laughed, as she pointed her finger at the source of her trouble. "She ate the bed linen that I hung to dry. I was on my way to try and trade her for a block of soap. She isn't worth much more than that. She causes too much trouble, and a block of soap would be a good trade."

"Will you trade the goat to me? I have a block of soap that I am willing to trade," Lara happily responded. "I have a small pen at my cottage that is suitable for a goat."

"Are you sure?" Aslev replied. "She gives good milk, but she has to be watched to keep her out of trouble. You cannot chase her in your condition."

"If you will push your cart to my cottage, I will gladly trade my block of soap for her," Lara replied. "I am good with animals. They seem to like me."

"Show me the way," Aslev replied. "I need to be home before dark, and the sun is beginning to lower in the sky. You never know what kind of creatures roam the forest at night."

"Follow me," Lara said, as she stood and brushed the dirt from her woolen skirt. "I will be ready for a cup of tea once I reach my cottage. In return for your trouble, will you join me?"

"I would love to join you," Aslev said, as she slowly turned the cart and began to follow Lara back to her cottage with a broad grin upon her face.

* * *

Frustrated from days of searching Cumberland Forest, Thomas slammed his satchel down against the stone floor of the Command Center. His mind was reeling over Lara's absence, and he could feel what remained of his sanity starting to slip away. He didn't understand why he couldn't reach her. The last time he was unable to reach her, she was held against her will by Jario in the Canyon of Obscurity. Both brothers believed that Jario was responsible for Lara's disappearance. If not directly responsible, he was the reason she was gone.

Seeing Tate and Gavenia enter closely behind Thomas, Preston could tell by the look on their faces that volunteering to accompany him on the search did nothing to calm his nerves.

"Tate, did you find anything?" Preston shouted, knowing full well that they had come up empty again.

"Nothing," Tate replied, as he took the quiver of arrows from Gavenia's back. "We searched the entire forest, and Gavenia searched it from the air. We found nothing."

"We did speak to Lord Cumberland. He knew of the old ties between Evergreen and Cumberland and honored our request to speak with him," Thomas said. "He has promised to send a messenger if anyone should find her."

"How soon will you be going out again?" Preston asked. "With Lady Lara gone, we need you here at the castle. I have heard the people whisper in the hallways. They are afraid without you here."

"Do they not understand?" Thomas sternly asked, as he ran his hands over his face and through his hair in frustration. "Lara is missing. She is the Lady of this castle. She is what makes this castle survive, and we need to find her. She could be held against her will or worse, tortured." Thomas lowered his eyes for fear they would show Preston the tears that were about to run down his face. "She is my mate, and it is my responsibility to find her."

"Thomas, let Gavenia and I search the area around Crimson Claw Castle," Tate offered. "Jario has a fascination with Gavenia's white hawk. She may be able to find out if Lady Lara is in his castle."

"Gavenia, you would do that?" Thomas asked. "You would put yourself in danger for Lara?"

"Of course," Gavenia responded. "I wed your brother and that makes her my sister. She is family. If I can help, I will gladly do so."

"We will go tomorrow," Tate looked at Gavenia to see if she agreed. Seeing her nod her head, he put his hand on Thomas' shoulder. "Stay here with your people. Let them see you. Make them feel safe. We will find out what we can about Jario and his castle."

Thomas stepped forward and hugged his brother and then Gavenia.

"Go," Thomas ordered. "Get some rest. Tomorrow will soon be here."

✳ ✳ ✳

The castle was quiet and Gusty stood staring out the window of his chamber. He felt he had regained enough of his strength and was ready to face Jario. Before he left, he needed to speak with Gautier. First to thank him for his gracious hospitality and then to ask how he could be of service to Black Thistle Castle. Finally, he wanted to know what he knew about Lady Lara. He had overheard the servants whispering about her disappearance and that the Evergreen Army was searching for her. He wanted to know if Jario was involved. Hearing that Gautier was in the library, Gusty made his way through the hallways to speak with him.

Seeing the door to the library was open, Gusty quietly approached the doorway being careful so as not to surprise the wolf. Gautier stood bent over the large wooden table looking at parchments. Seeing that he was alone, Gusty rapped against the open door. Gautier looked up and motioned for him to enter.

"What can I do for you?" Gautier asked.

"I thought I should tell you that I will be leaving for Crimson Claw Castle tomorrow," Gusty replied. "I wanted to thank you for your hospitality."

"I am sorry to hear that you are leaving," Gautier responded. "You may always return if you find Jario's hospitality lacking."

"I have no plans to stay at Jario's castle," he replied. "I am interested in your offer to stay here at Black Thistle. I need to know your plans for me, if I do."

"I would like you to be my commander," Gautier said, as he tossed the small stone he was holding onto the corner of the parchment. "I have seen the kind of man or vampire, if you prefer, you are and feel that you would be a responsible leader for my army. An army designed for protection instead of vengeance. Is this appealing to you?"

"Very much," replied Gusty. "This recent war, Jario's war, has brought me to my senses. It has changed me. I no longer require the feeling of death within my hands to enjoy my existence. I must face Jario first, but on my return, I will gladly take the position of commander."

"Good," Gautier said, as he clapped Gusty on his shoulders. "I had hoped for this answer to my request. Take the chestnut stallion, Aspen, and visit the wicked vampire. I must warn you to be careful. He is still desperate for power."

"I will return as soon as my mission is complete," Gusty replied. "Again, thank you."

Chapter 3

She was humming as she stood facing the flame in the hearth twirling the end of her long braid between her fingers. The strands of her wheat colored hair made her think of the softness of silk. Her skin was smooth and free of the ugly age spots and deep wrinkles she had tried to ignore. She had seen a youthful reflection in the clear pond as she strolled through the forest. The glassy pond had shown her delicate curves that no longer sagged and caused her to bend frequently upon a walking stick. It had been well over a century since she had taken her true form, and Velsa was considering keeping it.

Tossing the block of soap onto the table, she thought about how easy it had been to fool Lady Lara with her new appearance. By simply reversing the letters of her name, she had a beautiful new name that still satisfied her and one she considered keeping.

Protecting Lady Lara had kept her busy using her magic to help provide the things she needed. Lady Lara was not without skills and could be quite resourceful, but she was in a difficult position. Now that her time was near, Velsa felt an unusual and unexpected desire to help. If a little help would ensure she would receive her required payment, she would do whatever was needed to benefit herself.

After meeting Lady Lara on the path to Primrose Pond, she had graciously invited her back to her cottage for tea. It was a thoughtful gesture, and Velsa found her conversation delightful, as well as, the clover tea she had given her. She had taken stock of the almost empty cottage. Lady Lara had done what she could to make it livable. The floors and wooden furniture had been scrubbed clean and fire wood had been stacked by the hearth. She had seen wooden bowls were filled with berries, wild onions, and mushrooms. Velsa could smell the rabbit simmering in the black cooking pot hung over the fire in the hearth. A basket sat on the floor by her chair with a small linen gown that had been partially hemmed. Her new surroundings were simple, but she seemed to be comfortable and happy.

Looking toward the window, she was pulled from her thoughts as she heard the sound of running toward her cottage. Velsa waved her hand and immediately changed from Aslev back into the old hag. Knowing who was approaching, she huffed with disgust and angrily chewed on her bottom lip. Opening the door with a flick of her wrist, she waited for her visitor to enter.

"Jario," Velsa smirked. "I see your hands are empty. You do remember that your debt has not been paid. I am not a patient woman."

"I have not forgotten," Jario nervously replied. "It will be difficult, but I will accomplish your request."

"What brings you to my cottage?" Velsa asked, as Jario saw her raise a suspicious eyebrow.

He knew that she could read his thoughts, knew all of his desires, and he never paid a visit to her cottage unless he wanted something.

"Have you heard the rumors? The Evergreen Army is searching for Lady Lara. She is missing," Jario stated, while he watched to see Velsa's reaction.

"I know of the rumors," she smirked. "I have heard a great deal of conversation floating on the wind. It would surprise you what I have heard."

"Where is she?" Jario asked, hoping for some clue to lead him to Lady Lara.

"You are very bold today. You sound a little desperate. What is wrong, dear Jario? Are you afraid that someone else may have gotten to her before you?" Velsa responded, as she began clucking her tongue and shaking her head in disgust.

"You know where to find her, don't you?" Jario gasped, as he stepped closer to Velsa. "Tell me, please!"

"Concentrate on obtaining the tail of the white wolf for me," Velsa sneered. "You have too many unpaid bargains. Bring me the tail. I will give you a clue, but not until that white tail is securely in my hand."

Jario's anger flared, and he stormed from the cottage. He could hear Velsa's cackling laugh as he ran through the trees. Finding Ash tethered where he had left him, he quickly mounted his stallion. If he hurried, he would have just enough time to find a stable or empty cottage where he could spend the day out of the sunlight. He would then make his way to Hunter's Point for a much needed cup of ale and a meal before heading on to Crimson Claw Castle.

* * *

Sitting in the corner of the tavern at Hunter's Point, Jario stabbed a piece of venison with the tip of his dagger and stuck it into his mouth. He had paid for a room and was watching the noisy group of men while he finished his meal. Throwing back the last of the ale, he stood and tossed a coin onto the table for the young woman that had served him. She was too young to appeal to his interests, and he smiled at her as he headed for the stairs.

Making his way upstairs, he found his room and slid the bolt to secure the door. A single bed, a chair, and a small table with a bowl and pitcher graced the pathetic room. He pulled the blanket from the sagging bed and covered the window. Sitting down on the edge of the bed, he heard it creak as he pulled off his boots and his tunic. Tossing his tunic onto the back of the chair, he leaned back with his arm bent behind his head and closed his eyes.

His thoughts drifted to the stone cottage in the Canyon of Obscurity and the feel of Lady Lara's body pressed against his. His arousal stirred as he thought of the few precious droplets of blood that he had whisked away from her neck with his tongue. He remembered her pressing her mouth to his wrist and drawing his blood. It was the most intimate feeling he had ever experienced. He could feel his arousal straining against the leather laces of his breeches and started to loosen them to give himself some much needed comfort.

A sudden burst of laughter filled the hallway beyond his door. Jario stood and opened the door wide to find two women standing before him ready to rap upon his door.

"What do we have here?" Jario asked, as he folded his arms against his bare chest and leaned against the frame of the doorway.

"I am Gert and this is the lovely Falla. We saw you were alone," the buxom brunette replied, as she lowered her shawl revealing a bare shoulder. "We thought you might like some company. Falla is real friendly, and I have been known to make many a man forget his troubles."

"Is that so?" Jario smiled and stood back allowing the women to enter his room. "What will this visit cost me?"

"One coin each," Falla replied, as she untied her brown hair and let it fall around her shoulders.

Jario closed and bolted the door. He stood watching the women undress and sit down on the sagging bed. Lifting their arms and wiggling their fingers, they beckoned him forward. Smiling, he untied the laces he had loosened earlier and freed his manhood from its misery. He let his breeches fall to the floor as he watched the women's eyes travel over his body. He ran his tongue against the points of his fangs and anticipated the taste of their blood. Stepping toward the giggling women, he knelt down next to the bed.

"Look at my eyes," Jario asked, as he lifted both of their chins. "I want to see you look at me."

The women raised their eyes from his bare chest and looked directly into Jario's eyes.

Using his compulsion, he gently stated, "You will enjoy everything I do to you, and you will do as I say."

* * *

Tate pulled the door to the tavern open and let Gavenia pass through ahead of him. They had spent the prior evening in their treehouse, and Tate still had visions of Gavenia's red hair covering his chest as she slept. It was their special place, and a stolen moment they had decided to take on the way to Crimson Claw Castle.

After bathing in the cool stream, they rode most of the day and were ready for a hearty meal before taking a room in the tavern at Hunter's Point. Finding an empty table next to the stairs, Tate signaled to the woman behind the bar as he pulled the stool out for Gavenia. Taking the stool next to hers, he sat down and lightly kissed her cheek.

"What can I get you two lovebirds?" The gray haired woman asked.

"I smell the rabbit stew," Tate replied. "Is there enough left for the two of us?"

"My Frederick made a new big pot for the evening crowd," she said, as she smiled at Gavenia. "Anything else?"

"Bread, ale and a room for me and my sweet Gavenia," he requested, as he picked up her hand and kissed her fingertips. "I thought my bride should have the comfort of a bed instead of the hard ground tonight."

"The rooms are not fancy, but they are clean," she laughed and looked over at her husband that was coming from the kitchen. "We have one room left. I will get the key and your stew."

She turned and left the table heading for the kitchen. Tate looked about the tavern after hearing the boisterous laughter of a very large man with a full beard and a bald head. He didn't recognize anyone in the tavern and wondered if anyone knew Jario. Carefully scanning the eyes of each person in the room, he determined they were all human.

Hearing the kitchen door open, he watched the woman carrying two bowls of rabbit stew, two ales, and a half loaf of bread on a pewter tray. The large tray reminded him of Lulu, and it caused him to laugh a little. Setting the tray down, the woman removed the bowls, mugs and bread from the tray. She reached into her pocket, pulled out a key, and handed it to Tate.

"That will be three coins for the meal and one coin for the room," she said, as she looked at Tate. "The room is at the far end of the hall."

Tate opened a small pouch that hung on his belt and handed her four coins.

"Have a good evening," the woman responded, as she dropped the coins into her apron pocket.

Tate and Gavenia ate their stew and talked about their dreams. Away from Evergreen Castle and alone, they took advantage of the time they had to share their hopes for the future.

Jario stood at the top of the stairs and froze in place. He had heard those voices before, somewhere. Listening carefully, he realized he knew them from the dungeon at Black Thistle Castle. It was Thomas' brother, Tate, and his new mate, Gavenia.

They must be looking for Lady Lara, he thought, as he looked about for a way to escape without being seen.

Almost forgetting about his gift of haze, he shook his head and pulled it quickly as he stepped down the stairs. He made his way through the crowded tables of people toward the door.

"Sir," Tate shouted. "Can you pass me the bowl of salt?"

Jario gasped quietly. He thought he had been caught and then remembered he was invisible. Pulling the door open, he ran from the tavern to the stable without looking back.

"Could someone shut the door?" Fredrick shouted. "The wind blows it open, but the wind isn't kind enough to close it before it leaves."

Gavenia giggled at the funny words from Fredrick. Tate looked over his shoulder at the open door. He sensed a strange presence and knew it wasn't the wind. Glancing around the tavern, he looked for danger. Seeing none, he turned back to Gavenia and took in her lovely smile.

Chapter 4

Aslev approached the tiny cottage carrying a wooden cradle within her arms. She could hear the sound of muffled moaning floating on the wind and hurried through the gate. Rapping softly on the door and hearing no answer, she cautiously opened the door. Looking about the empty room of the cottage for Lara, she made her way to the small bedchamber. She found her lying on the bed holding her belly.

"Lara, it is Aslev. Do you need help?" she asked, as she placed the cradle on the floor and moved toward the bed.

"The baby is early," she said, as she gripped the bed linens tightly and groaned through a contraction. "Please help me. Do not let my baby die."

"Hush now, do not speak of death. I will help you, my dear. I have delivered many a baby," Aslev replied, patting her on the arm. "Do not worry."

Aslev pulled Lara's nightdress up over her knees and could see the crown of the baby's head. She mumbled a few short words and watched as she slowly closed her eyes. Hearing the sound of deep restful breaths, Aslev looked about the room for a blanket. Folded neatly on the bench were a woolen blanket and two folds of linen. Taking the linen, she spread it over her hands and began to quietly chant. The room warmed, and the hair on her arms stood on end. Slowly the baby moved from Lara's body into her waiting hands.

Wiping the blood from her tiny face, Aslev nodded and the baby was released from the afterbirth. Hearing the sound of a tiny gasp, she whispered a single phrase under her breath, and the baby was clean and lying within a piece of fresh linen. She pinched the baby's ankle between her fingernails, and the baby began to cry. At the sound of the baby's cry, Lara slowly woke. Seeing Aslev holding her baby, she sighed in relief.

"You have a baby daughter," Aslev said, as she handed the baby wrapped in linen to Lara. "She is beautiful. What name have you chosen for her?"

"Laralynn," she replied, as she pulled the linen down away from her daughter's face to get a better look. "Laralynn, after her great grandmother."

"A beautiful name for a beautiful baby. She is perfect," Aslev said. "Laralynn has all ten fingers and ten toes. She has the sweetest little red birthmark on her left ankle. It looks like a teardrop."

Lara pulled the linen away from her daughter's feet and looked at the red mark. It did look like a teardrop. She kissed her ankle and recovered her feet.

As Lara cuddled with her new daughter, Aslev removed the soiled linen from the bedchamber and left the cottage to dispose of it. Digging a hole behind the cottage, she emptied the linen into the earth and threw a flame from her fingertips setting it on fire. Watching it burn, Aslev swayed and chanted until the flames slowly receded and only ash remained. Covering the ash, she spit upon the mound of earth and returned to the cottage.

Entering the bedchamber, Aslev moved the cradle next to the bed.

"What have you brought me?" Lara asked, as she looked at the wooden cradle and then up at Aslev's smiling face.

"I thought you might need a cradle for the baby," she replied. "I see you have a basket ready for the baby. If you prefer to use the basket, I will not be offended."

"No, the cradle is lovely," Lara responded, grateful for the fine gift. "Could I bother you to move the linens into the cradle for me?"

"Of course," Aslev smiled, as she removed the woolen blanket and linen pillow stuffed with feathers from the basket and settled them down into the cradle. "Would you like some tea or something to eat? I am sure I can find something to prepare for you."

"Tea would be lovely," Lara replied, as she ran her fingers over the very fine apricot strands of Laralynn's hair. "There are two pieces of bread left from this morning and a small cup of honey on the table. I seem to be famished."

"I am not surprised," Aslev laughed. "I will get you fed and then you and the baby can rest."

Lara could hear Aslev as she poured the water from the pitcher into the pot. She was lucky that Aslev dropped by her cottage. The pain seemed to disappear after her arrival. Aslev had given her enough comfort to forget the pain. It had all happened so quickly, and she was very happy to have the company.

Aslev entered the bedchamber carrying a plank of wood with two cups of tea and two pieces of bread smeared with honey. The honey smelled heavenly and Lara couldn't wait to taste its sweetness upon her tongue. Aslev set the plank upon the bench and moved toward the bed.

"If you are going to eat, I will need to move Laralynn to her cradle," she said, as she reached for the baby. "Once you have finished, I will return her to you."

Lara reluctantly gave her baby over to Aslev and watched her lay her gently into the cradle. Laralynn made a soft sigh and continued to sleep. She gently tipped the cradle to make it rock. Seeing Lara smile, she then helped her sit up and lean against the wooden frame of the bed.

"Here is your tea," she said.

Aslev handed Lara a cup and then placed a small piece of linen with a slice of bread on her lap. Taking the other cup of tea and bread, Aslev sat on the foot of the bed. She sipped her tea and ate the bread as she watched Lara and the baby. It brought sadness to her mind. She had never had a child. Seeing the baby made her regret that she never mated with Gautier. Thinking of him made her hands tremble, and she quickly put him out of her mind.

"I will help you with a bath after you have rested. Later, I will fix your evening meal. It might be good for me to stay the evening to watch over you," Aslev said. "You are still weak and will need help with the baby. I am sure the people of Primrose will be by to offer their help. They are all good people."

"I would like that," she replied, as she drank the last of her tea and wiped the crumbs from her mouth. "You have been so kind to me. How will I ever repay you?"

"Not to worry," Aslev replied. "We all need help now and then. When the time is right, you will know how to repay me."

Lara smiled and watched Aslev lift Laralynn from her cradle. Feeling her back in her arms, Lara felt a calmness settle over her. She was finally a mother and looked forward to caring for Laralynn. With Aslev's help, she hoped everything would be fine.

* * *

Baxter had decided to travel by horseback since flashing with Thomas to any location left Thomas unconscious for hours and sometimes days. The sound of the horse's hooves thundered across the meadow as Thomas and Baxter raced each other toward the village of Peaks View. Thomas could no longer sit within the castle walls and wait for word about Lara. He knew that he was needed at the castle, but he had to try and find her. Baxter had suggested that he ride with him to the village, and he jumped at the chance.

The village was south east of Evergreen Castle and west of Cobb Cove. A number of cottages and small farms filled the inlet village. This inlet was one of three waterways for ships to unload their goods and for travelers to board a ship to leave the island. The village got its name from the spectacular view of sunsets against the tall peaks that stood near Cumberland Castle. Within the tall peaks of the mountains, multiple waterfalls spilled over the rocks. The falls had long been called Witches Weep. No one was sure why, but it started flowing after the War of the Witches. Villagers believed the witches that survived the war made it rain to put out the fires. It rained until the peaks filled with water and spilled over the rocks, continuing to flow to this day.

Seeing the smoke rising from the stacks of the cottages, they knew they were getting close to the village. Baxter had known a few of the farmers in Peaks View and hoped they could get their help in searching for Lady Lara. Growing up across the cove in Primrose Pond, Baxter had crossed the waterway to Peaks View many times to find work. He had helped fishermen clean fish, held sheep for farmers to sheer, and learned to lay the thatch on roofs. It was when he had learned to hold a crossbow that he decided to travel to Evergreen Castle to join the army.

Dismounting their horses outside of the tavern, Thomas and Baxter tethered them to the wooden railing before entering the old stone building. The room was crowded and smoke from pipes filled the air. Baxter looked about the hazy room for anyone that might remember him. Seeing a short man with a wooden peg for a leg, he made his way to his table.

"Master Whale, it has been a long time," Baxter addressed the man seated at the table. "Do you remember me?"

"Come closer, my eyes are not as good as they used to be," the man replied.

Baxter bent down and let the man look upon his face. He watched the man's eyes brighten with recognition.

"You have grown into a handsome young man," the man grinned, as he reached to shake Baxter's hand. "What brings you back to Peaks View?"

"We are looking for Lady Lara, the Mistress of Evergreen Castle," Baxter said, as he stood up to face everyone at the table. "She is missing, and we fear harm may have come to her."

"The rumors are true," he replied, as he shook his head. "We had all hoped it was only a rumor. It is sad to know that it is true. She is a fine lady."

"Yes, it is true," Thomas said, as he moved closer to the table. "She has been gone over ten moons. The people of her castle are worried. We would ask for your help to send word to us if you should see her."

"She left the castle suddenly," Baxter added. "We suspect that she was running or hiding from someone."

"Can we count on you to help us?" Thomas asked, as he looked about the table.

The group of men nodded their heads, and Thomas felt comfort from their response.

"We will send a messenger to Evergreen if we should find her," he responded. "We are sorry for your people and hope that she is found soon."

"Thank you, Master Whale," Thomas replied.

Baxter reached for Master Whale's hand and gripped it in appreciation. Waving to the men, they left the tavern and mounted their horses to start visiting each of the cottages in the village.

*** * ***

As she lifted above the trees, Gavenia's hawk reveled in the sight below her. Racing through the air, she played among the gentle currents of the wind. She could see the three red stone towers capped with gray stones that she knew belonged to Crimson Claw Castle. It was beautiful in the glow of the warm afternoon sun as it sat tucked among the trees and faced the Dragon's Tear River. Seeing the reflection of the sun upon the windows, Gavenia looked for a balcony door that Jario might have left open. Not seeing any, she flew low along the river feeling the spray from the cool water upon her back as it crashed against the rocks. Hoping that Jario might be watching, she swooped up into the air and spiraled down toward the water. Turning at the last minute, she continued to glide through the air forgetting she was anything other than a hawk.

Jario sat in his private chamber leaning his head back against the soft leather of the high-backed chair. He had been dozing more from boredom than from anything else. Hearing the squawk of what he thought was a hawk, he jumped up and stood as close to the window as he could get without doing himself harm. Off in the distance, he could see a white hawk flying low above the water. He hurried to the balcony door and opened it slightly allowing the sun to reflect on the glass but keeping him protected. Moving the door back and forth, he could see the sun's reflection on the glass shimmer against the water. Stepping back to the window, he searched for the hawk, but he couldn't see it anywhere. Suddenly, he heard the sound of strong wings flapping outside of his balcony door.

"You found me, my beautiful white hawk," Jario cried with excitement. "I feared that when I moved from Black Thistle Castle that you would never find me." He pushed the door open wider to allow room for the hawk to enter.

Gavenia recognized Jario's voice and entered the chamber. He had never hurt her, and she felt she would be safe within the chamber. Perching on the top of the post at the foot of his ornate bed, Gavenia folded her wings against her body.

"This is wonderful," Jario sighed, as he paced back and forth in front of the bed. "You are truly my hawk. Good things have always happened when you are near to me. I want you to stay with me always."

Hearing his desire for her to stay with him, Gavenia raised her wings and spread them out before him. She needed him to understand that it would not make her happy to be imprisoned in his castle.

"I fear I have upset you," Jario said, as he lowered his eyes to the floor. "It is my only desire to have you close, but I understand your need to be allowed to fly free within the sky."

Gavenia lowered her wings and settled herself securely on the post.

Moving back to his chair, Jario started to sit down when he heard a knock upon his door.

"Enter," Jario loudly ordered.

The door opened and a young woman stood in front of a tall figure as she spoke, "Lord Jario, you have a visitor. Gusty is here to see you."

"Yes! Yes! Show him in Claudia," Jario replied, clapping his hands. "He is an old friend."

Claudia moved into the room to allow Gusty to step forward. Jario moved quickly toward him and offered his hand to him as Claudia moved from the room and closed the door. He reluctantly accepted Jario's hand and stepped further into the room.

"Gusty, it has been some time since I have seen you," Jario stated. "I watched you leave with the army and feared you were lost to me. I am grateful you have returned."

"I was the only survivor of your war," Gusty sadly declared. "I was near my final death and have been recovering since that day. All of your army was lost."

Jario turned his back on him for a moment as he remembered his failure. Satisfied that he could easily start over with a new army of vampires, he turned to look at his friend.

"They were mere humans and not worth worrying over," Jario smirked. "They are easily replaced. In fact, I have a dungeon full of vampires waiting to be trained. They need a good strong commander."

Waiting to see if he picked up on his implied offer, Jario noticed his furrowed brow.

"It was a waste," Gusty stated, unable to ignore Jario's lack of interest. "Because of your ego, the army was lost. Good men that were brave enough to march on your command died for your cause. Do you not feel any sorrow for them?"

"What has gotten into you?" Jario asked, as he stared at Gusty bewildered at his chatter. "This is not like you. You must still be ill and in need of more rest."

"My mind is clear even though my body is weak," Gusty replied. "I have come here to tell you of the loss of your army and to see your reaction. It is clear you have no interest in hearing of their failure and your own."

"No, I do not," Jario angrily shouted. "Enough of this talk. If this is all you have to say, I insist that you leave my castle. Leave now before I harm you. Our previous friendship is the only thing that prevents me from giving you your final death."

Gusty turned and walked toward the door. Pulling the door open, he stepped through to the hallway and started to close the heavy door.

Before he did, he looked at Jario and said, "You are being blamed for the disappearance of Lady Lara. They are searching for her and for you."

"I know that she is missing," Jario responded. "She is not here. If she was, you would find her within my bed linens."

Jario walked back toward the bed and leaned against the wooden post below his hawk as he tried to control his temper.

"I visited Velsa, and I believe that she knows where to find her," he continued. "She has offered me a hint if I can conclude our bargain and the payment that I owe her."

"I also bring a warning from Gautier," Gusty said, as he saw that Jario was angered and walking toward him. "He has told me that he will bind you forever if you dare to tread at Black Thistle ever again. If you value your freedom, stay away from his castle."

"How dare you? I do not fear him," Jario screamed. "Get out of here. You have changed. War has made you weak. I have had my fill of you. Leave my presence before I turn you to stone."

Feeling Jario's madness within his threat, Gusty slammed the door and left running through the hallway. Once outside, he mounted Aspen and raced to the shelter of the forest. After feeling the shade of the trees, he felt his body finally relax. He slowed his stallion and started his journey back to Black Thistle Castle to join Gautier's army.

I am no longer the vampire I use to be, he thought. I am no longer Gusty the malicious killer. That vampire is gone. I have come to realize that Gustavo has taken his place. He is vampire of truth and honor.

Feeling certain he had chosen the right path for himself, Gustavo headed back to Black Thistle Castle and a new life.

* * *

The tall grass swayed between the legs of Tate's stallion, while he grazed on the tender dandelions sprinkled amongst the blades of grass. Tate sat on a blanket under the shade of a tree as he waited for Gavenia's hawk to return to him. Hearing the sound of her rather unladylike squawk, he stood and pulled her clothing from his satchel. Turning to the sound of leaves crushing, Tate watched as the white hawk disappeared and Gavenia stood before him.

"I will never get tired of looking at you," Tate said, as he smiled and ran his eyes over her naked body one last time before he reached to pull her close. "Are you tired after your flight and visit with Jario?"

"Never too tired for your affection," Gavenia responded, as she ran her fingertips across his forehead and kissed his chin. "Before we lie down on your blanket, I need to tell you that Jario does not have Lara. He is looking for her, too. Velsa has offered him a hint if he completes their bargain."

"What is the bargain?" Tate asked, remembering the dreadful result of his brother's bargain with the old witch.

"He did not say," Gavenia replied. "Gusty came to see Jario while I was in his chamber. It was a very interesting and short conversation. Gusty was shaming Jario over the attack on Evergreen. It sounds as though Gusty has changed. Seeing all the death from the war must have had an impact on him."

"No doubt," Tate replied. "Jario's war had very little benefit. Men died because of his arrogance and hatred."

"What do you think has happened to Lara," Gavenia asked. "Since Jario does not have her, could she be hiding? Could she be hiding from him? He said he was coming for her."

"She may be hiding," Tate answered Gavenia with concern in his voice. "I fear what her absence is doing to Thomas. We need to bring her home. Since Lara is not here, we need to continue our search."

Gavenia pulled Tate toward the blanket spread out under the tree.

"I agree, but first things first, my love," Gavenia whispered, as she knelt down on the blanket and waited for Tate to join her.

Chapter 5

The long ride back to Black Thistle Castle left Gustavo exhausted. He leaned against the gate of the stall pressing his hand to his forehead. The pain had left him long ago, but a fog lingered behind his eyes making him feel weak. Leaving his stallion in the stable, he made his way to find Gautier. He decided he needed his help to completely heal. He had tried on his own with rest and blood, but he never seemed to complete the healing process. As he entered the castle, he was greeted by Lady Kayleigh. He was surprised to see her instead of her wolf. As she approached, he bowed slightly and said, "My Lady."

"Gusty, how was your journey?" Kayleigh asked, noticing the tired look within his eyes. "I feared for your safety while in the company of the evil Jario, and I am very glad to see that you have returned."

"The ride was long," Gustavo replied. "It has left me in need of rest, but I accomplished my task and have returned to join Gautier's army. It would please me if you would no longer address me as Gusty. I have given up that name, as well as, the death I once offered others. It would please me if you would call me by my given name, Gustavo."

"As you wish, Gustavo. It is a fine name," she replied, as she watched a bit of happiness fill Gustavo's eyes. "It is wonderful to have to back. Gautier will be very pleased. He is expecting you," Kayleigh offered. "Follow me, and I will take you to his private courtyard. He knew that you were to arrive and prepared a meal for you."

Gustavo followed her through the twists and turns of the castle's hallways. As she reached the large door, she stood back and waited for him to open it for her. He gripped the ornate handle and pulled the door open to reveal a courtyard filled with stone statues, finely trimmed greenery, and a stone wall that protected it from view. He was surprised something this beautiful existed at the castle. Everything he had seen that surrounded the castle was black, dead or poison. He realized that had been by design.

Gautier had heard Gustavo's request of Kayleigh and was pleased that he had given up the darkness. Hearing them make their way toward the courtyard, he anxiously awaited the conversation with his new commander. As the door opened, Gautier stood and made his way toward Gustavo.

"Welcome back," Gautier said, as he greeted Gustavo with an outstretched hand and nodded his appreciation to Kayleigh before she left them. "It is nice to have you back. I hope that Jario was not too hard on you."

"He was his usual arrogant self," he replied. "He threatened me with words, but I managed to leave before he grew angry enough to show me physical harm. He would have turned me to stone had I stayed any longer."

"Come and sit with me," Gautier said, as he moved toward the table. "You must be hungry after your journey."

"I find that I am more tired than hungry," he replied. "I have not been able to heal properly since giving up human blood. I am in need of your assistance, if you are still offering."

"Of course," Gautier said, as he moved behind Gustavo and pressed his hands upon his back and head. "You will feel some warmth beneath my hands and some pressure." Gautier could feel Gustavo's back tremble slightly. "I feel your worry. I will not harm you."

Gautier searched his body for the damage that had yet to heal. Finding a shattered mass above his eyes, Gautier focused the energy to reassemble the shattered bone that had pierced his brain. Slowly the bone began to pull itself from the tissue and mend. As the healing completed, the warmth gradually left Gustavo's body.

"How do you feel?" Gautier asked.

"Good," he replied, as he rubbed his hand over his forehead. "The fog has cleared and the throbbing has stopped. Thank you."

"Now, sit and we will speak of my army over our meal," Gautier said, as he pulled out his chair and offered his hand toward the other chair for Gustavo.

Nodding, Gustavo joined him at the table.

"Have you given any thought to building my army? How should we proceed to acquire good skilled men?" Gautier looked directly at him waiting for a commander's response.

"I had much time to think on my way back from Crimson Claw Castle. I will post your need within the villages," he replied. "I believe a competition would be the best way to evaluate the skills of those that apply. A fair competition over several days without the need to administer death would draw more candidates. We will choose the best."

"Yes, Commander," Gautier said, as he raised his cup to Gustavo. "This is a fine plan. I see that you have given this much thought. Yes, you will make a fine commander of my army."

* * *

Frustrated, Lara looked at the little goat she had affectionately named Trouble. It had taken quite a lot of practice to master milking the wicked little animal. She still received the occasional tantrum from the four legged beast, but thankfully, she was good enough to provide five buckets of milk to every two she spilled. Milking the goat this morning had produced a half a bucket of milk. A half a bucket that would be wasted since it also contained Trouble's hind leg before she kicked it across the pen.

"Having trouble with your goat?" a woman's voice asked, as she tried not to laugh.

Looking up, she noticed two young girls holding on to a woman's skirt.

"That goat has a mind of her own," she replied, as she bent down to retrieve the bucket.

"I thought I should come introduce myself to you. My name is Mollie McCash and these are my daughters, Nollie and Lettie," Mollie said, as she looked down toward her daughters. "Girls, say hello to Madame Thomas."

"Hello Madame Thomas," the girls shyly responded and then hid their faces behind their mother's skirt.

"Hello," she responded. "My name is Lara Thomas. It is very nice to see you again. I had hoped that you would visit me." Looking back up at Mollie, she smiled and was glad to have the company. "Mollie would you like to come in for some tea?"

Mollie nodded and waited for Lara to exit the pen and hang the bucket on the post of the pen's gate.

Following Lara to the door of the cottage, Mollie spoke softly to her daughters, "Madame Thomas has a baby, and you must be very quiet so as not to wake her."

Making their way into the cottage, she took a moment to check on Laralynn and found her sleeping soundly in her cradle.

"Would you girls like to take a peek at Laralynn?" she whispered, as she stood over the cradle. Seeing the girls smile as they nodded their heads eagerly, she beckoned them to the wooden cradle and pulled back the woolen blanket that Hazel had given her.

"One day, she will be big enough to play with you," Lara said, as she tucked the blanket back under Laralynn's chin.

The girls ran back to their mother and sat on the small mat that separated the two chairs. Lara poured water into the pot and hung it over the fire in the hearth.

"How long have you lived in Primrose Pond?" she asked, as she opened the wooded box that contained the dried clover.

"Six years," Mollie replied. "Kenneth, my husband, and I moved from Wintergreen Mountain to Primrose Pond. It was much too cold in the mountains. The weather is milder on this side of the island."

"Is your husband a tradesman or part of an army?" Lara asked.

"He works at the mill," she replied. "He cut down the trees in the forest. Now, he cuts the trees into pieces to be sent down Wood Cutter's Water to the ships that dock in Woods Bay."

Lara carefully pulled the steaming pot from the hearth and poured the water into the cups. Slicing two small pieces of bread, she spread a small amount of honey on each piece. Placing two pieces of bread on a plank, she made her way to Mollie and the girls.

"Nollie, Lettie, would you like a piece of bread with honey," Lara asked the girls, as she bent down to offer the sweet treat.

The girls looked at their mother for approval. Seeing the nod of her head, they carefully took the bread and began licking the honey.

Lara returned to the table setting the plank down and retrieving the cups of tea.

"You are new to Primrose Pond," Mollie said, as she took the cup of tea from Lara. "I have not seen a husband. Are you alone?"

Sitting down with her cup of tea, Lara knew someone would ask her a question she would struggle to answer. Taking a sip of her tea, she thought for a moment before she responded, "I came to Primrose Pond to escape harm that was done to my family. I hope to make a safe life for me and my daughter."

Mollie sighed after hearing her sad reply. She knew the island was never completely safe, and if she could keep her and Laralynn safe, she would gladly help.

"Primrose Pond is quiet," Mollie replied. "I am sure you will like it here."

"I have enjoyed the small village," Lara replied. "Everyone I have met has been friendly. I am glad you came for a visit and hope to see more of you."

"Me too," Mollie replied laughing, as she looked down at her girl's sticky fingers. "They seem to have enjoyed the visit, as well."

* * *

Jario wandered among the trees looking for Velsa's cottage. She never left it in the same place twice and cleverly kept it hidden. He knew if he waited long enough, she would know that he wanted to speak with her and reveal herself.

Hearing the sound of a branch snap, Jario spun around not realizing he had let his guard down. A young woman dressed in black velvet approached him. He was surprised to see her walking alone in the forest. Feeling his senses take over, he examined her scent and found that she was not human.

"Jario, what are you doing here?" Velsa asked. "Have you finally brought me the wolf's tail?"

"Velsa, is that you?" Jario asked, as he closed his eyes and opened them again trying to focus on the person before him. He couldn't believe what he was seeing. "How can this be? You are beautiful."

"I believe that I am," Velsa smirked. "I have always been beautiful. I chose to hide my beauty, but I will hide it no longer."

"May I escort you to your cottage?" Jario asked, as he offered Velsa his arm.

"You have come for a visit and what else?" she laughed, as she took Jario's arm and led him in the direction of her cottage that slowly appeared before them.

After seating herself by the fire, she watched Jario try to sit upon the small milking stool.

"You really need to get a chair for your visitors," Jario said, as he placed his hand against the floor to secure his balance and lean away from the fire.

"My visitors never stay long enough for them to need a chair," Velsa replied. "Stop the small talk and tell me why you are here."

"I am being blamed for Lady Lara's disappearance," Jario stated. "Gautier sent Gusty to warn me. Am I being blamed for something that you did to her?"

"I do nothing unless I am asked to make a bargain, or I am provoked with anger," Velsa said, as she stood and looked down upon Jario. "You certainly gave Lady Lara reason to vanish. You took her to the Canyon of Obscurity, after all. You are not blameless."

"So you are a part of her disappearance," accused Jario. "I knew it."

"You know nothing," Velsa shouted. "And, you will know nothing until I receive the tail of the wolf that you promised to bring me. Now get out of here and leave me alone. I was having a pleasant evening until you arrived."

Jario stood and angrily kicked the milking stool. He watched it hit the stones of the hearth and shatter.

Heading toward the door, he turned and shouted at Velsa, "You may be beautiful now, but you are still ugly inside."

As he ran from the cottage, he feared for his life. Suddenly, he felt intense pain. Grabbing the sides of his head, he knew the pain was caused by the witch. He closed his eyes and slumped to the ground. With his face against the floor of the forest and unable to move, he watched a toad leap from a hollow log. The pain took him to a dark place and left him screaming in the darkness.

* * *

Maps yellowed with age were spread out upon the large table in the Command Center. Thomas had been reviewing them for hours, and he had placed small black stones on the locations that had been searched, and he added marks for the new villages that had been found. After searching each and every farm and cottage in Peaks View with Baxter, the thought of searching every cottage within every village was daunting. He never realized how large the island was until now.

"My Lord," Preston said, as he approached Thomas. "You have a visitor from Black Thistle Castle."

"Is it Gautier?" Thomas asked, as he looked toward the door to see a tall man with dark hair standing in the doorway.

"It is Gustavo," Preston responded. "He comes on behalf of Gautier."

"Show him in," Thomas ordered. "I can speak with him here. There is no need to move to the Council Chamber."

Preston nodded to Gustavo to come forward. Thomas watched him approach and offered his hand in greeting.

"My Lord," Gustavo said, as he bowed slightly. "I have brought a message from Lord Gautier. I have been charged with building an army for Black Thistle. A competition will be held at the castle to draw the most skilled men for enlistment. Lord Gautier would be honored if you and a few members of your army, those of your choosing, would attend to assist with the judging."

Surprised and a little taken back by Gautier's message, he looked at Preston for guidance.

"My Lord, I believe this is worthy of a discussion," Preston said.

Agreeing with Preston, Thomas replied, ""I will discuss this with my Council and send word to Gautier. When will this competition be held and for how long?"

"Lord Gautier feels that allowing six moons to pass would give time for word of the competition to spread," Gustavo explained. "Word will be sent to the surrounding villages and posted at the docks of Echo Bluff, Cobb Cove, and Woods Bay. It will be a four day competition. The fifth day will be the announcement of the winners. The list will then be posted of those that are chosen. It will be made clear that this is a skills competition and not a challenge to the death."

"I am glad to hear it. We have all had enough bloodshed lately," Thomas replied feeling a little more relaxed from Gustavo's words.

"However, my army has been deeply involved in searching for Lady Lara. It will be our focus until she has been found and returned to Evergreen."

"My Lord knows of the search for Lady Lara, and he offers his small army to help in the search. You need only ask. He has tried using his magic, but he has not been able to find her within the island," Gustavo responded, as he looked at the map littered with stones. "It would be good if you would speak to him. He might be able to tell you more."

"Thank Gautier for his offer," Thomas replied. "For now, tell him we consider his request to attend the competition and will send word of our decision. Once my brother returns to Evergreen, I will make my way to see him."

"I will relay your message to Lord Gautier," Gustavo said, as he gave Thomas a slight bow. "Peace be with you, My Lord."

"And with you," Thomas replied, as he watched him turn and leave the Command Center.

Thoughts of Lara filled his mind, and he was anxious for Gavenia and Tate to return to the castle to allow him to visit with Gautier.

"Preston, what do you think of this competition?" Thomas asked.

"It will bring many to his castle," Preston replied. "With numbers comes trouble, and we have seen this type of trouble before. We will be prepared for the trouble it will bring, and the trouble Jario may add to the competition."

"Aw, Jario," Thomas sneered. "Will the trouble he causes ever end?"

"I fear it will end when Jario has seen his final death," Preston replied. "Until then, we stand ready to defend Evergreen."

"Lady Lara chose you well," Thomas responded, as he reached for Preston's hand. "It is an honor to be by your side."

"My Lord," Preston replied, as he bowed and then placed his fist over his heart. "It is I who am honored."

Chapter 6

Preston heard the door slam as Tate and Gavenia made their way into the Command Center. They dropped their gear at the door and immediately approached him.

"Glad to have you back," Preston said. "Your brother is anxious to see you. He has had a request from Gautier and wants to speak to you about how to respond."

"Where is my brother?" Tate asked.

"He is where he always is at this time of evening. He is in Lady Lara's courtyard awaiting the light in the tower," Preston replied. "Any news about Lady Lara?"

"Gavenia confirmed that she is not at Crimson Claw Castle," Tate responded, as he glanced at Gavenia. "Jario still delights in entertaining her hawk. It has allowed her to enter his chamber and listen to his conversations."

"He had a visitor while I was there," Gavenia added, as she took hold of Tate's hand. "Gusty shamed Jario over the loss of the brave men in his army. Jario was not moved by the loss of the humans. Gusty also brought a warning from Gautier that angered Jario. Before he left, he told Jario that he was being blamed for Lady Lara's disappearance. Jario told him if she was at Crimson Claw, she would be in his bed. After that, Jario basically threatened him and Gusty left."

"We will continue to search," Tate said. "At least she isn't held by Jario."

"Some good news came from your search," Preston replied. "Now, go see your brother. He needs you."

Tate and Gavenia left the Command Center and headed for Lady Lara's courtyard. Almost to the courtyard door, they saw Charlotte approaching them.

"Good evening, Charlotte," Tate said, as he stopped and waited for her to come closer. "How is he tonight?"

"I see the same distant eyes; however, he slips away a little more each evening. Before long, he will be completely gone," Charlotte replied. "I have not seen a smile since the tower came to light on its own. It troubles me."

"Until Lady Lara is returned, I fear he will never feel happiness again," Tate replied. "Thank you for caring for him."

"It is my honor," Charlotte replied, as she left them heading to find Thomas.

Stepping into the courtyard, Tate saw his brother picking blooms and tossing them into the water. Hearing his brother's boots, Thomas turned and strode toward Tate.

"Any word?" Thomas asked, as he embraced Gavenia and kissed her cheek.

"She is not at Crimson Claw Castle or with Jario," Tate replied.

"You know that to be true?" Thomas searched Tate's face to see if he was holding anything back.

"It was confirmed by Jario, himself," Gavenia said. "He told Gusty that she was not at the castle."

"Gusty?" Thomas barked. "Is he working with Jario? He came to see me with a message from Gautier."

"No, he was at the castle to shame Jario and give him a warning from Gautier," Gavenia replied. "Jario was angered by Gusty's words and thought of turning him to stone."

"For a moment, I thought I was being tricked," Thomas replied, letting his shoulders relax. "Gustavo brought a request to me from Gautier. He wants to build an army for Black Thistle. They have decided to have a skills competition to enlist men into his army. Gautier has asked that we help him judge the competition."

"A competition?" Tate said, smiling. "This could be interesting. However, it could bring trouble to the surrounding villages."

"Preston is already working a plan to handle the influx of men and any trouble that comes along with them," Thomas replied.

Looking up, Thomas watched the tower come to light and sighed before giving his attention back to Tate.

"Who would you take to the competition with you?" Tate asked. "You could count me in on this assignment."

"You, Elda, Oliver and Baxter would be my choices," Thomas replied. "Unless you feel their absence would leave Evergreen too vulnerable."

"No, this is a good choice," Tate offered. "We can all walk in daylight. I assume the competition will be held during the day."

"I will present this to the Council tomorrow and get their agreement," Thomas replied. "Your absence will impact the protection of Evergreen. I want to be sure that Preston has enough of the army prepared to handle what might arise."

"If there is nothing else, I would like to take Gavenia to our bedchamber and get some rest," Tate said, as he took hold of Gavenia's hand. "I look forward to the softness of our bed. I found nights on the hard earth uncomfortable."

"Off with you two," Thomas said. "It is good to have you back."

Thomas watched Tate and Gavenia leave the courtyard. Looking up, he stared at the glow from the tower. As long as the light came to life each night, he knew that Lara was still alive. It was all he had to hang on to right now. That and the fact that she wasn't with Jario.

* * *

Lara sat at the table and opened the leather bound journal. She had written a letter to Thomas almost every day since waking from the *Protection Spell*. The few days she missed were the days she was kept in bed by Aslev after giving birth to Laralynn. Lara wanted this journal to be a gift for Thomas. It would be a record of the years he would miss of his daughter's life. For her daughter, it would be a way to show her how much she loved her father and let them both know of the sacrifice she had made to protect her. With her quill in hand, she began to write:

Thomas my love,

Nearly one year has passed since the birth of our daughter. She is a good baby and loves the attention Mollie

McCash's daughters, Nollie and Lettie, show her. She smiles and laughs when they talk to her. Her red hair has softened and looks more like mine. Now that she has begun to walk, she requires my constant attention. She sits with me in the garden and watches me work. Thomas, I wish with all my heart that you could be here with us. I miss your touch, your sweet kisses, and your words of love. I think of you every day and will every day until I am gone. I love you, Thomas.

Yours for all eternity, Lara

She wiped a tear from her cheek as she closed the journal and placed it back into the chest for safekeeping.

A soft sigh and then a whimper caused Lara to move toward the large basket that sat in her bedchamber next to her bed. Laralynn had long outgrown the wooden cradle, and Lara replaced it with the larger basket she had found in the loft. As she entered the bedchamber, Lara could see little fingers reaching over the top of the basket.

"I see you are awake," Lara cooed, to her daughter. "Let's get you fed and dressed. We shall go to the market and see Ian and Hazel."

After readying Laralynn, she carried her wrapped in a blanket and placed her in the cart that Aslev had left with her. It had been very useful to carry her daughter and the items she needed to take to the market, as well as, the items she needed to bring back to the cottage. The cart was loaded with a basket of mushrooms, two rabbit pelts, and two bundles of wild onions. A cup of honey was carefully covered and wrapped in linen. The beehive she had found provided beeswax for candles and a bit of sweetness for her bread and tea. Keeping the wax for herself, she knew the honey would be worth a very good trade. She had also found a small nest with four eggs, but decided to keep them for her supper and left them on the table.

Pushing the cart up the path to Primrose Pond, she talked and sang to her daughter along the way. Stopping to point out birds and a big toad that bellowed as they passed, the walk seemed to go by quickly. Arriving at the market, Lara lifted Laralynn and carried her inside.

"Hazel, Madame Thomas is here with the baby," hollered Ian. No sooner had the words left his mouth than Hazel hurried into the room. "Do not scare the child, Hazel."

Upon seeing Hazel, Laralynn held up her arms and anxiously reached for her. Allowing Hazel to take her into her arms, Laralynn laughed as Hazel bounced her on her hip. Lara left to retrieve her items for trade and returned with her arms full. Setting her items on the counter, she waited for Ian to examine them.

She noticed Ian look up from his task as she heard the sound of boots on the wooden floor. Lara turned to see who had entered the market. Stunned and frozen in place, she was shocked to see Baxter standing before her. Quickly, she turned her face away from him.

"Good day sir," Baxter said, as he looked at the child in Hazel's arms.

"Good day," Ian replied. "Do I know you? You look familiar."

"I lived in Primrose Pond a long time ago," he replied. "My name is Baxter. My father was Henry Marsh."

"I knew your father," Ian said, as he searched Baxter's face. "You were just a wee lad the last time I saw you. I see that you are in the army."

"Yes, the Evergreen Army," Baxter replied. "I am charged with looking for the Lady Lara of Evergreen Castle. She is missing, and we fear that she has been taken by someone. Have you seen her?"

"We know of the Lady Lara, but we have never seen her," Ian replied.

"Has anyone new taken residence in Primrose Pond?" Baxter asked. He looked at Hazel and then at Ian for a response.

"Only Madame Thomas and her child," replied Hazel. "They are the only new residents of the village."

"Where can I find Madame Thomas?" Baxter asked.

"She is here before you," Ian responded.

Standing very still, she listened to the conversation and hoped he would not want to speak to her. Hearing Ian point her out, Lara took a deep breath and turned around to face Baxter. Since her hair was covered, she hoped he would not recognize her.

Baxter stepped forward and directed his question to Madame Thomas, "Have you seen Lady Lara or anyone new in your village?"

"No sir," she replied, shocked and relieved that he had not recognized her.

Do I look different, she thought? Has Velsa changed my appearance to keep me safe?

"I thank you for your time," Baxter replied, as he bowed slightly and started to leave the market. "Wait, I smell apples. I do not see them in the bins. Do you have apples today?"

"Yes, we received two large baskets of apples this morning from a farm beyond Fallon Castle," Ian replied. "They are in the back. Would you like one?"

Baxter dug into his pouch and pulled out a coin and placed it on the counter.

"I would," he replied, as he ran his tongue over his upper lip. "It has been some time since I have had fresh apples."

Ian walked to the back room and took an apple from the basket. Bringing it out to the main room, he dunked it in a pail of water and wiped it with a clean cloth before handing it to Baxter. Baxter quickly took a bite and closed his eyes with a sigh.

"Thank you," Baxter said, with his mouth full. "I'll be on my way. If you hear of Lady Lara, send word to Evergreen Castle."

"I surely will," Ian replied, as he watched Baxter leave the market and mount his horse.

Rattled, Lara took Laralynn from Hazel and pressed her lips against her forehead. She was truly protected. Taking another deep breath to settle her nerves, she stepped to the counter to watch Ian continue his tally of her items.

"What are you in need of today?" Ian asked, as he emptied the containers and set the cup containing the honey aside."

I need salt, flour, carrots, a block of soap, a spool of thread, and string to make candle wicks," Lara replied.

She had taken stock of her items and determined their value. Waiting for Ian to bicker, she gave him a glare that challenged him to try and cheat her. Waiting for his response, she glanced at Hazel and tried to hide a smile. Hazel stood with both hands on her hips as she glared at Ian. Watching Ian look at Hazel out of the corner of his eyes, she knew he would weaken.

"As always, you drive a hard bargain, Madame Thomas," he replied. "I will help you load your cart."

Still feeling a little shaken from seeing Baxter, she made her way to her cart and watched Ian and Hazel fill the cart around her daughter. Once everything was secure, she waved goodbye and made her way back to the safety of her cottage.

Chapter 7

The fire roared in the Great Hall and Thomas could feel the heat as it warmed his body. He hadn't been back to Black Thistle Castle since his encounter with Magna in the cell of her dungeon. He had mixed emotions over his return. Magna's crime had allowed him to regain his sight, but it made him remember the attack on Lara that almost gave her a final death.

Thomas turned as Gautier entered the hall and stepped forward with an outstretched hand to greet him, "Gautier."

"It is nice to see you again," Gautier said, as he clasped Thomas' shoulder. "Kayleigh and I were saddened to hear that Lady Lara is missing. If I can be of help to you, you need only ask."

"Thank you," he replied, dropping Gautier's hand. He turned to face the fire to feel its warmth and collect his thoughts. "I am not sure what you can do if your magic has not been able to find her."

"It is true, I have tried to find her using my magic and failed," Gautier said. "Without her blood or a personal object, it is difficult to make a connection to the soul of the missing. If you could bring me something, I would certainly try again."

"I will send a messenger with an article," he replied, as he turned back to face Gautier. "It has been over a year since she fled. I do not believe that she was taken. A spell provided by Meadow would have prevented it. What caused her to flee the safety of her home has me confused. If we knew why, it might help us find her."

"You realize that this could not have been accomplished without the help of magic," Gautier looked intently at Thomas. "This alone makes me suspect Velsa. Since Gustavo's return, I have since discounted the possibility that Jario had a role in this."

"Why would Velsa hurt Lara?" Thomas asked. "She has never tried to do harm to the witch. Even after her part in the loss of my eyesight, she never condemned the witch."

"It could have been a favor asked by the Lady Lara," Gautier offered for Thomas to think upon. "Velsa does not interfere. She makes bargains or attacks if she is angered. Believe me, I know her quite well. Of those options, I believe a bargain was struck."

"What can we do to break the bargain?" Thomas asked.

"If it was a bargain, there is nothing that can be done to undo it," Gautier replied. "A bargain is made and agreed to by both parties. If Lady Lara agreed to a bargain, it stands until a loophole can be found."

"Then we are back to where we began," Thomas shook his head in frustration. "We are left to search every cottage in every village, every dungeon in every castle, and every hollowed out tree in the forest."

"Let us not give up," Gautier replied. "She will be found and returned to you."

Thomas nodded, but he wanted to scream. It all felt hopeless.

"Have you given thought to my request for you to help judge the competition to be held here at Black Thistle Castle?" Gautier asked, trying to draw Thomas out of his saddened thoughts.

"I am sorry," Thomas replied. "I completely forgot. Yes, we would be honored to judge your competition. I must say that this was a very good idea."

"Good, this pleases me. I had hoped that you would agree to my request," Gautier smiled and bid Thomas to follow him from the hall. "Let me show you where this competition will take place."

Now distracted from his thoughts of Lara, Thomas followed Gautier from the hall and headed for the quad.

* * *

News spread quickly about the competition to be held at Black Thistle Castle. It was the topic of discussion among men at many of the taverns and at the harbors. Reaching well beyond the island, men saw the notices that had been nailed to posts at the docks and taverns.

Standing among a small crowd, Killian read the notice along with the rest of the men. The first ship would leave the harbor for Alltree Island in four days, and there would be two more ships that would depart in time for the competition. He had longed for a good reason to leave Wren Woodland behind. A fresh start was what he needed. Killian decided, then and there, he would take the first ship.

Life for Killian had been rough in the beginning. He had been abandoned as a child. The butcher and his wife had taken him in and raised him as one of their own. They were good people. He loved them, but he was ready to strike out on his own. He was tall with pale blue eyes and a head of dark brown curls. He had gained much needed muscle once he started working with the large slabs of meat in his father's butcher shop. His mother often said that his good looks would catch a woman's attention, but his temper would push them away. She was right. He caught the eye of many a young woman, but he could never keep their attention for long. His temper had always gotten in the way.

Racing back toward his room behind the butcher shop, Killian noticed his mother sitting on the porch mending his father's shirt. She looked up when she heard him and smiled.

"I left your dinner on the table," she scolded. "It would be good of you to be home on time for dinner."

"I am sorry mother," Killian replied, as he sat down on the wooden porch next to her. "I was at the dock. A notice has been posted for a competition for the Black Thistle Army. I have decided to try my hand at it. I am good with a sword and dagger. It is time for me to make it on my own."

"Oh, I feared this day would come," she said, as she tried to keep from crying. "I will miss you, my boy."

"I will miss you too, mother," he whispered, as he stood and wrapped his arms around her and kissed her forehead. "It is time. I will tell father and ready myself to make my journey to Alltree Island."

"What is this?" asked his father. "You are leaving us?"

"Yes father," Killian responded with his back straight and determined. He waited for his father to warn him of the dangers and try to talk him out of his decision.

"If you must go, I will not stop you," his father replied. "You will soon be eighteen and a grown man. I ask only to have a private talk with you before you go."

"Of course," Killian replied. "Shall we walk?"

Nodding, his father kissed his wife and followed Killian from the porch along the path to the forest. His father was quiet and appeared to be deep in thought. Reaching the edge of the forest, he stopped and looked at Killian.

"Son, we have kept a secret from you for many years," his father said, as he rested his hand upon Killian's shoulder. "We had hoped to help you when the time came. Now, that you are leaving us, you need to know what will become of you once you reach your eighteenth year."

Killian was confused and started to speak, but his father stopped him before words could leave his mouth.

"You are a shifter, my son," his father said. "A wolf shifter."

"What? Are you crazy?" he laughed. "I am no wolf."

Killian stepped back from his father and looked at him waiting for him to laugh and tell him he was only tricking him.

"It is true," his father said, stepping forward to grasp his son's arms. "If you go to the island, you will shift with the first full moon after you arrive. You will be a danger to everyone until you learn to control it. If you stay, we can help you."

"What are you saying, father?" shouted Killian, as he pulled away from his father's grasp. "This cannot be true. You are lying to me. You are wrong. There is no way that I could be a wolf."

The more he thought about his father's words, the angrier he became. He bolted from his father and raced into the forest. He could hear his father call his name, but he kept running. He ran until his legs gave out, and he slumped to the ground.

This cannot be true, he thought, as he clutched at his chest trying to breathe. I won't turn into a wolf. My father is lying.

Chapter 8

The excitement over the upcoming competition was evident. Men pounded targets into the bark of thick trees to practice the crossbow, axe, and bow. Women watched as men stripped down to their breeches and cheered as they wrestled in the sun on the soft grass of the meadow until their bodies glistened with sweat. The taverns were full of bragging and betting on who would be standing on the final day. Names of the tavern's favorites were scrawled upon parchment nailed to the wall. There wasn't a day that went by without hearing of the Black Thistle Castle competition.

Jario had heard the blustering men in the taverns and found it all very interesting. He knew he couldn't attend without feeling Gautier's wrath, but he could attend as someone else to hide his identity. He had yet to decide if he would attend as a spectator or add his name to the list of challengers. There were disadvantages to both, and he had to be sure no mistakes were made after his decision.

Bringing his thoughts back to the matter before him, he watched as two men dug a pit within the forest. He found two men that were willing to perform the task for a small pouch of coins. They were swift with the chore and did not waste time muttering with one another. Once completed, he would compel them to forget everything they had seen and done.

After the last of the tree limbs were placed over the pit and pine needles were spread over the pit to disguise it, the men stood waiting for Jario to make his inspection of their work and hand over the pouch of coins.

"Is it to your liking?" asked the young man. "It will surely trap the wild boar that you have seen within the forest."

"Yes, you have done well," Jario replied. He stepped forward and handed the young man the pouch. Drawing both of the men to look at him, Jario compelled them to forget.

"You will not remember me or your work in the forest," he stated. "You will walk into the woods until you find a hollow log. You will remember that you found a pouch of coins hidden there and will split the coins evenly between you."

With their pouch in hand, Jario watched the men shoulder their farm tools and head for the forest.

The trap was finally ready. All he needed now was the unsuspecting wolf to fall into its depth. He had seen the white wolf run through the forest, alone. The first time it was quite by accident. He had been returning from Cobb Cove during a full moon and had seen her standing in the forest before she had transitioned into her wolf. After that, he made a point to hide in the forest every full moon. She came alone and ran through the forest. He knew her path, and the placement of the pit was perfect. He only had to wait for the full moon, and he would have the wolf and her tail for Velsa.

* * *

Killian watched as the silhouette of the island came into view. The ship headed toward huge cliffs, and the top of two castle towers appeared to be jutting from its top. As the ship maneuvered into the harbor, he could see the thatched roofs of the small village off in the distance. It was not unlike his own village.

Leaning over the railing, Killian saw the men lower the wooden planked walkway onto the dock. He could feel nervous excitement making his stomach flutter. Killian knew he was on his own now. It was up to him to prove he was a man worthy of joining the army.

The horses that drew the wagon were tethered to the worn wooden posts. Gustavo jumped from the wagon and stood on the dock waiting for the men to gather their belongings. Fifteen men had made the journey from Wren Woodland and fourteen had survived. A fight over dried meat had claimed one man, and he had been quickly thrown overboard without the benefit of a ceremony or a prayer.

Killian stood with his quiver against his back and his pack over his shoulder. He was listening to Gustavo holler out instructions for the camps. He addressed those that had coins, to tell them of the taverns that had beds for a fair price. Knowing he would be sleeping at the camp, he made his way to the wagon and readied himself for the long ride to Black Thistle Castle. Looking up at the moon, he tried to forget the things his father had told him. He would soon find out if his father had told him the truth. If it was the truth, he would shift into a wolf the night before the final competition was over. For now, he would take one day at a time and hope his father had lied.

* * *

Seeing Baxter coming through the door, Tate hurried to greet him. He could tell by the look on Baxter's face that he had not found Lady Lara or any leads to follow.

"Nothing?" asked Tate. He knew before he asked and then saw Baxter shake his head. "I don't understand. It is like she has vanished from the island."

"If that is true, we will never find her," Baxter replied. "I took in the Primrose Pond area and found nothing there. A woman and a small child were the only new members of the village."

Will and Elda noisily entered the Command Center and approached the pair. They had taken up patrols around the harbor and the village since Baxter and Tate had been searching for Lady Lara.

"The first group of men heading for Black Thistle Castle arrived today," Will said. "It was a small group, and the men appeared to be young. The ship came in from Wren Woodland. I was told there would be two more ships coming from that area. Wren Woodland will be their last stop before the ships arrive here on Alltree."

"We have seen the meadow starting to fill with small canvas tents," Elda added. "The men must be coming from local villages or ships docking at the harbors to the east. It reminded me of the camp of men that worked to repair Black Thistle Castle."

"I forgot," Tate grabbed Baxter's shoulder. "We have a new assignment. We have been asked to judge the competition at Black

Thistle. Thomas, you, Elda, Oliver and myself have been given the assignment."

"This should be entertaining," Baxter laughed. "What is to be gained by the competition?"

"Gautier is building an army," Tate replied. "Since Jario lost his men during the war, Gautier wants to build a new army. One that is loyal to him and keeping the peace."

"We could use some of that around here," Baxter responded. "Where does that leave Jario in all of this? If we find him at the competition, what do we do?"

"I hope we find him without his head," Tate replied. "It would be his just reward for attending."

"Where is Thomas?" Baxter asked. "I need to report to him."

"He should be back anytime," Elda replied. "He went to see Gautier to discuss finding Lady Lara with magic. Then, he was going to see Zeb. He wanted to make assurances that we would make sure any trouble around the tavern would be resolved."

Preston and Thomas made their way back to the Command Center. Holding a linen bundle, they approached the small group.

"Good, you are here," Thomas addressed Baxter. "I need you to take this to Gautier. There are some personal items belonging to Lady Lara inside. His magic needs her personal items to help locate her. Since you can flash, I need them delivered now."

Thomas handed the bundle to Baxter and watched him immediately vanish.

"I take it there was no news from Primrose Pond," Thomas said, hoping someone would find him wrong.

"No news, I'm afraid," Tate replied. "We aren't giving up. We still have the whole west side of the island to search, as well as, the mountain. We will find her."

"I am starting to think she doesn't want to be found," Thomas sighed, as he felt his brother grasp his shoulder. "Gautier thinks magic is hiding her and that Velsa may have helped her disappear. It seems to make sense. After my encounter with Velsa the night Lara vanished, I am sure of it."

"Do we make a visit to the witch's cottage?" Tate asked. "Not to make bargains, mind you. We ask her questions."

"We will see Gautier within a week's time," Thomas replied. "If he finds her with his magic, I am sure he will let me know. I haven't had good luck with Velsa. I hate to think what she would take from me if I asked for her help."

"Then we wait," Preston said. "There are patrols to make before some of you leave Evergreen for the competition. Make sure all areas are in good order. I do not want any surprises while you are away."

Elda nodded in response and looked at Will.

"We need to patrol the towers Will," she said. "The last one there cleans the other's boots." Before she could move, Will was out the door.

***

Pulling the door open, Lara greeted Aslev. Seeing her at the door, Laralynn dropped her cloth doll and waddled to Aslev's waiting arms. She squealed as Aslev lifted her up and spun her around before resting her on her hip.

"How is my favorite little girl?" she asked, as she watched Laralynn grin with a few front teeth peeking through. "You are growing so fast. You won't be a baby much longer. Before you know it, you will be all grown up."

"Oh please, Aslev," Lara said. "Let's keep her little as long as possible. There is no need to make her grow up too soon."

"You are right," Aslev replied. "You should enjoy this while you can. She will not be little forever."

"I made some tea. Would you like some?" Lara asked, as she walked toward the cupboard to get Aslev a cup.

"That would be lovely," Aslev replied.

"What brings you by my cottage today?" Lara asked.

"Have you heard of the competition that is to be held at Black Thistle Castle?" Aslev asked. "It is rumored that those from Evergreen Castle will be judging the men."

"From Evergreen, you say?" asked Lara.

She felt her eyes begin to water when she heard her home mentioned. Quickly turning to avoid Aslev, she poured the steaming water into the cups.

"Why a competition?" she continued.

"The new Lord of Black Thistle Castle, Lord Gautier, is building an army," Aslev replied. "The prior army was lost during a war, and the old Lord of Black Thistle left in shame."

"I have never understood the need for war," Lara replied. "It brings more death than peace and a waste of life."

"Until everyone can live in peace," Aslev said. "There will be war and death."

Making her way to Aslev with her cup of tea, she waited for her to set Laralynn down. Watching Laralynn waddle to her doll, Aslev took the cup and softly blew on the edge of the cup to cool the steaming tea. Taking a sip, she followed Lara and sat down to watch Laralynn play with her doll.

"I am so glad that you came for a visit," Lara said. "I have been a little lonely, lately."

Aslev smiled and took another sip of tea.

Chapter 9

New banners baring the original boar and thistle were draped over the stone columns on either side of the entrance to Black Thistle Castle. The rumbling of wobbling wooden wheels could be heard coming from the vendor's carts as they were pushed over the drawbridge and through the courtyard. Curious men and woman lined the dirt path to get a glimpse of the castle that had been rumored to be haunted and had stood in ruins long after the War of the Witches. Children ran about pretending to defend the castle as they swung their swords made from small limbs that had fallen from the trees. Everyone could feel the excitement in the air, and it seemed to all to be a sign of good times ahead.

Wooden stands had been constructed to allow the spectators a good view of the competition, and they were being filled quickly. The midday sun hovered directly over the castle, and many of the women had starting waving their hats to try and cool their faces. Surprised by the large amount of spectators, Gautier ordered that the archery event be moved to the outside of the quad. Moving them behind the barracks, he felt it would keep the people safe by lining the targets in front of the forest.

The men stood around Commander Gustavo to hear the instructions and receive their colored strip of cloth that indicated what event they had entered. Two hundred eighteen men were lining up to sign the competition roster and some made it known that they wanted to enter more than one event.

Killian chose to compete in three events and signed his name under Archery, Dagger Throwing and Medley. Receiving his colored strips of cloth, he handed the quill to the man behind him. He had never seen anything like this before. His home in Wren Woodland was a very small village, and other than the crowd of people at the harbor, he had never seen so many people in one place. Looking about for the location of his first event, Killian noticed a man dressed in black with an emblem across his chest displaying a boar and thistle. He was holding a large piece of blue cloth. He made his way over to the small group of men that stood around him holding the same colored cloth.

"I am Samuel," he gathered the men's attention as he spoke. "You will be competing in the first Medley event of the day. The object of this event is to gain control of your opponent's flag while protecting your own flag. You will each have a length of rope and a wooden sword. A blow to the heart is considered a death blow, and if you receive one, you will drop to the ground as if dead. If you impede anyone's progress after you are down, your group will be disqualified. A reminder to you all, this competition is to display your skills of strategy, not the skill of the sword. Your first opponent will be the Red group. If you win today, you compete tomorrow. Each win allows you to advance. Do you understand?"

The men all nodded and then looked across the quad to the men that gathered under the red cloth. They were an ugly group of overweight men. Seeing that most of the weight hung about the middle of their bodies and not about their chest and shoulders, Killian surmised that they spent time wielding a cup of ale instead of a sword. He gathered the men together to make a plan.

Gautier and Thomas stood watching the crowd gather in the stands. Tate and Elda wandered around looking for any sign of trouble.

"While the sun is out, we do not need to worry about Jario's interference," Thomas said. "He has no gift of walking in daylight."

"I expect him to make an appearance but using the gift that I so foolishly granted him," Gautier replied. "He can change his appearance, but he can only appear as a man or a boy. Since he was not here to sign the roster, he will not be competing."

"That gives us less people and places to watch," Thomas said, as he saw Tate coming toward him.

"Gustavo informed us that the first event is ready to proceed," Tate said. "If you are making an announcement to the crowd, you should do it now."

Gautier nodded and walked slowly to the center of the quad. He raised his arms to draw everyone's attention.

As the crowd became silent, Gautier began to speak, "Good day to you all. My name is Gautier, and I would like to welcome all of you to Black Thistle Castle. As you know, this castle stood in ruins for a very long time. It suffered terribly from the War of the Witches. My brother was Lord of this castle until his death. I have taken his place and will rule this castle fairly. These men before you will compete for positions in my army. Those that are chosen, will protect the castle, align with the castles within Alltree Island, and help protect the surrounding villages from crimes committed by humans and immortals."

The crowd began to cheer and Gautier raised his arms again to request quiet.

"I see that this pleases you, and it makes me glad," Gautier continued. "I have asked for the assistance of Lord Thomas from Evergreen Castle and representatives from his army to help with the judging of these men. I know that they will be fair to all. Also, I have noticed that several vendors have arrived to sell their wares. Show them respect and take part in the refreshments that they offer. If you are all ready, let our competition begin."

Gautier turned and walked back to stand by Thomas as the crowd roared with approval.

The men to compete in the first Medley walked to the center of the quad. The men had tied their colored cloth around their arms and stood in position ready to begin. Samuel waved the banner drawing everyone's attention and quickly dropped his arm to start the event. The Reds ran forward waving their wooden swords and ropes above their heads. The Blues moved forward with five men standing close to each other and two staying back to defend their own flag. As the Reds passed the center of the quad, the five men quickly moved out stretching their ropes that had been tied together to make one long rope. They circled around the Reds and easily trapped them altogether. One of the Blues dashed for the red flag. Taking it from its stand, he grasped it and waved it in the air. Without taking a loss the Blues had won the first Medley.

The crowd cheered their success and shouted Blues, Blues, Blues. The men cheered and slapped Killian on the back. He had made the plan, and it had worked perfectly. Grinning from ear to ear, he walked with his group from the field to watch the next Medley. He would soon have his first session with his bow at the Archery event, and he stood listening for his name to be called.

The day went by quickly with one exciting event after another. The sun slowly began to set, and the many torches were lighted around the quad and along the row of vendors. Children tired from a day in the sun, leaned their heads in their mother's laps and slept through the shouting and cheering.

Hearing the boisterous crowd, Jario casually walked among the heavy crowd of spectators. He appeared to be a young man of fifteen and had made a quick friend of a young girl, a daughter of one of the vendors. Taking a liking to Jario, Stella accepted his request to sit in the stands and watch the night's events. The two made their way to the stands, and Jario helped her climb to the highest plank for the best view. They leaned back against the wooden railing and settled in to watch the last of the Medleys.

* * *

Aslev tethered her palomino horse named Butter at the post outside the cottage. Hearing the cottage door open, she looked up to see Lara standing in the doorway with Laralynn standing beside her. She walked toward the door as Laralynn ran into her arms.

"Lara, are you ready to go to the competition?" Aslev asked.

"Are you sure it will be safe to take Laralynn?" Lara nervously asked. "We will have to spend the night along the way."

"I believe that we can make it by evening," Aslev replied. "I know a shortcut through the forest around Primrose Pond that will allow us to cross Whistler River. Once we cross, it will be a short ride through the forest to Black Thistle Castle."

Aslev brought Laralynn back into the cottage, and they began to bundle her up for the ride to Black Thistle Castle to watch the competition. Lara filled her basket with bread, cheese and honey for Laralynn, as well as, blankets, clothes and linen squares. She felt safe now that Baxter had not recognized her at the market. There was still a risk, but she needed to see Thomas. If only for a moment, she needed to see him.

"Are you ready little lady," Aslev asked Laralynn and listened to her squeal.

Lara pulled the door closed behind her. She looked over at the mischievous goat and hoped that Mollie would be able to milk the goat without too much trouble. She watched Aslev mount her large golden mare and handed Laralynn up to her waiting hands. Stepping on the large rock by the post, she straddled the mare and took Laralynn and placed her between herself and Aslev. She felt Aslev nudge Butter as she guided her up the dirt road. They were on their way to the competition. She was on her way to see Thomas for the first time since she fled the castle.

Chapter 10

It had been a good first day, overall. There were a few drunken skirmishes to break up and one boisterous archer that lost by the width of a hair, but Preston and Elda quickly had everyone's tempers under control. Day two of the competition drew an even larger crowd than the day before. The stands were filled quickly, and everyone seemed eager to watch the men compete.

The groups of men that had won the first round of the medley were anxiously waiting to receive their strips of colored cloth. Fifty-six men remained from the one hundred twelve that had entered the medley event. Strategy rather than skill had allowed the groups to advance to the next round. Strength and skill would play a role in today's medley, and the men took the time to assess their competition.

After handing out all the colored cloth, Commander Gustavo stepped onto the field and began to shout out the order for the medley, "The first two groups will be the Reds and Browns followed by the Blues and Greens. The next two pairs will be the Whites and the Blacks followed by the Grays and Mustards.

Killian watched the commander back away from the field as the first two groups made their way to the opposing ends of the field. The crowd stood and cheered their appreciation.

"Red, Red, Red," shouted a child that stood in the stands.

Not to be out done, another child yelled, "Brown will win!"

Happy with the strip of blue cloth he was handed, a sign of good luck, Killian gathered the men to take a good look at the groups of men that had entered the field. They all appeared to be equal in size and strength.

"Watch their feet," Killian whispered. "You can tell where they are headed from the direction of their feet."

Gustavo stood with a small flag raised. He waited until he had the attention of the men and then dropped the flag to start the event. The men moved cautiously toward each other. As their wooden swords were raised, the sound of wood smacking against wood echoed through the field. Ropes were tossed at men's ankles, causing some to trip and fall to their knees. A few men fell after receiving a strike to the heart and lay motionless upon the ground. The "Reds" were outnumbered and eventually succumbed to the speed and strength of the Browns. The Browns retrieved the flag and hoisted it in the air. The crowd jumped to their feet and cheered their approval. The winners slapped each other on their backs and made their way off the field to watch the next two groups of men.

Killian and his group of Blues, ran onto the field. The Greens were taller than most of the men in his group. Huddled together, Killian and the rest of the Blues whispered to one another and then took their positions to watch for Gustavo to start the event. Seeing him drop the flag, they readied their ropes and wooden swords as they watched the men approach. The Greens had left their flag unprotected. Seeing the opportunity offered by the men, Killian and two other Blues threw their ropes at the Green's swords. The loops at the end snagged the swords and pulled them from their hands. Rushing the men with their own swords, they were able to take down three of the men with a blow to the heart. Jumping over the body of one of the Greens, Killian dashed for the flag and pulled it from the stand raising it above his head. They had won the event and the right to advance. Killian listened to the sound of cheering and greeted his group of Blues with his own shouts of approval.

Gustavo stepped onto the field and announced, "The next event will be the Tent Pegging. Please bring the horses forward onto the field."

Gustavo watched as four horses were led to the edge of the field by four men. Four boys stood on the opposite side of the field with large pumpkins at their feet. Four more men made their way to each of their horses and were handed a lance.

"Will one of you boys place a pumpkin in the center of the field?" Gustavo shouted, as he looked over at the boys with pumpkins at their feet.

One of the boys picked up a pumpkin and carried it to the center of the field. He turned his back to the horses and walked a good twenty paces before he stopped. Setting the pumpkin down on the ground, he ran off the field and stood next to the other boys.

"You will have one chance to pierce the target," Gustavo addressed the men standing by their horses. "You must give speed to your horse. If you fail to pierce the target, you are out. If you are successful, you will continue. Each round will present a more difficult target. This will continue until only one of you remains."

The first man mounted his horse and anxiously waited for Gustavo to signal him to begin. Seeing the nod of his head, he nudged his horse with the heels of his boots and swiftly approached the target. Raising his lance, he carefully aimed and threw it at the target. It sailed through the air and pierced the pumpkin, splitting it in half. The crowd stood and shouted their appreciation for his success.

Killian watched another rider pierce his target and then made his way out of the quad and around to the back of one of the barracks. He had stowed his bow and quiver of arrows inside a barrel for safe keeping. Retrieving them, he approached the men that stood waiting to align themselves with the archery targets. Each man had their own bow and quiver of arrows slung against their backs and faced a target. Killian stepped forward to face an empty target and waited for instructions.

"You will each have three attempts at the target," Preston addressed the men. "Your best arrow will be measured against the others. The best of those arrows will be the winner." Waiting for questions and hearing none, Preston continued. "Place all but three arrows on the ground. This way I am certain that you will only release three."

He watched as each man removed all but three arrows from their quivers and placed them on the ground in front of them.

Seeing the men were now facing the targets, he shouted, "Ready . . . Take Aim . . . Release."

Killian aimed and released each of his three arrows toward the target that was made from a bale of hay with a red circle painted from animal blood. Once everyone's quivers were empty, they all walked toward their targets. Preston followed the men and watched as each man withdrew two arrows, leaving their best. Only two men, Killian and a man called Hedge, had arrows that had pierced the red center of the target. Hedge had the better arrow and won the event. Killian pulled his arrow from his target and then congratulated Hedge on his victory. He was happy to have pierced the target and happy for the winner.

Returning to the quad, Killian watched the White and Black Medley before he made his way to the vendor's carts. He had brought a small pouch of coins and pulled one coin free, keeping it tight within his closed fist. Seeing a woman selling bread and cheese, he approached the cart and pointed to the slices of bread and hunks of cheese.

"One coin for one slice of bread and one slice of cheese," the woman said, as she watched Killian lick his lips. "For you, young man, I will add a ripe fig and a cup of water. I may need you one day. We take care of our army."

Killian handed over the coin and took the bread, cheese and fig from her hand. He watched her fill a cup with water and set it on the wooden plank before him.

Taking the cup with his other hand, he said, "I thank you for your kindness. I hope that I will be chosen for the army and will do my best to protect you."

The woman smiled at him and then quickly turned to the next person offering coins for her wares. Killian walked to the shade of the barracks and sat down to eat his meal. He had completed his events for the day and would spend the remainder of the day watching his competition. In the quiet, he let his mind wander. He had tried to forget what his father had said to him before he left for Alltree. Seeing the sun beginning to set, he started to fear what would happen if he did turn into a wolf. In case it really happened, he had to make a plan.

How do I plan for turning into a wolf, he thought?

Shaking his head, he tried to ignore the thought as he tasted the sweetness of the ripe fig upon his tongue.

* * *

Now that the sun's light had disappeared, Jario stood within the forest and willed his appearance to change again into the young man of fifteen. His disguise had allowed him to walk freely about the grounds, and he was anxious to return to the stands in hopes of seeing the wolf. Even though he had not seen the white wolf the prior evening, he knew she would eventually leave the castle grounds. With the coming of the full moon, she would take to the forest to run. His trap was set, and it was waiting for her.

Approaching the stands, Jario looked about for Stella. She had kept him company the prior evening and had been a source of entertainment when she followed him into the forest after the events had concluded. Her father's shouting had interrupted a single kiss and left Jario wanting for more.

"Jack," Stella called to Jario. "I am up here. Come sit with me."

Scanning the stands for her voice, Jario spied the young woman's waving hand. He quickly made his way up to her side. As he sat down, she handed him a fig.

"They are really sweet and juicy," Stella said, as she lifted the fruit to her mouth and took a bite.

He watched as she raised the fruit to her mouth. Seeing the juice that remained on her lips made him release a soft growl. He was here to scout for the wolf and not to be distracted by Stella. Quickly he turned his head to the center of the quad and tried to calm his arousal.

"Look," Stella shouted. "The men on the horses have burning torches. What will they be doing with the fire?"

Out of the corner of his eye, he spotted Velsa in the crowd coming toward the stands. If he had not seen her recently, he would have never recognized her. Now beautiful, she would draw the attention of many of the men at the competition.

They will run for their lives once they get to know her, he thought, as he *watched a man stand with his mouth gaping open.*

As she made her way up the wooden stands, he noticed a woman carrying a small child. She seemed to be following closely behind Velsa. Not recognizing the woman, Jario watched Velsa and the woman settle in to watch the competition. The woman bounced the child on her lap, and Velsa handed the child a piece of bread.

"Hum, they are together," Jario whispered softly to himself.

The woman looked about the quad as if searching for someone. Following her gaze, Jario saw that she kept her eyes focused on the men that huddled at the far corner. They were Evergreen men.

"Look Jack," Stella shouted, as she gave Jario an elbow to the ribs and distracted him from watching the woman's gaze. "They are tossing the burning torch through a ring. Isn't it wonderful? I have never seen anything like it."

Jario turned his head to see the horse and rider circle around to take another torch. As the horse turned to gallop back across the field, a flicker of white caught his attention. He followed it as it moved slowly behind several men. As the white object reached the last of the men standing alongside the field, he saw Kayleigh. Dressed in white, she stepped into full view and walked toward Gautier. He had rarely seen her in this form before leaving the castle. He watched her grasp Gautier's arm, and Gautier leaned down and kissed her forehead.

The little wolf and her master, he thought. Very soon, you will be a broken wolf.

"He is going to do it again," Stella yelled. "Watch him! Jack, watch him!"

Jario was distracted again by Stella's shouting. He watched the rider and smiled at Stella. He decided Stella was becoming a distraction. He needed to focus on the wolf. All her shouting was making his head hurt.

"Would you like to take a walk?" Jario asked, as he stood to find that Kayleigh had disappeared.

Seeing her nod, he turned to find his way down the stands. Passing in front of Velsa, he looked up into her eyes. She lowered her brows at him, but she did not appear to recognize him. Looking closely at the woman beside her, he saw a young woman with dark hair and brown eyes. It seemed peculiar to him that he had never seen her before, but there were many women that lived in the villages surrounding Black Thistle. Jario assumed that her husband had entered the competition, and she had come to watch his event. Dismissing her from his mind, he was suddenly stopped as the child reached for his tunic and grasped it firmly between her fingers.

"I am sorry," Lara said. "She is sometimes too friendly."

"No worries," Jario replied, as he spotted the tiny red mark upon her ankle. "She is a happy child. I have enjoyed seeing her smile."

Lara pulled the tunic from Laralynn's grasp and nodded her thanks, as Jario and Stella turned to leave. Once they reached the bottom of the stands, Jario looked back up at the woman and then at Velsa. Velsa looked directly into his eyes and smirked. His new appearance had not fooled her. She knew who he was.

Chapter 11

The morning light streamed through the hole in the canvas above his head. Not ready to face the day, Killian rolled over covering his eyes with the inside of his arm. As he tried to creep back into his dream, the angst of the coming full moon gripped his chest so tightly that he could hardly take a breath. Sitting up, he rubbed his chest trying to ease his discomfort to no avail. Crawling from his shelter, he stood and started to pace back and forth gasping for air. Bending over at his waist, he grabbed his thighs and began to cough and gag until he finally regained his breathing. Wiping a thin film of perspiration from his face and neck, Killian looked across the field toward the forest. It was dark and would provide protection from unwanted eyes. If by chance what his father had told him was the truth, he would run to the forest before the moon rose in the night's sky and wait. He would hide and face the curse alone. Taking a deep breath, Killian sat down and watched the sun slowly rise and its rays fill the sky.

* * *

Gautier stood facing the fire in the hearth when he heard Thomas and Tate enter the Great Hall. He had sent word for them to arrive early so that he could speak with them in private. He had performed a *Locator Spell* and wanted to tell them what he had discovered.

"Thomas, Tate," Gautier said, as he greeted the men with his outstretched hand. "It was good of you to come early."

"Do you have good things to tell us?" Thomas asked. "Have you found her?"

"I performed the *Locator Spell* with the items that you sent me," Gautier replied. "It has revealed that Lara is on the island, but she is hidden by a powerful *Blocking Spell*. I was unable to break through the spell but discovered a shadow image."

"What is a shadow image?" Tate asked. "Is she kept in the dark? Is that why you cannot see her?"

"A shadow image can be created if two people are hidden together in the spell," Gautier explained. "Since this is unlikely, I believe that her appearance has been changed by a *Transformation Spell*. This would allow her to be hidden in plain sight. You would not recognize her if she stood before you."

"Would everything be changed?" Thomas asked. "Would her voice or her scent change too? I could always find her in the castle by following her sweet scent."

"This spell was powerful," Gautier tried to clarify his statements with an example. "It has sealed her behind a barrier. I see only what I would see behind a smoked window pain. It is possible that her voice or scent could seep through the barrier, if the barrier is not completely solid."

"Well, we can't go sniffing every woman that we meet," Tate shrugged. "Can you do anything to help us find her voice or scent?"

"I have not done what you are asking," Gautier replied. "I will search for a spell that might be able to find her scent."

"Whatever help you can provide would be appreciated," Thomas said, as he reached for Gautier's hand. "I am sure you understand my worry. I need to find her."

The sound of soft footsteps drew their attention as Kayleigh entered the Great Hall. Stepping to Gautier's side, she offered Thomas and Tate a smile before she spoke, "Tonight I run with the full moon. My senses will be at their peak. Is there something that I should pay particular attention to, as I run?"

"Lara always smelled of lemon and mint. It was her favorite bath oil," Thomas replied, as he closed his eyes for a moment. His lips pressed firmly together when he remembered the moment they lost her scent in the forest the night she disappeared.

"I will follow the scent if I should run across it during my run," Kayleigh replied, as she touched Thomas' arm. "We all feel her absence and hope she will be home soon."

Thomas could not speak. He was overwhelmed. Nodding his head in thanks, he turned and left the Great Hall. Again, his hopes of finding Lara were dashed.

* * *

It had been decades since Lara had slept under the stars, and she found that she loved the dark glittering cover of darkness. It reminded her of the nights she had sat in the courtyard under the stars with Thomas. She had taken all those nights for granted. Eternity was their future, and now, it was gone.

Waking, Lara sighed softly. She had dreamt again of Thomas. His strong arms had kept her warm, and his words of love had comforted her. Now that she was awake, the lovely moment vanished, and the reality of his absence was present.

Seeing him standing across the quad from her yesterday was wonderful. She wanted to run to him and throw her arms around his neck. It had been difficult to hide her constant gaze upon his face. Aslev had asked a number of times if she had seen someone she knew. She always responded no and that she found everyone interesting to watch. She was glad to see that her faithful friends never left Thomas alone. Someone was always with him. She watched him scan the crowd and then drop his eyes to the ground when he realized he had not found who he was seeking. After seeing Baxter at the market, she knew that he had been looking for her. It pained her to think of him all alone.

Laralynn grasped a strand of her mother's hair and pulled her from her thoughts. Feeling her daughter snuggle closer, she closed her eyes and tried to return to the dream that had given her so much comfort.

* * *

Aslev could not sleep. Lara's thoughts of Thomas had been crashing through her mind all night. Trying to distract herself from Lara, she pondered the surprise appearance of Jario. After seeing him sitting in the stands as a fifteen year old young man, Aslev stewed over what he was doing with the young woman or what he was going to do. The sun was just starting to rise when she realized that she was just a distraction. Jario was at the competition to watch the wolf. Smiling, Aslev was happy to know that Jario was not going to renege on their bargain. The moon would be full tonight and that meant that the white wolf would be out for a run. She would be close if Jario needed her help in slicing her tail from her body. She would enjoy hearing the little wolf howl in pain. The wolf deserved it for taking Gautier from her. Excitement caused her to giggle out loud. She had something to look forward to, at last.

Chapter 12

The events that Killian had entered were completed with an excellent outcome. The Blues had won their medley and would compete against the "Mustards" tomorrow for the final event. He had also come in one behind the leader in the dagger throwing event. To his surprise, it had been a moving target, and he had no experience throwing a dagger at something that moved. He had only missed one target and left the quad with a feeling of accomplishment.

He leaned back against the wooden plank of the stands and tried to relax. The sun was hours away from setting, but he kept looking up at the sky. His body felt no different to him. He had no idea what to expect, but he knew the process of changing would have to be painful. The idea of a man changing into a wolf was terrifying. Standing, he decided to move to the lowest plank of the stands. He concluded that this would allow him a quick exit if he started to feel pain.

Why am I thinking about this, he thought? This is impossible. My father didn't want me to leave the island. He told me a story to keep me home working in the butcher shop.

Satisfied that his father's story had been a trick, Killian made his way to the vendor carts to find something to eat. He was famished.

***

Lara sat in the stands watching Thomas and Tate walk past the spectators. He was close enough to allow Lara to see the silver-gray of his eyes. They were no longer bright and happy eyes. The look of great sadness filled them. She looked away not wanting to see the hurt on his face. Laralynn suddenly squealed, and Thomas turned to look up into the crowd. Seeing the child, he smiled. Turning back toward Tate, he kept walking.

"That was your father," Lara whispered softly into Laralynn's ear. "You will know him one day. He is a wonderful man and will love you very much."

Aslev could hear Lara's whispers to the child. She would make sure that Thomas found his daughter, but not until she was sixteen. He would be grief stricken when he discovered that his Lara had died, but he would have to endure it. Everyone had some kind of pain to endure. Aslev knew that firsthand. After all, the beat of Lara's heart was the bargained payment. A bargain was a bargain, and she had never let anyone out of their payment. She had held up her part and then some; however, she had seriously thought about taking this payment early. If she did, she would be able to raise Laralynn as her own child. Biting her lip, she pushed the thought from her mind. Laralynn would be too much work. She had no time for work. Clucking her tongue, she noticed that the sun was dropping lower in the sky and started watching for Jario and the white wolf.

* * *

Kayleigh could feel the excitement race through her body as she watched the sun drop lower in the sky. She had removed her clothing and stood by the open door to the balcony watching the sky turn from blue to a soft rose. Untying the ribbon that secured her hair, her soft golden curls fell about her shoulders. The sound of the chamber door being pushed open made her smile.

"I wanted to see you before you left for your run," Gautier said, as he moved toward Kayleigh. "It will be dark soon. You must be careful."

"Do not fear for my safety," Kayleigh replied, as she stroked the side of Gautier's face and then kissed his chin. "I am a wolf. Others fear me. I will let my wolf run and chase the creatures that live in the forest. I will let my wolf run free tonight. She will delight in the sounds and scents of the forest. It will be a glorious night."

"You will call to me if you find trouble," Gautier ordered, as he tipped her chin up so that he could look into her eyes. "I will be only a moment away."

"I will," Kayleigh replied. "My wolf will keep her mind open to you. You will see everything that she sees, if you wish to watch."

Gautier took Kayleigh's hand and walked her back to the open door to watch the sunset and wait for the full moon to appear high in the sky. As they watched the sky darken, she rested her head against his chest and waited for the moment she would let her wolf take control.

* * *

Killian stood at the edge of the forest and then stepped into the shadows to hide. He had decided he would wait among the trees to see what would happen. He watched the sky change from blue to rose and then to a vivid orange. His stomach churned, as beads of sweat ran down the side of his face. As the sun moved from view, the sky began to darken, and the darkness made his hands begin to shake. Pressing them against the rough bark of a tree, he watched the clouds drift across the sky until the full moon, in all its glory, hung proudly in the sky. Keeping his hands pressed against the tree, he anxiously waited for something to happen. He could hear a nervous laugh leave his mouth. He was still a man. Pulling his hands away from the tree, he brushed his palms over his breeches. Relaxing his shoulders, he started walking through the forest and began to laugh.

This is silly, he thought. A man turning into a wolf, I have never heard of such a thing. If my father could see me now, he would be laughing at what a fool I was to believe him.

He could hear the chirping sounds from crickets and the crushing of pine needles beneath his boots. It had all been a trick to make him stay at home. Shaking his head, Killian picked up a small stone and threw it deep into the forest. Kneeling down to pick up another, he yelped in pain as he gripped his knee and fell forward. Feeling a sharp rock beneath his knee, he stood and tried to rub the pain away. Kicking the offending rock with his boot, he cursed it for wounding him. Walking further into the forest, he could feel the cool breeze against his damp face, and it made him shiver. Feeling his knee throb, he sat down on a downed tree and started to pull up the leg of his breeches. His hands began to shake uncontrollably. Pain shot through his body, and the force of it threw him to the ground. The sensation of his tunic rubbing against his back caused heat to race down his spine. He yanked his tunic over his head to try and relieve the pain. His bones began to pop, and the force of their movement caused Killian to scream as his vision blurred and the forest began to spin.

Lifting his body from the ground, he stood panting for breath. He could see his shredded breeches on the ground next to his boots. The pain that had consumed him was finally over. His vision was crystal clear, and he was bombarded with every sound and scent within the forest. It had happened. His father hadn't lied to him. He was a wolf. Angry, he let his wolf take over. He could do little to control it. He watched as his wolf raced into the forest. He ran for miles. He ran until his anger left him, and the joy of the race took him by surprise.

Overcome by thirst, his wolf stopped by a pond to drink. He looked into the glassy water at his reflection. At first, it startled him. Bright yellow eyes stared back at him. His thick coat was black as the night with a bit of silver at the tip of each ear. Dipping his mouth into the cool water, he drank to soothe his throat. Refreshed, he lifted his head and howled. Off in the distance, he heard another howl.

Could there be another wolf like me, he thought, as he backed away from the pond and turned toward the sound.

He heard the howling again and recognized the sound of distress. A wolf was injured. He charged through the forest and followed the howling until he came to a large opening in the ground. His wolf could hear the sounds of panting, whimpering, and snarling. Peering into the deep pit, he saw a white wolf caught among tangled branches and leaves. He could smell blood. The wolf was caught among the branches and wounded.

Crushing leaves and twigs made him step back away from the pit. He watched as a young man walked toward him. Feeling threatened, he leapt forward in a defensive stance and began to growl. The young man stepped back and raised his hands.

"I'm not here to harm you. Leave this place," the young man ordered. "I only want the white wolf."

Feeling this man was a threat to the trapped wolf, he lowered his head and exposed his teeth. He stood ready to attack the young man if he came any closer to the pit. He didn't understand why, but his wolf would not allow this man to harm the white wolf. He had to protect her. As he moved forward, the man moved back keeping his hands in the air.

Off in the distance, he could hear boots running through the forest. The young man turned toward the sound and then raced away leaving him alone with the white wolf. His wolf frantically paced around the pit listening to the whimpering. His mind filled with her cries for help. Baffled from what he was hearing, he continued to pace around the large opening until a tall man with dark hair stepped from the trees. He looked toward the black wolf showing no threat or fear and made his way to the side of the pit and knelt down.

"Kayleigh," Gautier shouted. "Are you hurt?"

"A branch has pierced my leg," she screamed into his mind.

Confused, his wolf backed away from the pit. He had heard the white wolf speak into his mind. Recognizing the man, he realized the man had come to help and not harm the wolf. He continued to move back away from the pit and then turned and raced into the forest.

When will this night end? My life has changed forever, he thought, as he continued to run through the forest and from himself.

* * *

The sun was just beginning to rise and Killian woke to the sound of a skunk waddling through a pile of leaves. Slowly, he lifted his head once it had moved from sight. His naked body ached, and his mind reeled from what he had seen and heard during the night. Looking about for his clothes, he remembered pulling his tunic from his body and seeing his breeches fall to the ground in shreds as his body changed into a wolf. He had to get back to his camp before anyone saw him. His body swayed as he stood, and he leaned against a tree for support. He thought back to where he had been when he felt the pain of the shift. He remembered a small clearing.

Can I find it? Hopefully, there will be something left of my clothes.

Exhausted and confused, he ran in what he thought would be the direction of the clearing. He felt thorns and the rough bark of branches upon the forest floor scrape his legs and cut his feet. By the time he reached the clearing, his legs, ankles and feet were covered in blood. Finding his boots and his tunic, he pulled on his boots and wrapped his tunic around his waist to cover him the best he could. Shaking his head at his appearance, he ran for his camp in hopes of arriving there before anyone caught sight of his ridiculous appearance.

Chapter 13

Gautier sat by their bed waiting for Kayleigh's wolf to wake. He had retrieved her injured body from the pit and returned her to their bedchamber. As he washed the blood from her fur and wounds, he tried to make his love for her overpower the anger that was building within his mind. He had easily healed her broken hind leg and extracted the broken stake from her front leg. The stake had nearly missed her chest. If it had pierced her heart, he would have lost her forever.

She had called to him the moment she felt her wolf fall through the covering of the camouflaged pit. At first Gautier had thought the pit to be one dug by a hunter, but his senses had picked up on the scent of a vampire before leaving with Kayleigh cradled in his arms. Finding a vampire's scent near a pit could only mean one thing. The vampire intended to trap something. A coincidence that her wolf had fallen into it was unlikely. Sensing the scent was a tad too familiar, he knew of only one vampire that would dare to take his revenge against Kayleigh. The vampire he had banished from Black Thistle Castle. He was sure that Jario had been in the forest. If he had been in the forest, he had probably been at the competition.

Pulled from his thoughts, Gautier heard Kayleigh whimper, and he moved to sit on the edge of the bed. Stroking her thick white fur, he saw her open her eyes.

"Kayleigh, my dear," Gautier softly said, as he continued to stroke her fur. "You are safe."

He felt the shiver of her leg before she shifted back to her human form. Standing, he pulled off his boots and climbed into bed next to her. Pulling the bed linens up over both of them.

"How do you feel?" Gautier asked, as he felt her snuggle next to him.

Laying on her side, she placed her head on his chest and wrapped her arm around him.

"Tired. Thankfully, the pain is gone," she softly said.

"What do you remember?" he asked. "Were you running from someone?"

"No, I was just running until the ground gave way," she replied.

"I scented a vampire at the pit." Gautier barked, as he pulled the bed linens tighter about her shoulders. "I fear that Jario had a hand in this."

"I heard a man speak, but I did not recognize the voice. The pain I felt distracted me, and I was trying to concentrate on calling for you," she said, as she moved her leg over his. "I heard another wolf howl after I fell. I could hear it running toward me. Before I heard the man speak, he peered into the pit at me."

"Was he a shifter?" Gautier asked.

"I believe that I could sense he was new to the wolf form," Kayleigh replied, as she sat up looking down at Gautier. "He kept the man from me. Gautier, he protected me."

"I saw the black wolf pacing around the pit, but he ran off as I approached," he said. "We need to find him. Do you believe that you could sense him in his human form?"

"I could," she replied. "Do you think he has been at the competition?"

"It is a possibility," Gautier answered her. "Today, if you are well enough, try to find his scent. He will need your help."

Kayleigh leaned over and kissed Gautier. Pulling back she smiled.

"What was that for?" Gautier asked.

"Because, I love you and to thank you for saving me," she replied.

"I love you, too," Gautier responded, as he placed his hands on either side of her face and pulled her down to kiss her lips.

* * *

Jario stood alone in an abandoned cottage he had found on the way through the forest surrounding Black Thistle Castle. He could feel his body fill with anger. His plan had almost worked. He had heard the white wolf running through the forest and fall into the pit. She had been within his reach when a black wolf had unexpectedly arrived and taken a protective stance before him. He was livid over being interrupted. Jario knew he could have turned the black wolf to stone if the wolf had attacked, but he had to leave when he heard Gautier coming to the rescue. In the dark, his temper flared as he paced back and forth across the small space clenching his fists.

"Every time I come up with a plan, it fails," Jario screamed. "I will tolerate failure no longer."

A rap at the door drew his attention away from his rage. Making his way to the door, he stood and listened for any sign of danger. Hearing the rustle of a woman's skirt, he asked, "Who is there?"

"Open the door," a woman smirked. "Are you afraid?"

Bewildered more than fearful, Jario opened the door being careful not to stand in the sunlight. As the woman barged past him, he saw the deep red of a skirt before he saw her thin waist and long black hair. As he closed the door, she snapped her fingers and the few candles within the room ignited with flame.

"So, you are Jario," the woman smirked, as she looked him up and down. "I expected more, but you will do."

"And, you are?" Jario asked, as he cocked his head to the side. "How do you know me?"

"I am Desirae," she replied. "A friend of yours told me about you. I had to come and see for myself."

"Who is this friend you speak of?" he asked.

"His name is Buck," she replied, as she turned to look about the room. Waving her hand at the hearth, a crackling fire came to life.

"Buck is dead. He died in the war with Evergreen," Jario mocked her response. Jario looked from her eyes to the stone floor. He could not bring himself to look at the flickering flames.

"Ah, what he said was true. You have a great fear of flames," she laughed.

"If you had been burned like the logs in that hearth, you would have fear of flames, as well," Jario sneered. "It was pain beyond belief."

Seeing her nod her head in agreement, Jario watched as she made her way to the wooden chair by the hearth. She sat down and straightened her skirt neatly over her lap. Taunting him, she motioned to the only other chair in the room. She beckoned Jario to sit. Cautiously, he walked toward the chair without looking at the flames. Keeping his eyes to the floor, he sat down and nervously sighed.

"Why are you here?" he asked, as he felt the hairs on his arms stand on end with each flicker of the hearth's flames.

"My sister, Derora, was killed by a witch that lives in this forest," Desirae replied. "She was killed during the War of the Witches. I have come to seek revenge upon this witch."

"The only witch within this forest is called Velsa," Jario responded. "Is this the witch you seek?"

"Yes, I seek the witch, Velsa," she replied. "It took many years for the news of my sister's death to reach me and many more to find my way to this island. By chance, I met your friend. Buck told me of this island, of you, and of the witch, Velsa. He did not survive the war with the Evergreen Castle, he ran from the war. He boarded a ship and left the island. I might say, he has told me some quite fascinating stories. I am sure they were not all true, but they were fascinating. To hear him tell it, he has had quite a few ladies of royalty begging for his lips and his loins."

Hearing her speak of Buck made him laugh.

"He has always told those stories," Jario replied. "I doubt they are true. He is better at stealing gold rings from pirates than sweeping a lady off her feet into her bed."

"And you?" Desirae asked, with a grin on her face. "How are you with the ladies?"

"I have had my fair share," Jario snickered. "I have a lady that I seek for all eternity, but she is not within my grasp. She is mated to another; however, she is missing or hidden."

"Hidden?" Desirae looked at Jario strangely. "Is she hiding or has someone hidden her?"

"I believe that the witch, Velsa, has hidden her," Jario replied. "For what reason, I do not know. I have not been able to find her for well over a year."

"If I help you find your hidden lady, will you help me obtain my revenge against Velsa?" she asked, as she saw Jario raise his eyes to look directly at her.

"I will," Jario responded without hesitation. "I will most definitely help you."

* * *

Aslev had packed up her belongings and prepared Butter for the journey back to Primrose Pond. She felt they had stayed long enough. Lara had seen Thomas, and without him knowing it, he had seen Lara and his child. It was time to get them back to the safety of Primrose Pond and the cottage.

A sudden flurry of hot wind raced through her fingers, up her arms, and swirled round her head. Aslev knew the sign. Another witch had stepped foot upon Alltree Island. It was a sure sign that trouble was coming her way. Revenge was the message on the wind. The witch was seeking revenge for a death that was committed by her hand. It was revenge for the death of the witch named Derora.

"Lara, my dear," Aslev called. "It is time to leave. We must get back to Primrose Pond."

Helping Lara and Laralynn up onto Butter's back, Aslev climbed the rails of the fence and straddled the mare. Feeling Laralynn snuggle against her back, she smiled and patted the child's leg. Clucking with her tongue and giving Butter a nudge with the heels of her shoes, they started the journey back to the cottage. Looking over her shoulder, she felt eyes staring at her. Quickly, she quietly recited a *Cloaking Spell.* Assured they would be hidden by the spell's protection, she guided her horse toward the cool dark forest.

Chapter 14

Sweat dripped from Killian's face as he pressed his shoulder against a brawny man and knocked him to the ground. Feeling the man's rough calloused hand grab his ankle, he bent down to try and pry his fingers loose. Losing his balance, Killian fell to the ground landing on his back. Seeing another Blue running toward them, he rolled over and twisted his legs. This caused the man to roll and expose his chest. The Blue lunged forward and pressed his wooden sword to the man's heart making him release Killian's ankle. Jumping to his feet, Killian ran toward the flag. Grabbing the mustard flag, he raised it above his head. The crowd stood and cheered for their victory while chanting their appreciation for the Blues and the Mustards.

After huddling with his group of Blues in celebration and offering their hands of respect to the Mustards, Killian looked for a patch of shade to rest his tired and aching body. Resting his back and head against the barrack wall, he closed his eyes and drifted off to sleep. Visions of black fur and the sound of popping bones filled his dreams. He saw flashes of a man seeking a white wolf and heard the wolf's voice in his mind. He growled at the man to keep him away from the pit. Twitching awake at the sound of his own growl, he rubbed his face trying to remove the sleep from his eyes.

Looking down at the ground, just beyond his boots, he saw green velvet slippers and white billowing fabric. Raising his eyes, he stared at a woman with hair the color of golden flax.

"You were growling," Kayleigh stated. "Growling is best kept within the shelter of the forest."

Killian quickly stood up and brushed the dirt from the back of his breeches. Realizing she was the lady of the castle, he bowed slightly.

"My Lady, I was dreaming," Killian replied. "One does not have control over their dreams."

"True," Kayleigh confirmed. "However, one does not have much control of their wolf during a full moon, either."

"I do not know anything about wolves," he chuckled, trying to pretend it was all a witticism."

Seeing his stunned expression, she continued.

"You are a new wolf," Kayleigh stated bluntly. "In fact, you are the black wolf that stood bravely against what threatened me. I owe you my thanks and possibly my life. I think it best that we speak about this in private. Do you agree?"

Killian knew then that she was the white wolf that had been trapped within the pit. He nodded his head and watched her turn and walk toward the castle. Frozen in place, he saw her turn and look over her shoulder. She stood waiting for him to follow. His stomach jumped with rumbling nerves, but he quickly forced his boots to move and to follow her.

* * *

As the sun began to set, Thomas and Tate walked about the quad looking for any sign of Jario. After hearing from Gautier of the attempt to trap Kayleigh, they were suspicious of any young man that sat among the spectators. With Jario's ability to change his appearance, he could easily be an old gray haired man or a ten year old boy. Thomas felt comforted by the fact that Jario was not concealing Lara since it appeared he was busy trying to trap Kayleigh.

"Do you think he will come here?" Tate asked his brother. "Do you think he is brave enough to make an appearance?"

"Bravery has nothing to do with it," Thomas smirked. "Jario is arrogant. His arrogance will force him to stand among his enemies. He will delight in being here among us. I believe that his arrogance will eventually be the end of him."

"He is that," Tate laughed. "Kayleigh should be safe until the sun sets. Jario cannot walk in daylight. If he planned to retrieve her during the daylight, he would be risking a final death. Is he that desperate?"

"His plans have all failed, but I know that he won't stop trying," Thomas said. "Sun or no sun, he won't stop trying to kill me, take Lara for his own, or rule Evergreen."

"I still don't understand the need for Kayleigh," Tate said. "She is a wolf. She has no magical powers. What could he gain from capturing her?"

"Revenge against Gautier," Thomas shrugged. "Gautier made him leave Black Thistle Castle. He and Magna had made the castle their sanctuary. He had no place else left to go."

"He has his own castle," Tate stated. "Why risk the wrath of Gautier over Black Thistle?"

"There must be something else behind his need for Kayleigh," Thomas replied. "If Jario doesn't need her for himself, he must need her for someone else."

"Velsa!" Tate declared. "It has to be Velsa. Who else could it be?"

"That hag's name keeps coming up," Thomas growled. "That name gives me nightmares."

"Do you want to make a visit to her cottage?" Tate asked, knowing full well that Thomas never wanted to see her again.

"Not unless it is to end her," Thomas replied. "To end that hag's existence, we will need Gautier's and Meadow's help. We won't be able to do it on our own."

"He has suffered from the pain of her magic just as you have done. He will surely help us," Tate responded. "He will want his revenge against the old hag."

Seeing Elda, Baxter and Oliver coming toward them with their parchments, Thomas decided to include Velsa's name in their discussions with Gautier before they returned to Evergreen Castle.

"Are we finished here?" Oliver asked. "I am anxious to get back to Evergreen."

"You are anxious to get back to the tavern and that pretty lass," Baxter said, as he jabbed at Oliver's arm.

"That too," Oliver grinned. "I have missed the frisky lass."

Everyone laughed except Thomas. They all knew that he was thinking of Lara. Seeing Thomas turn and head for the castle, they all quieted and followed closely behind him. They needed to report to Gautier and head for home. They had done as he had requested and chosen the best of the men for Black Thistle's army and knew that Gautier would appreciate their selections.

* * *

Desirae watched Jario move away from the hearth and toward the covered window. She could see his tense body relax as he distanced himself from the flickering flames. Studying his demeanor, it was obvious that Jario was an ordinary vampire. He did have extremely dangerous powers, but he had not acquired anything of value without the assistance of someone else. She was sure that someone else had been the witch, Velsa.

"What are your plans for this evening?" Desirae asked, waiting for Jario to turn and face her.

"Since I was unable to obtain the article that I had hoped to collect, I will return to my home at Crimson Claw Castle," Jario replied, keeping his back to Desirae. "I find that I need to return to the comfort of my home."

"Do you have room enough for a visiting witch?" she asked, as she stood and walked toward him. Running her finger down his back, she felt his body tremble. "My needs are simple. I will not require much from you."

He felt his back stiffen as visions of Magna flashed before his eyes. He had not realized until that moment that he had truly missed her.

I do not miss the torture, he thought. Who in their right mind would miss the torture? I miss seeing her and hearing her voice.

"There is room enough for visitors," Jario turned to face Desirae. He started to move his hand toward her waist. Hesitating when he saw her smirk, he dropped his hand and turned back toward the window. "As soon as the sun is down, I will ready my horse to leave. Did you come by horse? I did not hear you approach."

"No, a horse was not needed for me to travel across land," she replied. "If you like, I can transport you, your horse, and myself to your castle with my magic."

"Splendid, I am anxious to return to my castle," Jario grinned. "The sun will be down shortly, and we can leave this dreadful cottage."

Chapter 15

The gray stones that capped the red towers of Crimson Claw Castle slowly came into focus. Ash pulled against the leather reins as they appeared outside the stone stable's wooden door. The gray stallion was skittish, and Jario stroked his neck until he was calm enough to be led to his stall for the evening.

Closing the stable door, Jario found Desirae looking up into the sky. She tilted her head as if listening to the wind.

"What has your attention?" he asked, as he moved to stand beside her and looked up searching the starry sky.

"I am listening to the messages that are carried upon the wind," Desirae replied, keeping her eyes closed and trying to concentrate. Exhaling a disgruntled sigh, she turned to face Jario. "There are too many voices on the wind tonight. Once the wind has rested, I will try again."

"In the meantime, let me show you to your chamber," Jario stated. He felt uncomfortable around the witch and resisted taking her arm to lead her through the castle. He was afraid she would gain some knowledge about him if she should touch him. "Follow me. There are only a few chambers that are suitable for visitors. They are all on the second floor above the Great Hall, the Chamber of Maps, and the Council Chamber. The castle had been abandoned for years, and I am trying to make it a brilliant gem befitting its name."

"Where is your chamber?" Desirae asked, letting a frustrated sigh escape her. She was disappointed that she would not be invited to share his chamber. "Is it far from mine?"

Jario thought to ignore her, but he knew that she would persist until he answered her.

"My chambers are on the top floor of the castle," he replied. "It overlooks the river and the forest. It is my favorite place to gaze at the stars and the reflection of the sunset upon the water." He kept the most important reason to himself. He was not ready to share his hawk with anyone.

Arriving at the chamber he had chosen for her, he opened the door and pushed it open allowing her room to enter. Waiting in the hallway, Jario motioned his hand toward the chamber and waited for Desirae to enter.

"I will send Claudia to your chamber," Jario responded. "She will help you get settled. Please let her know if you need anything."

"And if I need something other than what she can provide," Desirae moved toward Jario. "Will she send you to me?"

"Desirae, I am not at your beckon call. I am the Master of this castle. I have willingly allowed you to stay and will provide for your needs until you decide to leave. I know nothing about you. I have taken a great risk bringing you here," Jario said in a stern voice."

Seeing her take a deep breath, he waited for her to speak, but she stood quiet as she stared into his eyes.

"I have not always benefited from those that brandish magic," he continued. "If I am hesitant to trust you, I have good reason. We discussed an arrangement that would benefit both of us. Until that arrangement is completed, I ask that you refrain from tempting me with your womanly charms. I do not want to offend you by turning you down again."

"I see," Desirae replied. "You have more backbone than I was led to believe."

"I do not know what you have heard of me," Jario laughed, as he stepped back further into the hallway. "I do not know, and I do not care. I bid you good evening, Desirae."

Jario turned and headed toward the stone steps and his private chambers.

Desirae closed the door and took in the grand bedchamber. Feeling a chill from Jario's stern words, she flicked her wrist and filled the hearth with a warm fire. One by one, she brought the candles about the room to flame. Enjoying the warm glow, she walked toward the canopied bed. The large wooden posts of the bed were beautifully hand carved and draped in golden brocade embroidered with delicate white roses. The far end of the chamber was completely covered in heavy golden drapery.

A vampire requirement, she thought, as she ran her fingers over the soft fabric.

She heard Claudia's footsteps before she heard the soft rap at the door. Turning her attention toward the door, she called out, "Enter," as she walked toward the door to meet her.

"My name is Claudia. I have come to ready your chamber for the evening hour," she said, as she moved toward the bed. "Are you hungry after your journey? Shall I send a meal to your chamber?"

"I would like some berry wine to sip by the hearth," Desirae replied.

"I shall see that it is brought to you," Claudia said, as she moved toward the wall of fabric. "There is a lovely view of the river and the stars from the balcony. Shall I pull the drapes back for you?"

"I would enjoy seeing the night's sky," Desirae said.

As Claudia pulled the heavy fabric to the side, Desirae saw the beautiful stained glass doors that held images of two red dragons facing each other. The reflection of the flames within the glass made the dragons seem alive. Desirae forced herself to touch them to be sure they were only glass. Relieved, she opened the doors and stepped out onto the balcony. The sound of the water rushing against the rocks calmed her uneasiness. She had a history with dragons that she wanted to forget.

"There is a sleeping gown in the armoire. Shall I help you with your laces?" Claudia asked.

"No. I am not ready to retire," she replied, as she continued to look at the water below the balcony. "I need only the wine. I can manage on my own."

Claudia nodded and left the chamber to retrieve the wine.

Placing her hands upon the stone wall about the balcony and closing her eyes, Desirae listened to the wind. She swayed with its gentle movements searching for the path to Velsa's cottage. It led her beyond Black Thistle Castle and through the forest. She followed the wind as it began to weave between the trees and head for a dim light.

Holding onto the wind, she sped through the trees toward the light until the images suddenly went dark, and the wind had suddenly vanished. Desirae felt a strong surge of power push back against her vision.

"You know I am here," Desirae whispered into the night. "Yes Velsa, I have come to avenge my sister. We shall meet very soon, and it will be a delightful meeting."

Turning toward the chamber, she saw Claudia placing a goblet of wine on the small table by the hearth.

"Thank you Claudia," Desirae smiled as she looked at the goblet. "That will be all."

* * *

Thomas stood alone in their bedchamber looking at their bed. He saw that McDuff had turned down the bed linens, as he had done every day. Looking away, he clenched his fists and moved toward the chair by the hearth. He had not slept in their bed since Lara had gone missing and would not return to it until she was home. Sitting down, he removed his boots and dropped them to the stone floor. It had been almost two years since she had vanished. It had been two years of hunting for her, dreaming of her, and missing her. He was no closer to her now than he had been the night she vanished. The light in the tower and Gautier's assurance that she was on the island was the only thing that kept him going. A life without her was no life at all. If the light in the tower should ever go dark, he had made up his mind to end it. He would go to the Canyon of Obscurity and stand in the sunlight. It would turn him to ash, and the pain of her absence would be over.

The door opened and McDuff entered the chamber and walked toward Thomas.

"My Lord, Gautier has sent a messenger," McDuff said, as he gently touched Thomas' shoulder to draw his mind away from the sadness. "Shall I ask your brother to receive him for you?"

"No, McDuff," Thomas replied. "I will meet with him. Where is he?"

"In your Council Chamber," McDuff responded. "He requested that the message be delivered in private."

Pulling on his boots, Thomas stood and followed McDuff to the door.

"I will have Charlotte bring a meal to your chamber. You need to eat," McDuff fussed, as he had done every night for weeks. "You aren't sleeping. You need to eat."

Thomas nodded as he kept walking. He heard McDuff scolding him, and he knew that he meant well. He would have to answer to Lara if his responsibilities were not met.

"Yes, McDuff," Thomas groaned, as he kept walking. "I will eat the meal that Charlotte brings to my chamber."

"Good," McDuff firmly said. "Now, go meet the messenger."

As Thomas entered the Council Chamber, he saw Gustavo holding a folded parchment.

"You have a message for me?" Thomas asked, as Gustavo stepped forward and handed him the parchment.

Turning it over, he saw Gautier's mark imprinted in the wax that sealed the message. Breaking the seal, he opened the parchment expecting the worst. He read the note slowly. Confused, he read the words again. Looking up at Gustavo, he saw him shrug his shoulders.

"Do you know of this?" Thomas asked him. "Did Gautier tell you what he wrote within this message?"

"No, My Lord," Gustavo nervously replied.

"Tell Gautier that I have read his message," Thomas ordered. "Thank him for me, and thank you for bringing this message to me. Can you find your way out?"

"Yes, My Lord," Gustavo responded, troubled by Thomas' strange reaction.

Thomas turned and headed toward the Command Center. Elda and Baxter looked up and stood when Thomas approached them.

"Have you seen my brother?" Thomas asked.

"Tate and Gavenia are dining in the courtyard," Baxter said. "What is wrong? Has something happened?"

Without answering, Thomas ran to the courtyard. Throwing the door open, he looked about for his brother.

"Tate," Thomas shouted. "Tate, are you here?"

"Yes," Tate replied, as he and Gavenia stood and walked from behind the fountain. "What is wrong?"

"I have received a message from Gautier," he gasped, trying to get the words out as quickly as possible. "It has me confused. I do not understand how this could be possible."

Tate could see Elda and Baxter enter the courtyard and stand quietly behind Thomas. Thomas' hands began to shake as he handed the parchment to his brother.

"Read it for yourself," Thomas requested.

Tate took the parchment and began to read it as Gavenia took hold of Tate's arm. Reading it over Tate's shoulder, she gasped as she realized what it meant.

"Gautier believes this?" Tate asked, as he looked up at Thomas and then back at the parchment.

Thomas,
I have discovered more from the spell I offered.
It has shown me what I believe to be a child.
Two shadows - Both hidden
One from within the other
Two hearts - Both protected
One marked without the other
When time passes - Two will be released
Gautier

"I have a child," Thomas whispered, as he moved to sit upon the edge of the fountain. "Lara has hidden my child. Why? Why would she do that?"

"Protection," Gavenia said, as she pointed to the parchment. "To protect the child from what?"

"Jario," Thomas said, as he gritted his teeth and felt his fangs descend. "She did this because of Jario. I am sure of it. She fears what Jario would do to the child."

"We will find them brother," Tate said. "We will find them and bring them home."

Finally seeing Elda and Baxter, Thomas stood and barked out orders, "Elda take a group to the village near Wintergreen Mountain and start searching for a woman and a young child. Baxter, I want you to lead a search starting at Woods Village and move west to Shepherd's Grove and Primrose Pond. We have to find them. Tate, you and Gavenia search the forest around Black Thistle Castle and

Peaks View. I will search the Cumberland Forest and Hunter's Point."

"It is too dark to start searching," Tate said to Thomas. "Get some rest. We will start at sunrise tomorrow. I know what you are thinking. Stay away from Velsa. My gut tells me that she is involved. If she is hiding Lara, she will never tell you where she has hidden her."

"If she has harmed her, I will burn that witch alive," Thomas shouted.

Chapter 16

Walking among the trees letting the palm of his hand graze the rough bark, Killian tried to comprehend what Lord Gautier had asked of him. He had personally offered his thanks to him and his wolf for the bravery they had shown in protecting Lady Kayleigh's wolf. Then, he had asked him to become her personal guard. A place among the Black Thistle Army had been his only thought when entering the competition, and now, he had been asked to protect the Mistress of Black Thistle Castle. It was a post of great distinction, but the thought was overwhelming.

Am I really strong enough or brave enough to protect Lady Kayleigh.

Seeing a patch of wild berries, he picked a handful and sat down cross legged in the thick pine needles that littered the ground. Leaning back against a large smooth rock, he threw the berries into the air and caught them with his mouth. The childish motion seemed to relax his mind, and he laughed as remembered doing the same thing with a childhood friend.

His body was still sore from the change, and he tried to ignore the constant nudging from his wolf to set him free. Closing his eyes, he could feel his wolf begging to be released. Remembering the pain, Killian pushed back against his wolf, but the wolf pushed back harder. Relenting, Killian found a cluster of small evergreens and hid behind them as he removed his boots, tunic, and breeches. He had recalled his breeches being torn to shreds and didn't want to return to his blanket in only his tunic wrapped around his backside.

Kneeling down, he turned his body over to his wolf and felt the sudden pain of his popping bones. The change was painful, but much faster than before.

"The pain will lessen the more often you give yourself over to the wolf," the white wolf sent her voice into his mind. Standing before him, her white fur glistened in the moonlight that seeped through the trees. "You will begin to enjoy the feeling of freedom."

"How can I hear you in my mind?" Killian asked.

"It is an ability wolf shifters share," she replied. "I tried to explain everything to you before you met with Gautier. If you have more questions, you can ask them later. For now, let's run. My wolf is ready. Are you?"

Killian watched as she bolted through the trees into the thick forest. Not to be outdone by a female or a female wolf, his wolf raced after her. They ran for hours weaving through the trees, jumping over logs and through small streams. He had never felt such freedom. As they rested by the pond after a long cool drink, he noticed the flicking of her ears, and he realized that she was listening carefully to something.

"Gautier has requested that we return," she spoke softly into his mind.

Their wolves were disappointed that they had to leave the forest, but they both headed back toward the castle. Finding his clothing, Killian hid behind the clump of evergreens and felt his wolf release its hold leaving him naked. He quickly dressed and stepped forward to escort the white wolf back to the castle.

"You were right. I did enjoy the feeling of freedom," Killian grinned down at the white wolf.

Approaching the castle, Killian could see Lord Gautier standing by the stone wall. Kayleigh's wolf raced toward him and jumped to press her front paws upon his chest. Seeing Lord Gautier rub his fingers within her fur and the wolf lick his face, he knew that they loved each other.

"Killian, did you enjoy your run?" Gautier shouted.

"Yes, My Lord," Killian replied. "It gave me time to think on your offer. I would be honored to become Lady Kayleigh's personal guard."

"Very good, Killian, very good," Gautier responded, as he knelt down to lean against his white wolf. "Follow us, I will show you to your chamber."

***

Returning to her cottage, Velsa was relieved to be back among the comfort of her potions and herbs. Inhaling their pungent aromas, she felt her spine relax. Snapping her fingers, she watched the hearth flicker and then burst into flames. Untying the laces of her gown from below her breasts, she pulled the heavy gown off her shoulders and let it fall to the floor. Stepping from the pile of fabric, she reached for her silk robe and let it slide over her arms and about her shoulders. Enjoying its softness wrapped about her body, she sat down in her favorite chair by the fire. The warmth of the fire began to soothe her senses, and she closed her eyes to try and sleep.

Awakened by a sudden flurry of wind, Velsa listened as the wind battered against her window causing the shutters to flap and her door to rattle. She knew the wind wasn't a storm. The wind had a message for her. Opening the door and stepping out into the dark night, Velsa stood in the last of the moonlight outside her small cottage and listened to the chatter. It was buzzing with whispers, laughter, and sobbing.

Velsa paced the length of her cottage and raised her arms above her head letting the wind weave through her fingers. Her fingers began to warm and the heat raced down her arms to her shoulders.

"Desirae, I hear you. I welcome your visit. Your sister was no match for my powers and you will feel their strength the same as your sister. Enjoy your little adventure on the island, while you can," Velsa laughed, as she sent her message out into the wind.

Returning to her cottage, Velsa slammed the door and kicked the gown she had worn out of her way. Reaching for her kettle to make a much needed cup of tea, she saw a blue wasp land upon her hand. As she shook her hand, she felt a stinging sensation. Cursing the tiny creature, she picked up a bowl and scooped a bit of brown salve out and rubbed it on the welt the creature had left behind. The salve stung worse than the bite, and she felt slightly dizzy. Looking down at her hand, she saw her fingers start to turn blue.

"No!" she shouted. "Where is it? Where is the pest? I have to find it. Who sent a Hunter Wasp? I have to kill it before it can leave my cottage."

Velsa cursed and screamed as she searched for the Hunter Wasp. She knew the danger of receiving a bite from the magical creature. She had used them many times to gain knowledge for herself.

"Gautier is the only one strong enough to create a Hunter Wasp," she barked out loud. "What are you after? Who has asked you for help?"

Spying the creature on the sill of her window, she threw a handful of purple sparks toward it hoping to end its quest. Before they could make contact with the creature, it escaped through a crack in the glass. Furious that it got away, she clenched her fists and screamed causing the bundles of herbs to fall from the ceiling. Overwhelmed from the madness of the evening, she collapsed into her chair. Looking down at her blue throbbing hand, she spit on the welt. As she leaned her head back against the chair, her hand suddenly began to itch.

"Enough!" she screamed. "Enough!"

* * *

Lara listened to the soft sighs from her daughter as she drifted off to sleep. It had been a long journey home, and she was exhausted too. Pulling the leather journal from the chest, she placed it on the table next to her cup of steaming tea. Sitting down, she opened the cover and turned it to an empty page. Picking up the quill, she dipped it into the ink and began to write.

Dearest Thomas,

I saw your handsome face and wanted to run into your arms. I wanted to hold you in my arms and feel your lips upon mine. Your eyes were filled with sadness, and I know that I am the reason for it. I need you to know that I miss you. It breaks my heart every day to be without you. Your daughter is healthy and happy.

We saw you look up at us and smile. It was only a moment. A moment I will always remember. I told her that you were her father and that you would love her one day.

Stay strong my love, Lara

Closing the cover of her journal, she returned it to the wooden chest. Untying her apron, she removed it and hung it upon a wooden peg. Picking up the candlestick, she made her way to her bedchamber. Blowing out the flame, Lara sat in the dark with her arms wrapped around her body. Tears began to well in her eyes.

"I love you Thomas," she whispered into the dark. "I will always love you."

Chapter 17

Thomas stood in the Command Center looking at the maps that had been spread across the large wooden table. They were covered with marks of all the places they had searched for Lara and found nothing. Knowing there was a child, the army had retraced their steps and searched every village again to no avail.

A great sadness had taken over Evergreen and Echo Bluff. It hung like a heavy weight about the shoulders of everyone. Even the long hoped for marriage of Charlotte to Woodward had not brightened everyone's mood for more than a few days. Thomas had struggled for weeks about what to do. He had come to the only conclusion possible. He would end the search.

"Brother," Tate cringed, as he quickly noticed he had startled his brother. "I am sorry. Did I disturb you?"

"No," Thomas replied, as he reached for his brother's hand. "I am glad that you are here. I have decided to end the search for Lara and my child."

"Why?" asked Tate. "Have you given up?"

"More than a decade has passed since Lara went missing," Thomas replied. "A decade has passed since it was discovered by Gautier that I have a child. We have spent that decade searching every cottage, cave, ship and forest for them. It must end."

"Has there been any more news from Gautier?" asked Tate, as he noticed a slight red ring in Thomas' eyes.

"Nothing more," Thomas sadly replied. "She has been well hidden, and Gautier has not been able to find a loophole. I can only hope that she is safe, and my child is happy. One day, when it is time, she will come home to me."

"Did you know that Elda tried to find Velsa's cottage?" asked Tate. "She was going to trade herself for Lara, but she couldn't find the cottage."

"No, I did not," Thomas looked surprised. "She is brave and very foolish. We must all stay away from that old hag. Evergreen cannot afford to have anyone else taken from us."

"How long has it been since you had a blood meal?" asked Tate, as he forced Thomas to look at him. "It is clear that it has been too long. Come with me to the kitchen." Tate pulled on Thomas's arm and felt him pull back. "You need to eat, and if you won't come with me on your own, I will get Oliver to help me carry you to the kitchen. If Lara comes home and finds you in the Holding Room, she will banish me from Evergreen."

Knowing Tate was right, Thomas reluctantly followed him from the Command Center to the kitchen.

* * *

Since arriving at Crimson Claw Castle, Desirae had hidden herself away in Jario's Chamber of Maps to learn about Alltree Island and its inhabitants. The Hunter Wasp she had sent to spy upon Velsa had returned to her, and she had easily extracted every bit of knowledge that it had retrieved from Velsa's blood. She had painstakingly unraveled and documented every spell, bargain, and threat that Velsa had made. Tearfully, she had watched the moment her sister, Derora, had been blasted by a *Disintegration Spell* and heard her sister's vow of revenge drifting through the wind. It would be her responsibility to avenge her sister's death, and she would take her time. She wanted Velsa to know that she was coming, but she wouldn't know when.

Desirae heard the door open. She expected a visit from Jario. He had visited her every evening since her arrival. He would always ask the same question of her. What have you learned? She smiled as she heard Jario's hands rubbing together before he spoke, "What have you learned? You have been held up in this chamber for over a decade."

"I have finally finished recording Velsa's compassionate history," Desirae announced sarcastically. "Oh, she willingly helped anyone for a price. The price was always to her benefit. I find she has been greedy and hateful for most of her life. An interesting note, did you know that she once loved Gautier, and he returned her love?" She watched Jario's mouth drop open. "I was surprised too. His lovely Kayleigh came between them." Laughing, she stepped from the table and walked toward the large map of Alltree Island that had been painted upon the wall. "She has hidden Lady Lara, but there is something else. She has also hidden her child."

"What?" Jario exclaimed, as he stood stunned. "She has a child?"

"Yes, a daughter," Desirae nodded. "A daughter with a red mark upon her ankle. A red mark in the shape of a teardrop."

Jario's mind started to spin. He had seen a child with a mark upon her ankle. He had seen Velsa with a woman that held a child with that mark.

It was her. The woman that sat beside Velsa at the competition was Lady Lara.

"Where can I find her?" asked Jario. "Do you know where I can find her?"

"Primrose Pond," Desirae declared with her arms spread wide. "She is in a small cottage in Primrose Pond."

"I must leave at once," Jario shouted with excitement.

"Wait, you haven't heard the best part," Desirae smirked. "Your Lady Lara is no longer a vampire. She is a human."

"Human? She is a human?" Jario repeated, trying to comprehend everything he was hearing.

"Sadly, she will die when her daughter turns sixteen. Velsa is taking her heartbeat from her when her daughter turns sixteen," she snarled. "Velsa has somehow become attached to the child and the child to her. She will destroy this child just like she destroyed my sister."

Desirae watched Jario run through the door. She shouted after him, "Beware, Velsa has set a trap for your affections that will not end well."

✳ ✳ ✳

Loud laughter filtered down from the tiny loft. Laralynn and her best friends, Nollie and Lettie, had been playing all afternoon, pretending to be fairies with magical powers. For the past three years, they have been inseparable. Only the setting sun had managed to keep them apart.

"Mother, can we go to the pond to hunt for fairies?" Laralynn asked.

Seeing Nollie cross her fingers, she laughed and copied her by crossing her own.

"You may," her mother replied. "Be very careful and be home before dark. The girls have a long walk home. I don't want their mother angry with me if they should be late."

"Thank you mother," Laralynn clapped her hands and hugged her friends. "We will be careful."

The girls scurried down the ladder and out the door before Lara could hand them a basket filled with bread and berry jam. Opening the door, she called to the girls and held up the basket. Hearing her calling for them, Nollie ran back to retrieve it.

Thank you Madame Thomas," she said. "We will not be late. Do not worry."

Lara smiled and leaned over to kiss Nollie on her forehead. Nollie giggled and then ran to catch up with Laralynn and her little sister. Feeling a cool breeze, Lara pulled her shawl tighter around her shoulders. She could see gray clouds beginning to cover the sunlight, and she knew that rain was coming. Lara stood and watched the girls until they were out of sight.

"I'll race you to the pond," Nollie screamed, as she started to run.

Laralynn and Lettie shouted, "Wait for us?"

Stopping to take off her shoes, Laralynn scrambled after Lettie not wanting to be left behind.

The girls sat by the pond and ate their bread covered in sweet berry jam. They watched as a cluster of butterflies flew over the pond, and they each pointed at their favorites. As a patch of sun broke through the clouds, Laralynn moved so that she could feel it upon her face. Lettie picked flowers and showed Laralynn how to make a crown with the tiny flowers. As they each took turns making up a story about a beautiful fairy, they lost track of the length of time they had been at the pond. It was starting to get dark.

"It is past time to go home," Laralynn grumbled. "Mother will surely be worried. Is it safe for you to walk home? Will you make it home before it is dark?"

"If we hurry, we will be home before dark," Nollie replied. "Let's hurry Lettie. We need to run."

Laralynn hugged her friends and watched Nollie grab Lettie's hand as they began to run through the forest. Picking up her basket and shoes, Laralynn hurried through the trees and headed home to find her mother standing by the gate waiting for her.

* * *

After hearing of the magnificent discovery from Desirae, Jario left Crimson Claw Castle without giving thought to the remaining darkness. He had driven Ash to the limit and managed to reach the abandoned cottage just before sunrise. Securing his stallion to what was left of the rotten fence, he felt the first drops of rain and quickly entered the cottage. The darkness had always soothed his nerves, but he needed the light to be able to think. He needed a plan. He needed a plan that would not fail. Picking up the small piece of flint, he walked back and forth in front of the hearth. He had not brought a hearth to flame since he stood with his body burning. Watching his hand shake, he placed the flint back on the table, and he cursed the darkness as he sat back down in the chair.

"Why are you sitting in the dark?" a soft voice asked.

Startled, Jario jumped from the chair, "Why are you here?"

"I have come to ask a favor. Do you remember our bargain? It was three favors of my choosing to be paid at the time of my choosing," Velsa smirked.

"What do you want?" sneered Jario. "I do not have time for this?"

"You will make time or suffer the consequences," Velsa barked, as purple sparks shot from the tips of her fingers.

"Tell me what you want," Jario ordered. "I want to get on with it."

"I want you to go to the Canyon of Obscurity and retrieve Caper Spurge. It is a very poisonous plant. Bring it to my cottage. I will give you three days to complete this favor."

"I know nothing of Caper Spurge. How shall I find it?" asked Jario, as he clenched his thumb within his fingers and gritted his teeth.

"I will put the image in your mind. I find it interesting that you first thought of the plant and not the loss of your powers," laughed Velsa.

"I have had other things on my mind. Are you going to help me? I cannot stand within the sunlight," Jario stated.

"I have brought you a potion that will allow you to keep your powers within the canyon for three days. It will also keep you safe within the sunlight," Velsa said, as she handed a small bottle to Jario. "Do not betray me."

Taking the bottle from Velsa, he could feel heat seeping into the palm of his hand. A sudden burst of blue light blinded him for a moment. He could feel the heat of the burning hearth before he opened his eyes to see that Velsa had vanished. Left with no choice, he pulled the stopper from the bottle. Jario could smell the potion's rancid odor, and he hesitated before lifting the bottle to his mouth. Placing the bottle to his lips, he tilted it up and let the liquid pass over his tongue and run down his throat.

I have to hurry, he thought, as he made his way to his stallion. I have three days to find Lady Lara in the sunlight.

* * *

Tate and Gavenia secretly continued to search for Lady Lara. They knew that Baxter and Elda were still searching, as well. Thomas had ordered the searches to stop. He had lost all hope of finding her and receiving bad news at the end of each search tore at his soul. Knowing that Jario had been at the competition, they thought it worthwhile to have Gavenia's hawk visit Jario, again.

Standing in the shade of the forest, Tate watched Gavenia remove her clothing.

"Bring your hawk quickly," Tate ordered, as he clasped his hands and raised them over his head to grasp the back of his neck. "You are so beautiful."

Gavenia blushed and knelt down upon the soft moss. In an instant, her hawk appeared and spread her wings. Tate watched as she flew between the trees and up into the sky.

She could see that Jario's balcony door was not open. She flew back and forth over the water trying to draw his attention. Seeing the reflection of the morning sun against red glass, Gavenia circled lower to find a door moving slightly. It was too low to be Jario's chamber. Curious, she landed on the stone wall of the balcony. Afraid to enter the chamber, she squawked and scrapped her beak against the rough stones. She could hear the rustle of a woman's skirt before the glass door swung open.

"You are a pretty one," Desirae cooed.

Not recognizing the woman, her hawk moved away from her.

"I will not hurt you," Desirae softly said. "I am a friend to all of earth's creatures."

Concerned for her safety, her hawk took to the sky. The woman stood on the balcony and watched her soar through the air. She smiled and called to her to return. Still unsure that it was safe, her hawk landed back upon the stone wall.

"Do you visit Jario?" asked Desirae. "Are you his secret pleasure? He is not here. He has run to find a woman that has been hidden in Primrose Pond."

She ruffled her feathers upon hearing of a hidden woman and heard her hawk asking her what to do. Trying to control her hawk, she feared she would release her and turn her back into her human form. Jumping from the balcony, she swooped once more around the balcony and then headed for the tops of the trees. Landing on a sturdy branch, her hawk watched the woman leave the balcony and close the glass door.

Tate heard the flap of Gavenia's hawk and anxiously waited to greet her. She dropped to the ground and instantly released her hawk. Gavenia grabbed her clothes and hurried to put them on.

"What has happened?" asked Tate, as he took hold of Gavenia's arm to keep her steady.

"Jario has gone to Primrose Pond to find a hidden woman," Gavenia choked on her words. "It could be Lady Lara."

"How do you know this?" asked Tate. "Who told you?"

"A woman was in the castle, and she told me," Gavenia replied. "We need to hurry. We have to find her before Jario finds her."

"We will go back to the castle and get Elda and Baxter to come with us," Tate said, as he mounted Twiggs and pulled Gavenia up behind him. "Not a word to Thomas. He couldn't bare it if we told him and found nothing."

Chapter 18

To others, a curious blackbird sat on a low branch outside an abandoned cottage. As a child, Desirae had perfected the spell to hide herself within a blackbird and had frequently used it to spy on her sister and others. After seeing the hawk, it had given her the idea to follow Jario. She knew that he would never be able to find Lara and her child in the dark. Knowing that Jario had not thought beyond hearing of where Lara was hidden before he dashed from the castle, Desirae suspected that he would attempt to seek help from Velsa.

Desirae had seen Jario enter the abandoned cottage where she had first met him. Assuming he was hiding from the sunlight, she was surprised when she saw Velsa enter the cottage. Seeing there wasn't any smoke coming from the stack, Desirae flew to the clay stack and hovered over its opening as she listened to their conversation. Her feathers ruffled when she heard the witch mention Caper Spurge. She knew of the poisonous plant and the spells that needed it. Velsa was planning a *Death Spell* for someone. Certain it was to be used upon herself, she waited until their conversation was complete and quickly retreated to the shelter of the trees moments before she felt a blast of heat coming from the stack.

As Velsa left the cottage hidden within her blue smoke, a very faint blue tendril of smoke left a trail for her to follow. Keeping a safe distance behind her, Desirae followed the witch to her cottage.

So this is where you hide your cottage, Desirae thought, as she circled the area making note of its exact location. I will see you very soon.

As she flew above the cottage, she watched it slowly fade from view. Swooping down, Desirae sensed the roof's thatching and perched upon its peak. It was hidden from sight, but it had not vanished. Satisfied with her discovery, she blinked her eyes and instantly returned to her bedchamber within the castle. Releasing the spell, she laughed as she lifted the hem of her skirt and hurried from the chamber to find Claudia. She wanted a goblet of berry wine to celebrate her discovery and plot her attack on the witch that murdered her sister.

* * *

After Velsa's visit, he had immediately headed for Primrose Pond. Thinking about her threats, Jario quickly changed his mind and turned in the direction of the canyon. Suffering the consequences of another failure was not something he wanted to endure. He feared what Velsa might do to him if he did not fulfill his bargain. He owed her too many payments, and sooner or later, she would demand he make good on another one or all of them.

Even if I went to Primrose Pond first and found Lara, he thought, I have no place to keep her while I search for Velsa's damn weed. I was foolish to leave Lara and the woman alone in the cave, and I paid dearly for that mistake. I will not make that mistake again.

Dismounting Ash, Jario tethered his stallion and walked toward the rocks overlooking the canyon. The closer he got to its edge, the more it reminded him of his failed attempts at becoming the Master of Evergreen. One failure after another flashed through his mind causing his anger to flare. Bending down, he picked up an unsuspecting lizard that had dared to cross his path. Pretending he held Thomas' throat, Jario gripped its scaly body and tightened his fist as he watched it turn to stone. Smirking, he could feel the darkness of the canyon crawl under his skin as it drew him closer with each step. Standing before the deep dark gorge, he looked down at the small stone creature and laughed as he hurled it into the air, watching it fall to the floor of the canyon.

Focusing back on the obligation at hand, he hesitated for only a moment and then jumped off the rocky edge. He could feel the lightness of his body and was relieved that the potion had worked. Velsa had never given him a potion that had failed, but he was skeptical of her current mood, her closeness to Lara, and the affection she had shown to the child. She had offered them protection from something or someone. He was beginning to believe that he might be that someone, and he feared that would make him an enemy of Velsa.

Am I retrieving this poisonous plant for her to use against me, he thought?

Shaking his head, he closed his eyes and brought the image of the plant into view. Looking out over the floor of the canyon, he saw nothing but rocks, dead trees, and more rocks. Grumbling to himself, Jario started to walk the canyon floor searching for the plant that would cancel his debt.

* * *

The sun began to rise, and Laralynn had been too excited to sleep the night before. She had come down from her loft and had managed to milk her goat, Trouble, before her mother had come from her bedchamber. After helping her mother clear the table, wash the dishes, and put them away, Laralynn climbed the ladder to ready herself for the first day of the long awaited festival. She brushed her hair and carefully braided her long light copper strands.

"I am finished," she called, as she descended the ladder. "Are you ready? Mother, are you ready?"

"Yes, my dear," Lara softly laughed. "I am ready."

"I will carry the basket for you," Laralynn said, as she reached for the handle. "The berries, bread and goat cheese will be a good meal for us. We can sit in the shade of Ian's porch and watch the dancers. I cannot wait to hear the music. Do you think I will catch many ribbons? Do you think there will be any boys there?"

"You are too young to think about boys," Lara sternly said. "There is time enough for boys."

Laralynn frowned and opened the door for her mother.

They walked along the path to the village, and Lara tried to distract her by talking about what they wanted to plant in the garden. Inspired, Laralynn stopped several times along the way to gather seeds from flowers that had long spent their beauty.

"I will plant these by our door," she told her mother, as she pointed to the tiny seeds she held in her hand. "They will make our cottage look beautiful, and oh mother, these will be perfect next to the gate."

Lara smiled at her daughter. She enjoyed listening to her daughter's creative ideas and how much she loved nature.

She will enjoy the large garden at Evergreen, she thought. Flora will teach her many wonderful things.

Lara closed her eyes for a moment as she thought about the bargain. She knew her time with her daughter was running out, and Velsa would come to collect her payment. Shaking the sadness from her mind, she started to sing and Laralynn joined in taking hold of her mother's hand.

It wasn't long before they could hear the music coming from the village. Once Laralynn spotted Nollie and Lettie, she left her mother's side and ran to greet them. Laralynn could see the girls jumping up and down with excitement. This was Laralynn's first Festival of the Ribbons, and to be honest, she was excited too.

The girls walked around the village square listening to the music and watching the women dressed in brightly colored skirts sway to the beat of the music. Colored ribbons hung from crowns of flowers that sat upon their heads.

"Nollie?" Laralynn tilted her head and asked. "Why do they call it the Festival of the Ribbons?"

"You have never heard the story?" Nollie grinned. "I will tell you. It is a lovely story."

Long ago, a little girl became lost in the woods by Primrose Pond. The sunlight was dwindling, and she began to cry. She felt something tap her lightly on the shoulder, but when she turned around, she could not see anyone. Fearful, she looked about for a way out of the forest. Catching a glimpse of something moving on the smooth rocks, the little girl gasped when she looked down to see a tiny fairy with shimmering wings smiling up at her. She was dressed in green, and her hair was full of yellow curls. Seeing that she was beckoned by the fairy, the little girl knelt down. The fairy asked her why she was crying and was saddened to hear that she was lost. Smiling, the fairy untied several colored ribbons from her wrist and handed them to the little girl. She told her to hold them tightly and follow the blooming flowers to find her way home. The little girl thanked the fairy as she accepted the ribbons and looked about for the flowers. One by one, flower buds began to open. Careful to keep the ribbons within her hand, she followed the flowers for a short distance. Turning to wave goodbye to the fairy, she saw that the tiny fairy was gone. Hoping to see her again, the little girl turned and followed the path of flowers all the way home. The Festival of the Ribbons is celebrated every year to remember the kindness of the fairy and to remind us to be kind to one another.

"That was a wonderful story," Laralynn replied. "I hope we find a fairy in the forest. I would love to meet a fairy one day."

"I would too," Nollie replied.

Seeing Lettie pointing up, Laralynn followed her finger and looked up to see a man with a painted face that walked on tall wooden stilts. Hearing him growl at them, they screamed and ran toward the safety of a small crowd of people.

Noticing an apple in someone's hand, Laralynn remembered her mother buying apples from Ian's market and how wonderful they tasted. To everyone's delight, Lord Fallon had sent baskets of apples to the festival for everyone to enjoy. Laralynn stood in line to retrieve an apple for her mother and one for herself. Dropping them into her basket, she followed Nollie to watch the man that stood swallowing his sword. She clutched her throat when she heard women shrieking and men applauding his effort. It was a horrible sight.

The large bell that stood in the village square began to ring. It signaled the coming of the ribbons. Everyone turned and started moving toward the center of the square. Laralynn ran to her mother and handed her the basket for safekeeping. She needed two hands to catch the ribbons. Laralynn and her friends, gathered around the woman that held a basket over her arm. The musicians stopped playing and waited for the woman to nod her head. Laralynn raked her teeth over her bottom lip and anxiously waited for the music to start. As she heard the first note, the woman began to throw the brightly colored ribbons into the air. Laralynn and her friends scrambled to catch the ribbons. When the music stopped, Laralynn had four beautiful ribbons draped over her hand.

Smiling, she returned to her mother to show her the colorful prize. Sitting down next to her, she lifted the ribbons for her mother to see.

"They are lovely," Lara whispered. "They will look beautiful in your hair."

Taking a blue ribbon from her daughter's hand, she tied it around the end of her daughter's long copper braid.

"Thank you," Laralynn replied, as she selected a ribbon for her mother. "This one is for you."

Lara smiled and wrapped her arms tightly around her daughter.

* * *

The sunlight was beginning to fade, and Jario had not been able to find a single plant of Caper Spurge. He had searched nearly all of the eastern portion of the canyon and found nothing that even resembled the poisonous weed. The impending darkness would not allow him to search any longer. He could return to the abandoned cottage for the evening or stay in the canyon. Preferring the cottage over a cave, he remembered the stone cottage where he had held Lara. If he spent the evening there, it would allow him to get an early start to his search. Growing weary from his efforts, he decided to stay within the canyon cottage.

Racing through the dry shrubs of the canyon, he spotted the cottage hidden by the fallen tree. Memories flooded his mind, and he balked at entering the small structure.

I cannot stay here, he thought, as he peered through the cracked window. It reminds me of my many failures.

Looking across the canyon, he suddenly remembered the tavern where he had found the woman and the taste of her blood. Without giving it another thought, he raced across the canyon floor and began climbing its wall. Reaching the top, he anxiously made his way to the tavern for a cup of ale and his favorite meal. Opening the door, he inhaled the scent of human blood. Feeling his fangs descend, he spotted a woman with breasts the size of ripe melons and smiled as he ran his tongue over his lips. Sitting down at an empty table by the stairs, he signaled for the woman tending the bar. He watched her as she approached him and licked his lips again as she leaned over the table to let him see all she had to offer.

"What can I get for you?" she asked.

"Ale and a room for the night," Jario winked, as he watched the woman smile and wink back.

He smirked with the knowledge that he would have his fangs nestled between her plump breasts before the night was over.

* * *

Killian stood guard outside the large library. Every morning, Lady Kayleigh made her way to the library, and every morning, he stood guard just beyond the door to allow her privacy. He knew that being chosen to guard the Mistress of the Castle, was an honor. Lord Gautier had personally chosen him, and he wanted him to know that he had chosen wisely.

Hearing the sound of someone approaching, Killian turned to face the open hallway. A young woman, he had never seen before, stopped upon seeing Killian with his hand hovering over the hilt of his dagger and hearing his command.

"Halt," Killian ordered. "You have trespassed into the wrong hallway."

"My name is Alicia. Lady Kayleigh asked me to join her in the library. I am to help her document the scrolls and maps," she announced.

Hearing the sound of Alicia's voice, Kayleigh stepped from the library into the hallway.

"Killian, please let her pass," Kayleigh said, as she placed her hand upon Killian's arm. "I have asked Alicia to help me."

Kayleigh moved toward the young woman and took hold of her hand as she tried to reassure Alicia with her smile.

"Alicia, this is Killian," she softly said. "He is my personal guard. Do not be afraid; he will not harm you."

Looking at Killian, she introduced the young woman, "This is Alicia Wells. Her family is new to the castle. Her father, Adam, was accepted into the army, and I believe that he was part of the Blues."

She looked for Killian's recognition and was pleased to see a slight nod.

"Her mother, May, is probably busy in the kitchen. I discovered she has a talent with making delicate sweets. She accepted my request to teach the women working in the kitchen. I am ashamed to say that they are one of my weaknesses."

Killian bowed slightly. He lifted his hand from his dagger and returned to stand against the wall. He watched as Alicia followed

Lady Kayleigh into the library. Something about her voice and the way she walked made the hairs on the back of his neck stand on end. He didn't feel a threat from her, but he continued to watch her closely. He moved along the stone wall until he had a clear view into the library. Kayleigh noticed his movement and smiled, returning her attention back to her task at hand.

Lady Kayleigh and Alicia unrolled and rolled scrolls and maps for hours. He had watched the young woman lift the old leather bound books from the floor and speak in languages that he had never heard. Her voice seemed to sing in the air. He noticed the way she ran her fingers over the bindings and the embossed covers, and he could tell that she was delighted to be helping her mistress. Setting his concern aside, he felt the tension leave his body and his shoulders relaxed.

Kayleigh looked at the shadows that fell upon the wooden table and sighed, "We have done enough for today. Let's go see what your mother has taught the women in the kitchen. I would love to have a cup of tea and a delicate sweet."

Alicia smiled and put down the quill she had been using. Wiping the ink from her fingers, she followed Lady Kayleigh out into the hallway. She lifted her eyes to glance at Killian and felt her cheeks blush as she realized he had caught her glance. She quickly looked down and hurried to follow closely behind her mistress.

Killian caught her glance, and at the same time, he felt a shiver run up his spine. Clenching his hand before he rested his palm on the hilt of his dagger, he turned and followed Lady Kayleigh and Alicia to the kitchen.

Chapter 19

Jario felt the warmth of the sun upon his face for the second day in a row. He had lost all sense of that feeling since becoming a vampire and found that he enjoyed it. He made his way down the side of the canyon. It had been the same path he had led the young woman before he had compelled her. Smiling, he remembered the woman that had come to his room the prior evening. She had entertained him with her sassy wit and her talents. He had taken his fill of her blood and her body without having to use his compulsion. She was unafraid and bold as they come. She had even shown him a few talents he had never thought of in his long life.

Not paying attention to where he was walking, Jario tripped over a rotten tree root and landed face first on the ground. Pushing himself up, he noticed a cluster of green plants. It caught his eye since there were very few green plants in the dead canyon. Standing, he walked over to the plants and bent down to examine them. He retrieved a pair of leather gloves from his pouch and pulled them over his hands. Grasping the base of the stock, he yanked it from the soil. He let his mind show him the image Velsa had given him and he compared the blue-green stem and the leaves that were arranged in opposite pairs. The odd flowers had no petals. From everything that Jario could discern, he had managed to find the Caper Spurge. Pulling another plant from the soil to be sure he had enough, he spread the mouth of his pouch open and carefully placed the plants inside drawing the leather cords. Carefully removing his gloves, he dropped them on the ground and started running. He had the rest of the day and tomorrow to find Lady Lara, and he would try to find her before returning to Velsa's cottage.

She may take the ability to walk in the sunlight if I return too soon, he thought, as he started climbing the canyon wall. I will use what is left of the potion's spell to my advantage.

Jario pulled himself up over the edge of the canyon and untied Ash. Mounting his stallion, he gave him a quick jab with his boots and headed for Primrose Pond.

* * *

Baxter and Elda stood on the far side of the stable waiting for Tate and Gavenia. They knew they were disobeying Thomas' orders, but after hearing of Jario's search for a hidden woman, they knew they had to go to Primrose Pond.

"Horses or flashing?" Tate asked Baxter.

"We should take the horses and tether them in the forest," Baxter replied. "Thomas will think we are on patrol."

"Good idea," Tate said, as he looked at Gavenia. "Do you want to fly or flash?"

"I will flash with you," she said, as she gripped his hand tighter. If Jario is there, he may notice my hawk and wonder why it had followed him. It might make him jumpy."

"Do you know where you are taking us?" asked Elda.

"Yes, I will take us to the back of a market in the village. I visited it once when I was searching for Lady Lara. The market is set back against a crop of trees that will shelter our arrival from others," Baxter explained. "I have gotten good at flashing. I can take us all at once. Everyone hold hands."

Tate reached for Elda's hand, and Baxter took hold of Elda's hand and then Gavenia's. He closed his eyes. When he opened them, they all stood in a clump of trees behind a stone building.

"That was quick," Elda said, as she checked to see if her dagger was still within its sheath.

"I told you; I have gotten good at flashing," Baxter laughed, as he nudged her with his elbow.

Tate could hear music and looked back at Baxter. He shrugged his shoulders and followed Tate around the side of the stone building. People filled the square and two men stood playing stringed instruments.

"It's a festival," Gavenia exclaimed. "It is the Festival of the Ribbons. I remember attending this festival as a child. Do you smell the apples? Lord Fallon always sends apples to the festival."

"Grab an apple and spread out," Tate ordered. "Gavenia you stay with me. If Jario is here, I don't want him to harm you."

Gavenia took Tate's hand, and they walked through the crowd of people to find the apples from Lord Fallon. Seeing the crowd around the back of a wagon filled with wooden crates, they got in line to retrieve the sweet treat.

"Do you think Lady Lara will be here?" whispered Gavenia. "Do you think she will bring her child to the festival?"

"I hope she will," Tate replied. "I fear we will not be able to recognize her. If she is hidden with a spell, her appearance may have been changed. We need to watch for a look of recognition. She will recognize us and give herself away."

As they stepped forward, three girls burst from the wagon holding their apples. Accidently stepping on the toe of Tate's boot, one of the young girls stopped and stared up into Tate's eyes.

"I am sorry," she said, as her faced flushed. "Please forgive me. I was not watching where I was going."

"You are forgiven," Tate smiled, as he squeezed Gavenia's hand. "Enjoy your apple."

As she quickly left, an overpowering scent of apples filled his senses. He looked at Gavenia, and he could tell that she could smell it too.

"That was odd," Gavenia said.

* * *

The music drifted through the forest that surrounded the village square. Jario had tethered his horse deep in the forest. He didn't want to draw attention to himself as he arrived. Leaning against a tree, he tried to decide what form to take. He knew Lara's child would no longer be an infant. Counting the years that had passed, he surmised that she would be about fifteen. He determined a young lad of seventeen would be the perfect age for him. Pulling his power to change his appearance, he felt his body shiver as it transitioned into a young lad.

Releasing the pouch from his waist, he tied it to a branch that was far enough away from Ash. He ran his hands over the pouch to make sure it was closed. He didn't want to come back and find his stallion dead after nibbling upon the poisonous weed. Spying a worn path, he followed it toward the sound of the music and his hope of finding Lady Lara and her daughter.

Stepping into the crowd of people, he tried to control his desire for their blood. It overwhelmed him, and he felt his fangs descend. Covering his mouth with his hand, he closed his eyes for a moment and calmed his senses. Just when he opened his eyes, three screaming young girls ran past him carrying apples.

Have they any manners, he thought, as he shook his head.

Then realizing that he was probably looking for a young girl about their age, he started to follow them. They ran to a woman that sat in the shade of a wooden porch. He watched as one of the young girls dropped her apples into a basket and then kissed the woman on the check. As the woman turned her face toward her to receive her offer of affection, he suddenly stood frozen in place. It was the woman he had seen at the competition. She was older, but she was the same woman. He had found her. He had found Lady Lara and her child.

Searching the crowd, he looked for where her child had gone. Everyone clustered into the center of the square as a woman holding a basket requested silence. At the nod of her head, ribbons began to fly from her hand. He could hear the screams of young girls as they fought for the chance to catch one of the brightly colored ribbons.

Jario slowly walked in front of the porch and looked at Lady Lara. He smiled and nodded his head in greeting and watched her do the same.

She does not recognize me, he thought, as he made his way to the corner post.

He leaned against the rough wood as he watched the three young girls run back toward Lara and a woman that sat next to her. He listened carefully as Lady Lara called her child Laralynn.

Out of the corner of his eye, Jario saw Elda walking toward him. He panicked for a moment and then remembered that he was not in his true form. She walked around the crowd of people and then near

Lara. Lara quickly lowered her head. He knew that she recognized Elda. It was all the proof that he needed. He had truly found them.

Looking across the square, he noticed Tate and Gavenia looking at the faces in the crowd. He knew they were looking for Lady Lara, as well.

How did they find out she was here? Desirae, he thought. She must have told them.

As far as he knew, Desirae had not been to Evergreen Castle. She was the only one that knew of her being hidden. He decided that they had come on a routine search. He knew that Thomas would never stop searching until he found her. They would eventually give up and leave. He had nothing to worry about. Satisfied, he made his way into the crowd to mingle with the people of the village.

Looking over his shoulder, he spotted Laralynn looking at him. He gave her a smile and continued to walk through the crowd hoping she would follow him. Seeing the wagon and the apples, he got in line to receive one of the bright red orbs. Having one handed to him, he turned to see Laralynn standing before him.

"I have not seen you before," she said. "My name is Laralynn."

"I have not seen you before either," he replied. "My name is Jack. Do you live in the village?"

"Yes, I live with my mother," she smiled. "Our cottage is down the road. It is just past the small bridge on the left. It is the cottage with the noisy goat." He heard her laugh, and he laughed too.

Jario felt his hands begin to tingle. He had never felt anything like that before. He looked down at his hands, and it drew her attention to the same.

"Are you ill?" she asked.

"No, I gathered a plant for an old woman, and I fear that I must have touched it with my bare hands," he said, as his voice began to quiver. "It was poisonous."

"Are you in need of help?" she said, as she touched his arm. "My mother may be able to help you. She was taught some healing by a dear friend."

"I will be fine," he said, as he looked for an escape. "I need to go wash my hands."

"May I come with you?" Laralynn asked.

"No, you need to stay with your mother," Jario said, as he began to feel his eyes blur. "I must go. If you will be here tomorrow, I will meet you here."

"Are you sure?" she asked. "Are you sure you will be fine."

"Yes," Jario shouted, as he ran from the crowd.

Laralynn stood watching him leave. She looked over at her mother and then ran after him. Reaching the trees that lined the path to their cottage, she realized she had lost him and sadly turned to head back to her mother and her friends.

I met a boy, she thought, as she hurried back to tell her friends. I met a boy.

Chapter 20

Laralynn followed her mother down the dirt road toward their cottage. It had been a long day, but all she could think about was the boy she had met at the festival. He was just the right height and had the darkest brown eyes she had ever seen. If a person could fall in love at first sight, she felt she had done it. Reaching the gate of their cottage, she wasn't ready to go inside.

"May I go to the pond," Laralynn asked. "I won't stay long, and I promise to be careful. Today was an exciting day, and I want to relax by the cool water. Who knows, I might find a fairy."

"You may," her mother laughed. "It will be dark soon. Be home before dark."

Nodding her head, Laralynn dashed toward the worn path to the pond. Stopping to pick flowers along the way, she found herself daydreaming of the boy she had seen at the festival. Reaching the pond, she sat down on a smooth rock and removed her slippers. She walked barefoot along the edge of the pond and watched the dragonflies lightly kiss the smooth water. As they flew away, she noticed they left beautiful water rings rippling across the pond.

Just as she was ready to step into the water and cool her feet, she heard the sound of crushing pine needles off in the distance. Quickly running back to retrieve her slippers, she stopped when she saw the boy she had met at the festival step from the shadows.

"Did I frighten you?" Jario asked. "I am sorry, if I did."

"A little," Laralynn replied, as she took a deep breath to calm the flutter of her heart. "I thought it might have been a wolf. They say there are wolves that roam this island."

"Have you seen them?" he asked, as his mind drifted back to the white wolf for a moment.

"No," she said, feeling foolish. "My mother always warns me to be careful. I thought it was because of the wolves."

"Let's not think about wolves," Jario replied. "They scare me too."

Jario stepped closer to the pond and then jumped to a stone that was covered in damp moss surrounded by water. Looking up at Laralynn, he saw her cover her mouth as she gasped when he started to slip from the stone. Raising his arms, he madly waved them to regain his balance before he quickly stepped from stone to stone toward the pond's edge. Jumping from the last stone to the safety of the firm ground that surrounded the pond, he laughed as he bent over with his hands upon his knees.

"You are mad," Laralynn said. "You could have fallen."

He looked over at her bare feet and noticed the tiny red mark upon her ankle. He remembered seeing it at the competition and smiled.

"That was fun," Jario grinned, as he straightened and turned to face her.

"How are your hands?" Laralynn asked, trying not to appear flustered as she looked to see if his hands were red and swollen.

"They are much better. Thankfully, the stinging has stopped," Jario replied, as he lifted his hands for her to see. "I washed my hands in the cool water of the pond, and they feel much better. I must have accidently touched the poison leaves of the plant. I should have been more careful."

"Come sit by me," Laralynn shyly asked, as she sat down on a smooth stone and patted the stone next to hers. "I cannot stay out very long. I must go home before it gets dark, but I want you to tell me about yourself."

Jario made his way to the rocks and grinned as he sat down next to her, "I cannot stay long, either. I have to deliver the plants, but I can see you tomorrow."

"I would like that," she replied. "Will you be going to the festival? It is the last day. I heard that jugglers will be there."

"I'm not sure if I can attend until later in the day. I must work tomorrow," he said, as he watched her smile fade. "I can come once the sun starts to set. I could meet you here after the festival. This could be our secret place."

Laralynn's face brightened and she nodded. She felt her cheeks flush after hearing him speak of their secret place.

"I will look for you at the festival," she said. "If you are not there, I will meet you here when the sun starts to set."

"Until tomorrow," Jario said, as he stood and gave Laralynn a quick bow.

"Until tomorrow," Laralynn returned his bow with a curtsy.

Picking up her slippers, she turned to leave the pond. Hearing him walking toward the forest, she turned and shouted, "Jack, how old are you?"

"I am seventeen," Jario replied. "How old are you?"

"In three moons, I will be sixteen," Laralynn replied.

"We shall have to plan something special for your birthday," Jario said.

Feeling her stomach flutter, Laralynn shouted, "I am glad I met you."

Jario turned to face her and waved, "I am glad that I met you, Laralynn. More than you know."

* * *

Back among the shade of the Evergreen Forest, Baxter let go of Tate's hand. Feeling Elda yank her hand away from him, he headed toward the horses. They had found nothing that indicated that either Jario or Lady Lara were in Primrose Pond. There were a number of women and young girls at the festival, but the recognition they had hoped to see in someone's eyes was never noticed by any of them. Disappointed with the outcome, Tate clutched Gavenia's hand and pulled her into his arms. He kissed her forehead and tried to let her comfort take away his sadness.

"I saw you looking at the young girls," Elda taunted Baxter. "Did you find yourself a possible mate among the girls at the festival?"

"I wasn't looking for me," Baxter grinned, as he nudged her shoulder. "I was looking for your mate. Are men afraid of you? Is that why we never see them around you?"

"I will never take a mate until I can find one that is able to wield a sword better than me," Elda smirked.

"You might be left alone if you wait for that to happen," Baxter replied.

"She will find someone," Gavenia offered. "One day, he will sweep her off her horse, and she will fall instantly in love with him." She looked up at Tate and then pressed her face against his chest. "Just like I love you."

"Here," Baxter handed the reins of his horse to Elda. "Quick, mount my horse. Your mate might be somewhere in the forest. He is waiting to sweep you off your horse."

Elda jabbed Baxter in the stomach with her fist and quickly wrapped her arm around his neck. Gavenia began to giggle until she saw the sadness return to Tate's eyes.

"We need to get back to the castle," Tate grumbled. "I want to check on my brother."

Tate mounted Twiggs and pulled Gavenia up to sit behind him. Not waiting for Elda and Baxter to finish wrestling, he headed for the stable.

* * *

Jario stood in the forest looking for Velsa's cottage. It was long past sunset, and he was beginning to get angry. He had removed his tunic and carefully wrapped it around the pouch to keep his hands from touching the poison. He knew she could always feel his presence, and he was sure she knew that he was looking for her cottage.

"Velsa, I have your precious poison weed," Jario shouted, into the darkness. "I am tired of your game. You asked me to bring this to you, remember? I will leave the pouch here by this tree. If you desire to have it, you can come retrieve it when you are ready."

Instantly Velsa's cottage came into view. Cursing the witch under his breath, he stomped toward the cottage door. Raising his fist, he pounded on the door until it slowly opened. Stepping inside, Jario looked about the room for the witch.

"I see you are the pretty witch this evening," Jario smirked. "What name do you take when you are the pretty witch and visit Lady Lara?"

"I use my name," Velsa replied, as she squinted her eyes to glare at him.

Catching a delicate scent floating upon the night air, she raised her chin and inhaled the sweet fragrance. She knew immediately where he had been.

"You have seen the child. I smell her scent upon you," she said, as she accusingly pointed her finger at Jario.

Pressing her lips tightly together, she let sparks fly from her fingers. Jario quickly leaned out of the way of the sparks flying past his head.

"For your wellbeing, I advise you to stay away from the child," she shouted.

"I have seen her, and we have spoken," Jario replied, as he took a few steps backward toward the door. "It was a simple conversation. Does this worry you?"

"It should worry you," Velsa barked, as she stood from her chair. "If you harm her, I will bind you to the hollow of the tree next to my cottage. I might let the squirrels hide their nuts in your ears or wherever they can find a place to hide them."

"Why Velsa, you have become attached to the child," Jario sneered. "Have you a plan to do away with Lady Lara. Are you planning on taking the child?"

"Don't be foolish," Velsa grunted. "I have no need for a child. I have no room for a child."

"You could easily make your cottage larger," Jario said, as he walked toward the cot and sat down on the tattered fabric. "You are up to something."

"Enough about the child and Lady Lara," Velsa cursed. "Give me the plant."

Jario handed the pouch wrapped in his tunic to Velsa. She carefully unwrapped it and opened the pouch. Whispering a few words and spitting on the palms of her hands, she reached in and pulled out the plants. She smiled when she saw that he had brought her two plants.

"I hope this is enough to cancel the favor," Jario inquired.

"Yes, I was not expecting two plants," Velsa replied, as she laid the plants upon the wooden table. "This was kind of you. I will cancel the favor and an additional favor, because of this kindness." Hesitating for a moment, she stared at Jario. "I still expect to receive the tail of the white wolf. This bargain still stands. Don't forget that your payment is still outstanding, and don't make me wait too much longer. You know what I can do to you. I want the tail of that wolf."

Jario could see her face flush red with anger, and he lowered his eyes to the floor.

"I understand," Jario's shoulders hunched, and he kept looking at the floor of her cottage fearing to make eye contact. "It has been difficult to retrieve. I had her trapped in a pit, but a black wolf came to her aid. I was forced to leave her when Gautier approached. I will complete the bargain. Be patient, if you can."

Velsa began to study her plants and waved Jario toward the door without looking at him.

"We are finished," Velsa barked. "You may leave."

Jario stood and took a step toward the door. Turning he started to speak but changed his mind.

"Good evening," Velsa cooed, as she began to wring her hands. "I hope the next time I see you it will be when a wolf tail hangs over the palm of your hand."

He felt his body being drawn to the door. As the door opened, he was pushed out into the night air. The door slammed, and the cottage vanished. Jario stood in the darkness smiling. He had managed to cancel two favors. Relieved, he hurried toward Ash. As he made his way toward the abandoned cottage, he began thinking about Laralynn. He needed rest. He had plans for tomorrow evening.

* * *

The sun was beginning to set, and Gautier stood at the gate waiting for Killian's wolf with his white wolf by his side. Feeling uncomfortable about changing in front of Lord Gautier and Lady Kayleigh, Killian had gone to the privacy of the barracks to change into his wolf. As he exited the open door, he could feel how anxious the white wolf was to run. Their runs had become more frequent, and he had noticed that she was spending less time in her human form. She had told him of the *Binding Spell* that had kept her separated from her wolf, and he figured she was afraid they would be separated from each other again.

As he approached the white wolf's side, Killian's wolf sat and waited for orders from Gautier. The orders were always the same.

"Take good care of my wolf," Lord Gautier ordered. "If you find trouble, speak to my mind. I will hear you."

"We are wolves," Killian heard Lady Kayleigh speak into Lord Gautier's mind. "Do not worry. We do not fear the creatures in the forest. They fear us."

"I fear the pits that are dug in the forest," Lord Gautier replied. "I fear who digs the pits to catch you and what they will do to you if they catch you."

Lord Gautier knelt down and ran his fingers through her white fur. In return, she licked his hand and nuzzled his face. Seeing him stand, the white wolf didn't wait another moment and raced toward the forest. Not wanting to be outdone, Killian raced after her to the sounds of Lord Gautier shouting.

"Enjoy your run," Gautier shouted. "Be safe."

As Gautier turned toward the castle to return to the comfort of his bedchamber and wait for Kayleigh, a faint glimmer appeared before him. As the glimmer faded, a woman stood with her back to him. With a deep sigh, Desirae turned to face Gautier.

"I wondered when you would arrive," Gautier smirked, as he crossed his arms over his chest. "I have felt your arrival in the wind."

"And you did not come to greet me," she replied, as she looked about the castle grounds."

"You have taken up residence at the Crimson Claw Castle with someone that has been banished from my castle," Gautier barked. "He would not entertain a visit from me."

"I see there is bad blood between the two of you," Desirae laughed. "I am not here to mend your disagreement."

"What brings you to Black Thistle?" asked Gautier. "If not for Jario, for what?"

"I wish to speak to you about Velsa's death," she whispered, so that no one else would hear her.

"The witch still lives," Gautier stated. "I would know if the witch had passed on to the Otherworld."

"That is true, she still lives," Desirae frowned. "I have come to ask you to help me kill the witch. She killed my sister, Derora, during the War of the Witches. I am here to avenge my sister's death."

"Come inside, we will talk more of your interesting request," Gautier said, as he offered his arm to Desirae and led her slowly toward the castle. "Derora was my ally during the war. Unfortunately, we both received Velsa's wrath. Derora worst of all."

* * *

Thomas sat in the courtyard looking up at the light in the tower. Sadly, the light was his only connection to Lara. Hearing the door open and then close, he assumed it was Charlotte bringing him his nightly goblet of blood. The sound of boots filled his ears instead of the soft sound of slippers that greeted him every evening. Recognizing his scent, he knew he was receiving a visit from his brother.

"What brings you to my courtyard? Do you have news?" Thomas asked, as he gave his brother a nervous smile and waited for bad news.

"There is talk of a new witch on the island," Tate replied, knowing this was not the news Thomas was seeking. "She is staying at the Crimson Claw Castle."

"Another witch," Thomas muttered, as he closed his eyes. "It cannot be a good sign if she is taking shelter from Jario."

"It is the witch Desirae. It is rumored that Velsa murdered her sister, Derora, during the War of the Witches," Tate replied. "She is probably here to seek some kind of revenge on the old hag."

"Seeing the hag fall by Desirae's hand would give me great comfort," Thomas laughed. "I would enjoy her falling by anyone's hand, after what she has done to me and others."

"There are several among the island that would appreciate the death of Velsa," Tate said, as he sat down on the stone wall of the fountain. "Me being one of them."

Thomas looked up at the stars and closed his eyes wishing he had not done so. Shaking his head, he struggled to dismiss the stars she loved so much.

"Do the stars haunt you?" asked Tate.

Looking back at Tate, he studied his brother face and ignored his question.

"Were you searching for Lara today?" asked Thomas, as he waited for his brother to confirm his suspicions.

"Yes, we made a visit to Primrose Pond," Tate replied. "How did you know?"

"I went to the Command Center looking for you. I asked Preston where you were patrolling. You know that Preston would not lie to me. He told me you were not on patrol," Thomas said, as he watched Tate's eyes close. "I am correct in assuming that you found nothing."

"Brother, I am sorry that I disobeyed your order," Tate replied. "We did not find her. Gavenia's hawk tried to visit Jario at his castle hoping to hear information about Lara. Instead of Jario, she found the witch, Desirae. She told her hawk that Jario had gone to Primrose Pond to find a hidden lady. We assumed it was Lara. We went there to see if we could find her. If she is there, she is well hidden."

"She will stay hidden until she is ready to be found," Thomas barked. "Stop searching for her. The disappointment in not finding her is tearing me apart. I cannot sleep without dreaming of her running from me."

"Don't give up on her," Tate begged. "She didn't give up on you when Magna took you to her dungeon. She would have gone alone to fight her sister if we had not gone with her."

"This is different. She does not want to be found. She left me," Thomas angrily shouted.

"There must be a good reason, Thomas. She loves you. We all know that she truly loves you. If it is true that you have a child, she must have left to protect your child. A mother would do anything to protect her child," explained Tate.

"She left because she didn't think that I could protect her," Thomas whispered. "She had no faith in me."

"Stop blaming yourself," Tate barked. "Get out there and search for her. She would never give up searching for you. You know deep within your soul that is true. Stop making excuses. Did your vows mean nothing? Stop looking for everyone's pity and do something. Anything!"

Tired of listening to his brother's excuses, Tate stormed away from his brother and left Thomas alone in the courtyard.

Chapter 21

Laralynn sat at the table with her face resting against the palm of her hand. She had been staring at the beams of colored light that spilled through the small window above the door. Blinking her eyes, she realized that her mother had been looking at her.

"Laralynn, eat your eggs," her mother gently ordered, as she nodded toward her untouched meal. "It will be another long day. You need more than apples and figs to satisfy your hunger."

Laralynn poked her bread into the soft golden orbs of her eggs and twirled it around until the bread was saturated. Biting into the soft bread, she smiled back at her mother's watchful eyes.

"What shall we do for my birthday?" asked Laralynn. "It will be here soon. Aslev told me she had a very special gift for me."

Lara felt her heart still for a moment. The reminder of the coming deadline made her hands start to tremble. Seeing this, Laralynn quickly moved around the table to sit by her mother. She stroked her mother's hair and leaned her face against her arm.

"What worries you," Laralynn asked, as she continued to stroke her mother's hair. "Is it my birthday that worries you?"

"You will no longer be a child," Lara responded, kissing the top of Laralynn's head. "The time has passed so quickly. One moment you were my sweet baby girl and now you are all grown, ready to face the world."

"I will always be your baby girl," Laralynn said, as she lifted her mother's chin to look into her eyes. Seeing tears upon her face,

Laralynn kissed her mother's cheeks and wrapped her arms around her. "I love you, mother."

"I love you, Laralynn," Lara cooed. "Remember that I have always loved you."

"Enough melancholy, let's go to the festival," Laralynn said, as she quickly stood and started to clear the plates from the table. "Nollie told me that jugglers will be there today. This I have to see."

Lara gave her daughter a smile and hid the sadness she carried in her heart. She knew she needed to tell her daughter what was about to happen, but she couldn't bring herself to do it. She didn't want to see the tears in her eyes when she told her that she would never see her again.

* * *

Kayleigh was busy going through the books that had been found in the chamber behind the hidden door where Gautier had been bound. She had decided to remove the scrolls and books from the dark chamber and move them to the library. The morning light offered a better place to read, study, and determine their meaning. She knew there were others within the castle that would enjoy the poetry, drawings, and maps of distant lands and wanted to make them available. Three large crates sat on the floor next to the table and three more crates were waiting to be brought to the library.

Killian stood at his usual post outside the library door when he heard Alicia's soft footsteps approaching. With his hand on the hilt of his dagger, he stepped to see that she was alone and stepped back to allow her to pass. The same strange feeling that had made the hairs on the back of his neck stand on end had returned. He watched her walk through the door toward Lady Kayleigh. She seemed to glide across the stone floor. It was a soft stride that resembled the stalking of an animal. He worried that she might try to harm her. Concerned for his mistress, he moved closer to allow for a clear view of Lady Kayleigh.

When Alicia entered the library, she could see that Lady Kayleigh had already started working. She had hoped to arrive early enough to be hard at work before her mistress arrived. Picking up a book from the overflowing crate, she sat down and laid the book on the table.

"Alicia, Lord Gautier had a visitor yesterday that will join us later this morning," Kayleigh announced. She spoke loud enough so that Killian would hear her. "Her name is Desirae. She is a witch that practices white magic. She has asked to see our library, and Gautier has given his permission. Her sister, Derora, and Gautier were friends before she passed on to the Otherworld."

"I have found some books that she might be interested in reading," Alicia replied. "There are words written in the margins that are not familiar to me, but appear to be words for spells or chants. I will set them out for her."

Alicia busied herself with retrieving the books she had mentioned and arranged them on the far end of the table. Just as she had finished, she heard Killian's voice as he ordered someone to stop. Kayleigh made her way out into the hallway and returned leading Desirae into the library. Desirae looked at the stacks of books and smiled at Kayleigh.

"You have quite a collection," Desirae said, as she scanned the spines of the books.

Seeing Alicia, she walked toward her and reached for her hand.

"My name is Desirae," she said, as cold air began to circle their hands. She looked up into Alicia's eyes and then over at Kayleigh. "We have a very young shifter in our presence. So young, I am afraid that she doesn't realize it yet. Send for her mother, she needs to be told at once. This young woman is a wolf."

* * *

Thomas lifted his body from the cot that he had brought into their bedchamber for sleeping. His body ached from the thin mattress that gave him no comfort and allowed him very little sleep. He still couldn't bring himself to sleep in their bed. Just looking at their bed had made him yearn for his mate. Sleeping without her in their bed was accepting that she would never return.

This morning he didn't complain about his stiff muscles. His pain had been his reward for his behavior. He had stayed awake most of the night thinking long and hard about all the things Tate had said to him the prior evening. Tate was right. He had been making excuses and blaming Lara. He had been punishing himself instead of searching for Lara. He needed her back in his arms, and that meant, he had to search for her.

Determined to start again, he looked about for his breeches. As he picked them up from the floor where he had dropped them, he was greeted by McDuff as he entered the chamber.

"My Lord, I have brought you clean clothes," he grinned, as he walked toward the bed and spread them out upon the soft linen. "I have asked Tolin to ready your horse. It is good to have you back again, My Lord. We know you will find her and bring her home." McDuff headed toward the bath chamber, and as he did, he called to Thomas, "My Lord, let's get you ready."

Thomas followed McDuff without hesitation to the bath chamber. He was anxious to find Lara, and to do that, he knew he had to keep searching until he found her.

Dressed and feeling a new sense of resolve, he strode through the hallways and then through the Command Center without noticing the many mouths that dropped as he passed. Descending the steps two at a time, he made his way to the stable to retrieve his horse. As he opened the stable door, he was greeted by Tate and Baxter. They each held the reins to their horses and were quick to mount them as Tolin handed Thomas the reins to his black stallion, Midnight.

"We thought you would never get here," Baxter shouted.

"Brother, it is good to see you," Tate grinned. "Where do you want to start?"

"We will head for Woods Bay and work our way back to Evergreen," Thomas ordered. "We must be sure to search the mountain near Fallon Castle, as well. If we find nothing, we will search it all again until we find her."

Thomas nudged Midnight and headed through the open door of the stable.

"She is out there," Tate shouted, as he followed behind his brother. "We will find her and your child. We will bring them both home."

* * *

Laralynn had spent the day at the festival with her friends, Nollie and Lettie, but she had never stopped thinking about Jack. She had kept Jack a secret from her mother, but she had foolishly told Nollie about meeting him by the pond. As a result, Nollie had teased her all day about being in love with him.

It was finally time to return to their cottage, and Laralynn was glad to see that her mother no longer seemed sad. She held her mother's hand as they made the long walk back to their cottage and sang all the songs her mother had taught her.

Pushing the gate open for her mother, she looked over her shoulder at the path that led to the pond. The sun was still too high in the sky to meet Jack. She would have to wait until the sun began to set before she could go to meet him. Leaving her mother at the door, she went to the garden to pull carrots and onions for their evening meal. Finding a cabbage ready to be harvested, she carried the vegetables into the cottage and laid them on the table.

"After our meal, I would like to go to the pond," Laralynn said. "May I go?"

"It will be close to dark. Can't you wait until tomorrow when the sun is out?" her mother asked.

"I like to watch the dragonflies dance across the pond just before the sun sets," Laralynn replied. "They kiss the water and make beautiful rings that float across the pond."

"You may go but do not stay long," her mother warned.

Relieved that she would be able to see Jack, she helped her mother prepare their evening meal. They talked about all they had seen at the festival and how much they enjoyed the music. Once they had finished their meal and the dishes were washed and put away, Laralynn was anxious to make her way to see Jack.

"I am going to the pond," Laralynn called to her mother from the door. "I won't be long."

"Be careful," her mother replied.

Pulling her shawl from the wooden peg by the door, she threw it around her shoulders and left the cottage in hopes of seeing Jack. She felt her heart flutter as she hurried along the dirt path. Stepping around a clump of small evergreens, she saw him sitting on a moss covered log by the pond. Feeling a warm flush in her face, she pulled the shawl from her shoulders as she walked toward him. He stood as she approached and took hold of her hand to help her sit.

"I hoped you would be able to meet me," Jack said. "I am glad you are here."

"Me too," she replied.

Chapter 22

Velsa clutched the book of spells tightly against her breast as she paced back and forth. Catching her boot against the leg of the table, she stumbled and saw lights flash behind her eyes. Frantic for relief, she tried to focus on healing the painful sporadic intrusions. Carefully setting the heavy leather book down upon a piece of worn black velvet, she lifted her hands and pressed her fingers to her forehead. She had felt the strange throbbing pain when she woke and had not been able to dislodge it from her head.

As she felt the pain start to subside, she opened her book of spells and turned the brittle pages hunting for the perfect spell. She needed to counter the spell that had been cast upon her and push it back against the one that had delivered it. Unfortunately, she had not been able to discover the creator's signature. The frequent pain had not allowed her time enough to concentrate on the path from which it had come. Feeling the pain returning with a vengeance, Velsa grabbed onto the edge of the table and tried to force it away. Blood began to run from her nose, and she collapsed to the floor. She tried to lift her head but the agonizing pain allowed the darkness to consume her.

Not knowing how long she had been unconscious, she crawled to the bundles that were stacked against the wall. Balgair had brought her many important items, and she knew exactly what she needed. Opening one bundle after another, she finally found the precious item wrapped in a piece of linen. Forcing herself to stand, she leaned against the wall until the room stopped spinning. Grasping the stone within the palm of her hand, she closed her eyes and began to chant.

Stone of amber heal my pain;
Send it back to where it came.
Stone of amber block the path;
Keep it closed never to pass.

Velsa felt the spell vanish and slip away to find its creator. She had anticipated an attack from Desirae, but the spell of pain lacked creativity. Velsa knew of Desirae's talents and could feel her strong power upon the wind. When she was ready, she would unleash a spell that would light up the sky, and she would deliver it in person. This spell was an annoyance. A very painful annoyance, but an annoyance none the same. Someone was testing or practicing their powers, and she needed to find out who.

Feeling the pain slowly leave, Velsa swallowed the small amber stone and set to work to protect her cottage and herself from further attacks. She had no time for these interruptions. She had a spell of her own to create. A spell that required her undivided attention. One wrong phrase or word from her lips and she would cast herself into oblivion.

* * *

Laralynn ran to the pond. She couldn't wait to see Jack again. Her mother had kept her busy after their evening meal, and she was afraid that he would have thought she wasn't coming to meet him. Hearing the sounds of stones skipping across the pond, she sighed with relief. Knowing he was there, she still didn't relax until she saw him leaning against a tree.

"Jack, you waited for me," Laralynn shouted. "I thought you would have given up on me."

"I knew you would come," Jack laughed.

Laralynn ran toward him and threw her arms around his waist. Pressing her face to his chest, she whispered, "I missed you."

"I missed you too," Jack replied. "I cannot wait until you are sixteen."

"Why?" asked Laralynn.

"You will be old enough to wed," Jack said, as he pulled her away so that he could look into her eyes. He started to speak and paused for a moment. Changing his mind, he pushed his gift of compulsion away.

"Wed?" she said, as she swallowed nervously.

"Yes, wed." Jack replied. "There is something that I have not told you. I am the son of the Lord of Crimson Claw Castle."

"What?" Laralynn said, as she pushed away from him and stepped back to allow more space between them. "You lied to me? Why would you lie to me?"

Jack closed his eyes trying to think of something to say. He had hoped that she would have had a much different reaction.

"I did not want you to like me because of my wealth," Jack said, trying to sound convincing. "I wanted you to like me."

"I don't understand," Laralynn said, as she stepped further away from him.

"I love you, Laralynn," Jack lied. "I want you to come live with me at the castle."

"You love me?" she stuttered. Looking at him and then the ground, her knees buckled, and she slowly plopped down on the ground. "You love me?" she repeated.

"Yes, is that so hard to believe," Jack said. "I think I fell in love with you the moment I first saw you."

Laralynn closed her eyes and brought her hands up to cover her face. She could feel her skin flush. She wanted to believe him, but it had happened too fast. Her mother had told her about falling in love with her father. Her mother had felt heat race through her body when he touched her. She felt nothing like that from Jack.

"I need to think on this," Laralynn replied. "Give me some time."

"I will leave you to think about us," Jack said. "I will return the evening of your sixteenth birthday to ask your mother for your hand. If you decide you love me, I will bring you and your mother to my father's castle to live. I will take care of you. I will not bother you until then."

"Please don't be angry with me," Laralynn begged. "I thought this day would come but not so soon. I thought it would be more romantic."

"I am not angry, and I don't want you to be angry with me," Jack assured her. "I should have knelt and asked you to wed. Forgive me. Romance is new to me. You are my first love." He looked at her face to see if she understood. "I am use to giving orders and watching people obey me. I handled this badly." Frustrated, Jack bent down, picked up a rock, and threw it across the pond. "I have ruined this. I am sorry." Grasping his hands behind his back, he closed his eyes to calm the temper that wanted to escape. "I will give you the time you require to determine your feelings for me. Until then, I will patiently wait until you are sixteen."

Laralynn stood quietly listening to his excuses and apologies. Once he had finished speaking, she moved toward him. She saw him step back away from her and her heart began to ache.

"Goodnight," Jack said, as he turned to leave. "Be assured, I will come for you."

Laralynn felt her eyes fill with tears. Wiping the tears from her eyes, she saw that he was gone. He had left her alone. Sitting back down, Laralynn cried until there were no more tears. Feeling warm hands take her shoulders, she looked up to see her mother kneeling down next to her.

"Mother, I think I am in love," Laralynn said, as she leaned against her mother.

"I thought there might be a boy involved with your numerous trips to the pond," her mother cooed, as she kissed the top of Laralynn's head. "You will know when it is love, my dear. It will warm your soul. You will feel his love race through your body as it mingles with your own. Wait for that feeling. Don't accept anything less."

* * *

Killian had stood guard outside of Alicia's bedchamber every night since Desirae had discovered she was a wolf shifter. He had heard her cry every time Lady Kayleigh and Desirae had left her chamber. The sadness that spilled from her chamber was overwhelming. He knew she was confused. He knew exactly how she felt. He had been confused when his father had told him that he was a wolf shifter.

Seeing the door open and Lady Kayleigh move into the hallway, Killian was surprised to see Alicia step into the hallway after her. She kept her eyes to the stone floor, but he could see that her eyes were red and swollen.

"We are going to the library," Kayleigh announced. "We still have a great amount of work to do. Alicia has decided it will keep her mind off her wolf if she stays busy."

Killian nodded and stepped back to allow them to pass. He followed close behind them until they reached the library. Taking up his usual post at the door, he stood watching Alicia. Killian suddenly realized he had recognized her wolf the first day they had met. Her wolf had tried to contact his wolf the only way she knew how. The hairs on his neck, the shiver he felt, her voice, and her walk, they were all signs that her wolf was trying to reach out to him. Killian had heard Alicia's mother tell Desirae that she had turned eighteen shortly after arriving at the castle. That meant she would shift with the next full moon.

"I will take care of you," Killian softly whispered, as he tried to reach her wolf.

Alicia lifted her hand and touched her forehead with her fingers.

"Pardon?" Alicia said, as she looked toward Lady Kayleigh and saw that she was facing away from her. "Did you say something?"

"No, my dear," Kayleigh responded.

"Her wolf heard me," Killian quietly whispered.

Knowing he would have someone his own age to share this strange and wonderful circumstance with made him extremely happy. He wouldn't be alone anymore.

* * *

Thomas, Tate and Baxter had finally reached the far side of the island and looked about Woods Village. It was a bustling village with two tall ships anchored in its harbor as men unloaded its precious cargo. Scanning the ships for any sign of Lara, he saw only a few men that were busy preparing the ships for their next journey, and the wagons full of timber that sat nearby.

Spying the tavern that conveniently faced the dock, they tethered their horses and made their way to the door. They were all greeted by the smell of fish stew as they entered the tavern and eagerly stepped forward. Baxter eyed the men that sat with loaves of bread and wooden bowls full of the mouthwatering delight. The growling of his stomach told him he was more than anxious for a bowl for himself. As he licked his lips, he looked about for a table. Finding an empty table near the back, they took their seats and signaled for the tall man behind the bar to come to their table.

Tossing the cloth he had used to wipe the bar over his shoulder, he walked over to meet the men. He knew they weren't from the village and wondered why they were in his tavern.

"You are new around here. I'm Wade, and I own this place. What can I do for you?" he asked.

"We would all like some of that fish stew, a mug of ale, three rooms, and some questions answered," Thomas replied. "We are here from Evergreen Castle, and we are looking for Lady Lara. She stands a bit below your shoulder and has long strawberry hair. We fear she may have been taken and kept hidden by someone."

"I see a lot of folks pass through this village. Some are leaving this island and some are coming to stay," he said. "I haven't seen anyone as fine as a lady. If anyone knows of your lady it would be the widow. The Widow Maier owns the market. She sees all the women of Woods Village and hears all the gossip. She is sure to tell you all the latest news and the latest gossip. If your Lady is here in Woods Village, she is sure to know."

"You have been very helpful," Thomas replied. "We'll take the stew when you are ready."

Wade nodded to the men and headed back to the bar. Setting three mugs upon the polished timber, he turned and walked through the door to the kitchen.

"I'll go visit the Widow Maier and see what I can find out," Baxter said, as he stood from the table. Seeing Wade coming back with a tray full of bowls, he quickly changed his mind and sat back down. "I'll see her after we eat. It would be impolite to pass up a bowl of hot fish stew."

Chapter 23

Jario stood on his balcony looking out over the reflection of the full moon against the river below the castle. Oddly enough, his thoughts were on Lady Lara's child instead of Lady Lara. His plan had always been to retrieve her for his own mate and become the Lord of Evergreen Castle. Now that he had his own castle, his only thought of Evergreen was its destruction.

After hearing of her child, he had thought to use the child against Lady Lara. It would have been a simple matter of threatening her with the child's turning. A mother would do anything to protect her child, and Lady Lara would be no different. He needed a new plan. A plan that involved bringing both her and her daughter to Crimson Claw Castle. With the passing of the current full moon, he would have two moons to plan for his visit to their cottage and their return to his castle. Two moons were plenty of time to make a plan and prepare the castle for their arrival. He just had to decide which one would become his mate.

A soft rap at his door interrupted his thoughts of Lady Lara and drew him back into his chamber. As the door opened, he saw Claudia holding the door open to allow Desirae to enter.

"My Lord, Desirae has asked to see you," announced Claudia.

Jario nodded and straightened the cuff of his tunic as he watched Desirae glide effortlessly into his chamber. Feeling a bit of apprehension with her closeness, he stepped away from her and

146

leaned his elbow against the ornate wooden beam that hung above the lifeless hearth.

"I found your chamber empty and thought you had gone," Jario smirked. "I was told you have been gone from the castle for some time. Have you found accommodations more to your liking somewhere else?"

Desirae could feel Jario's unease and delighted in the way she made him flinch when she simply moved her hand. Walking toward the open balcony door, she stopped and sat down on the bench at the foot of Jario's bed. Crossing her leg over her knee, she straightened her skirt to cover all but the tip of her slipper.

"I made a visit to Black Thistle Castle," Desirae said, as she watched his face for his reaction. Seeing his jaw tighten, she knew she had struck a nerve. "I went to visit Gautier. He and my late sister were friends."

Hearing Gautier's name mentioned, Jario clenched his teeth and pursed his lips before he casually made his way to his chair and sat down. Anger started to seep into his mind, and he pushed it back trying to keep Desirae from noticing.

"How is the old warlock?" asked Jario. "Is he still being followed around the castle by his little wolf?"

"Lady Kayleigh," Desirae snapped, feeling resentment over his lack of respect for Gautier's mate. "I had gone through the books in your library and could not find what I needed. I remembered my sister telling me about the resources available in the library at Black Thistle Castle. I felt the need to visit it and see for myself."

"Do you find my library unworthy of your needs?" asked Jario.

"You must remember that the rumors of this castle are of lords and dragons," she replied. "I found many books documenting the history of the dragon that lived on the island, as well as, several books to assist me with my recent spells. I was looking for something specific. Sadly, I did not find it at Black Thistle, but I found something a little more interesting."

"The only thing I found interesting at that castle was the hidden chamber full of gold coins," Jario smirked. "Unfortunately, I read aloud from an old parchment that I found within the chamber. Uttering those worlds released Gautier and his wolf from a *Binding Spell* cast by Velsa. To my dismay, Gautier's appreciation for his release was short lived, and I found myself banished from the castle."

"My discovery was accidental, as well," Desirae laughed. "It seems Black Thistle is full of surprises. I discovered a young girl that should be shifting with the full moon for the first time this evening. Gautier will soon have a new wolf to add to the two wolves already taking up residence in his castle. The two new wolves are young, but they will learn a great deal from Lady Kayleigh."

Jario remembered the black wolf he had seen in the forest that stood guard over the pit that held the white wolf. He had disrupted his attempt to acquire the white wolf's tail.

If the wolf I saw is one of the new wolves living at Black Thistle, my assignment to retrieve the white wolf's tail has become even more difficult, he thought.

Desirae stood and moved toward Jario.

"I was going to have my evening meal in the garden tonight," she said. "Would you like to join me?"

Jario looked confused by her request. Before answering her, he stood and stepped around the back of his chair.

"I am not making advances toward you," she said, as she smiled trying to make him relax. "I want to know what you know about Velsa."

"Velsa?" asked Jario. "What of Velsa?"

"Yes, Velsa," Desirae replied. "I plan to drive her crazy before I kill her. I thought you might like to help me."

Jario's back straightened, and he became very curious to hear what Desirae had to say. Ridding himself of Velsa, his debts, and her demands of him would be of great interest to him. The task of retrieving the white wolf's tail would be eliminated. He would be free of her forever.

"You have captured my full attention," Jario chuckled. "By all means, let's have our evening meal in the garden. I find that our conversation might be very entertaining. That witch has delighted in driving me crazy for decades with her required payments for simple favors. I will get great pleasure in returning the favor."

* * *

Lord Gautier and Killian stood outside the Great Hall and guarded the door. Killian could hear Alicia crying as Lady Kayleigh tried to comfort her as she explained how her body would transform.

He knew the pain that she would suffer the first time she shifted. He had struggled through the pain, but he had learned to calm his fears during the transition. He had found that the fear enhanced the pain.

"Alicia," Kayleigh softly said, as she began to remove her linen sleeping gown. "Watch me shift. Do not be afraid of my wolf. She will not hurt you. You can see the full moon through the window. It is time for us to let our wolves free to run through the forest."

Lady Kayleigh knelt down and closed her eyes letting her wolf take over. Slowly she began to transform into her beautiful white wolf. Sitting before Alicia, she could see the fear in her eyes. Padding up next to her, she nuzzled Alicia's hand and felt her fingers brush against her soft fur.

Trembling, she followed her example. Alicia pulled her gown over her head and stood naked next to the white wolf. She knelt down and closed her eyes as Lady Kayleigh had shown her. Taking a deep breath, her bones began to move. Loud snapping and popping sounds filled her ears, and she began to cry out in pain as her body twisted and jerked uncontrollably. Alicia screamed for her mother until her voice disappeared. Pitiful howling replaced the screams within the Great Hall. Looking down at the floor, Alicia saw her front paws and padded backward.

"You are beautiful," Kayleigh's wolf softly said into Alicia's mind. "You are a beautiful gray wolf."

"I can hear you," Alicia replied. "How is this possible?"

"Our wolves can speak to one another in our minds," answered Kayleigh. "You will get used to it."

Yelping drew the wolf's attention to the door of the Great Hall.

"I am ready to run," Killian anxiously barged into their conversation. "The night is short enough. Let's go!"

Lord Gautier opened the door to the Great Hall and peered inside. Two beautiful wolves padded toward him.

"I see we have a new wolf among us," Gautier smiled, as he bent down to greet Alicia's gray wolf. "Enjoy your first run, but be very careful. There are dangers in the forest. Stay with Kayleigh and Killian. They will protect you."

Feeling her tongue upon his face, Gautier laughed and scratched behind her ears.

"Go," Gautier ordered, as he stood. "Enjoy your new freedom. I will sit with your mother to keep her from worrying. She will meet you upon your return."

Killian flicked his ears and watched as the white wolf headed toward the open door and out into the moonlight. Timidly, the gray wolf followed her. As Killian leaped through the open door and began to chase the female wolves, he could hear Lord Gautier's usual warnings of safety shouted after them. Letting his wolf take over, he raced after the two female wolves as they passed Commander Gustavo holding open the outside gate leading to the forest. Suddenly, his wolf's desire to make the gray wolf his own slammed into him, and he howled with all his might.

Chapter 24

Lara tossed and turned until she finally gave up trying to sleep. Sitting on the edge of her bed, she could see the bright light from the full moon shining on the floor by her feet, and she silently cursed its coming. She had always loved the moon, but the fullness of the glowing orb would soon bring death right to her door. Pulling the coverlet from her bed, she wrapped it around her shoulders and quietly walked into the main room of the cottage.

Standing alone in the darkness, her thoughts immediately went to Thomas. She had hoped she would see him one more time before Velsa took the beat of her heart. She had felt lucky to have seen Tate, Baxter and Elda at the festival and was disappointed that Thomas was not with them. She had determined it was probably for the best. The sheer sight of him would have been her undoing. She would have run into his arms, and he would have taken her home to Evergreen. There, he would have been left with the memory of watching her fade away as her heart slowly stopped beating.

Feeling the need to write in her journal, she opened the cabinet and lifted the lid of the chest. Retrieving her journal, she sat down at the table and lit a single candle. Dipping her quill into the ink, she began to write.

Dearest Thomas,

My one and only love, I am thinking of you this evening and hope that you are thinking of me. I looked up at the full moon tonight and fear it has brought tears to my eyes. For in two more moons, I will be forever gone. I will surrender my human heart beat as payment for a favor to Velsa. Do not be angry at her. I went to her willingly. She did not force me. It was I that requested her help, and she provided me a way to protect our daughter from the darkness that consumes Jario. Thomas, you have a lovely daughter. Laralynn is kind, a little mischievous, very adventurous, and best of all, loving. She has grown very close to Asher during our time here at Primrose Pond. Please allow their friendship to continue. She may need a familiar face to look upon. I find I must stop writing. My tears make it too difficult to see the page where I write. Please know that I miss your arms about me and your scent upon my pillow in the morning.

I love you Thomas, Your Lara

Lara placed the quill back in the wooden stand. As she closed the journal, she stroked the leather cover for a moment. Its surface had softened over the years of writing to her beloved Thomas. It seemed to pulse beneath her fingers with the love it held inside for him. She hoped he would be strong enough to read it one day. Wiping a tear from her face, she carefully wrapped the journal in the worn bit of lace and replaced it in the wooden chest for safekeeping.

Feeling the need to be close to Thomas, she opened the door and walked outside to stand under the stars.

"Are you looking up at the stars tonight, my love?" Lara whispered.

Looking up, she saw a shooting star race across the sky. Closing her eyes, she made a wish to be held once again in Thomas' arms.

"Mother?" Laralynn said, as she tiptoed outside to stand beside her mother. "Is something wrong? Why are you outside?"

"I did not mean to wake you. I could not sleep and wanted to look up at the stars," she replied, as she wrapped the coverlet around her daughter's shoulders. "I love to look up into the sky at night. The stars are one of my favorite things. They give me comfort."

"They are like tiny jewels sprinkled in the sky," Laralynn smiled, as she leaned her head on her mother's shoulder. "They are one of my favorite things too." Laralynn lifted her head and turned to look up at her mother's face. "Mother, you will always be my favorite. I love you more than the stars in the night's sky."

Lara wrapped her arms around her daughter and kissed her forehead.

"You are my very favorite too," Lara replied, as she felt the tears upon her face. "I love you to the stars and beyond."

* * *

The trip to Woods Village provided no insight to the whereabouts of Lady Lara. Between Tate, Baxter, and Thomas, they had visited every cottage, farm, shop, and tavern looking for her. They had even taken the time to search every stable and shed within the village and found nothing for their effort.

After hearing of Lord Thomas's presence in Woods Village and his desire to search the Wintergreen Mountains, Lord Fallon offered his help. He was sending a small unit of men from his army to escort them into the Wintergreen Mountains. They were to meet the men at the base of the mountains at a place called Rock Pile.

They all knew the mountains were difficult to climb and frequent rock slides lent much danger to anyone climbing alone. Many a poor soul had ventured into the mountains alone and never returned. Those that did return told stories of escaping from a mindless woman that roamed the caves. They spoke of seeing her feed upon the eyes of the lost to help her find what had been stolen from her.

Leaving the village behind, Thomas led Tate and Baxter through the dense forest that created a barrier between Fallon Castle and the mountains. As the sun began to set, they arrived at the base of the mountains to find Lord Fallon's men waiting for them. Seeing a large man walking toward him, Thomas dismounted his horse.

"Lord Thomas, I am called Hammer," he announced. "I will lead you and your men through the mountains to where there are known caves. This is the only area that would be suitable to hide from the many storms, wild animals, and from hunters."

"Send our appreciation to Lord Fallon upon your return," Thomas said, as he gripped Hammer's hand firmly. "I know these mountains are treacherous. We have long avoided this area, but I feel it is necessary to eliminate it from our search."

"What is that roaring sound?" asked Baxter.

"It is the waterfalls that flow from the mountains behind the castle," Hammer replied. "The many storms in the mountains feed the waterfalls and provide fresh water to the castle. You will eventually get use to the sound. Once the heavy rains stop, the sound begins to deaden."

"Don't you wish it would stop?" asked Baxter.

"Our fear is that the sound will stop, ending our water source," Hammer replied. "It is our only source of fresh water."

Baxter tried to ignore the thundering sound but could feel his head already starting to ache from the constant pounding. He could tell that Tate felt the same.

"Come sit by the fire," Hammer said. "Darkness will soon be upon us. We will make camp here for the night and start our climb early tomorrow morning. Ray managed to catch a few rabbits on the way here. He has skinned them and made them ready for the fire. You are welcome to join us."

"A good man at the tavern sent us off with a loaf of bread and some boiled eggs. We will share them with you," Thomas said.

"Save them for the climb. You never know what you will find on the mountain," Hammer replied. "Tether your horses and rest. It will be a long day tomorrow."

Thomas handed his reins to Tate and walked toward the group of men that sat around the fire. Sitting down upon the ground, he leaned back against a rock and looked up at the sky to see stars blinking back at him. A dark cloud was making its way across the sky, and he watched as it slowly covered the full moon.

"We may have some rain tonight. Dark clouds are covering the top of the mountain," Ray said, as he placed the rabbits over the fire. "Those clouds often fool us. Clouds often cover the mountains and then vanish as soon as they arrive. I fear they really aren't clouds, but unharnessed magic."

"I have had enough of magic," Thomas replied. "If magic is in these mountains, I suspect a witch is not far behind."

"For our sakes, I hope we don't find her, or the hermit that feeds on eyes," Ray stuttered. "I will keep my dagger at ready, and you should do the same."

Thomas knew that a dagger would be worthless against a witch. He had faced Velsa with his dagger, and she had vanished before his very eyes. He decided he would keep a good distance from the hermit, if they should meet. He had lost his sight by the magic of one old hag; he would not let another take it a second time.

Looking back up at the stars, he noticed a star shoot across the sky. Thinking of Lara's love of stars, he quickly wished to be able to hold Lara in his arms again. As he did, he felt a moment of comfort deep within his chest. He wasn't sure how, but he knew she had seen the same star and wished for the same thing.

Lara, I am going to find you and bring you home.

* * *

The wind was howling outside Velsa's cottage making the door rattle with every gust. She sat by the large pot of pigeon stew that hung in the hearth and listened to a strange sound that hovered over her cottage. The sound was not one found in nature, and she knew she was being harassed by another spell.

Velsa stood and made her way to the door. She pressed her hands against its surface and began to chant. Her hands were immediately pushed back, and the door burst open. The wind slowly calmed, and the strange sound turned into laughter. Velsa grabbed the door and slammed it closed.

"Show yourself," Velsa demanded. "Stop your silly games!"

Clenching her hands tightly at her side, she waited for a response. Complete silence was all she heard coming from the night's darkness.

"You are very foolish," she shouted. "It will take more than rattling doors to frighten me. Face me coward, and I will show you the power that is held within me."

The nuisance was gone. It had fled as fast as it had arrived.

Letting her temper fade, she returned to her meal that was boiling away over the fire. Ladling the fragrant stew into a wooden bowl, she sat down in her chair to enjoy her meal.

"Two more moons, two more moons," Velsa sang, as she waved her spoon in the air. "In two more moons, I will be one step closer to completing my spell. I will only need Jario to bring me the white wolf's tail. Her tail, her tail, her beautiful white tail."

Velsa kicked her slippers off and rested her feet upon an unopened bundle she had dragged in front of her chair. Closing her eyes, she envisioned the white wolf running about Black Thistle Castle looking for her tail. Velsa smiled and then burst into laughter.

Chapter 25

The faint morning light woke Thomas long before the others. He sat up and brushed his hands over his face as he wiped the sleep from his eyes. His dreams had been of Lara. They had always been of Lara, and they weren't the usual dreams of her beautiful face or the touch of her hand against his face. The dream he had was troubling. Lara was crying and needed his help. She was clutching her chest as a young girl knelt by her bed. Lara was dying. Shaking his head, he tried to clear the images from his mind. He knew it was a dream. Horrible things came to life in dreams, and this wasn't real. Trying to push the visions from his mind, he covered his face with his hands and pressed his fingers against his forehead.

"Brother?" asked Tate. "Are you unwell?"

"I had a nightmare," he replied. "I dreamt that Lara was dying."

"It was just a dream," Tate tried to reassure him. "We will find her. Elda would send a messenger with news if the light in the tower had gone out."

"Was it a nightmare, brother?" asked Thomas. "Or, was it a vision of the future? Was it a warning that I need to find her quickly?"

"Have you tried your gift of vision?" he asked.

"I have tried it every day, and it gives me the same result, nothing but darkness," Thomas replied. "This dream was different. It was vivid. I could hear the fear in the young girl's voice. She was crying. Do you think she was my daughter?"

"Gautier saw what he thought was a child," answered Tate. "Could this be magic? Could magic be helping you find Lara?"

"It seems only fair that magic should help me," Thomas smirked. "After all, magic took her from me."

"If magic is letting you see Lara and this young child, do you think magic is trying to tell you where you can find them?" questioned Tate. "You said she was in bed. There aren't beds in the caves of these mountains."

"What are you saying?" asked Thomas. "Are you saying we should forget about searching the mountains?"

"It seems like the dream may have been a warning," Tate suggested, as he noticed Baxter was sitting up listening to their conversation. "Baxter, what do you think we should do?"

"If we don't search the mountain and we never find Lara, Thomas will always wonder if she was hidden in the mountains," replied Baxter. "Tate, you go with your brother up the mountain. I will search Old Mill and Shepherd's Grove. I grew up near there. If I find her, I will speak into your mind to let you know."

"Baxter is right. I need to search the mountain for my own peace of mind," replied Thomas.

"After you are finished searching the mountains, I will meet you in Primrose Pond," Baxter said. "If she is dying, we need to hurry."

With a new plan before them, Baxter stood, rolled his blanket, and said his goodbyes to Thomas and Tate. Thomas watched him ride into the forest, and then readied himself for the climb.

"I see you are one man short this morning," Hammer stated.

"He has gone to search Old Mill and Shepard's Grove while we search the mountain," Thomas replied. "He grew up in that part of the island. I thought we could afford one less man."

Hammer nodded his head and pulled his bedroll over his shoulder. "Let's get moving," he shouted. "It is a slow climb, and it will be dark before we reach the caves. Be careful and mind where you step."

"He will take care of the horses," Ray pointed to a skinny young lad. "They will be here when you come back down."

Thomas gave the lad a nod and watched Tate throw his gear over his shoulder. Securing his own pack and weapons against his back, Thomas looked up at the dark cloud that was forming above the mountain.

"I hope we aren't in for trouble," Thomas said, as he pointed to the sky.

"If we wait for a day that brings a clear sky over the mountain, we will be old and gray," Hammer laughed. "Let's get moving."

Thomas fell in behind Hammer, the two other men, and Tate as they began to climb the gravel path to the caves. As the cloud darkened even more, Thomas' thoughts were on Lara, his child, and the nightmare.

* * *

"Mother, Aslev is here," Laralynn shouted. "She has brought us something."

Lara was wiping her wet hands upon her apron as she looked up to see Aslev and her daughter coming through the doorway. Aslev carried a large basket covered with a piece of linen.

"What is it?" squealed Laralynn. "What is in the basket?"

Aslev set the basket on the table and pulled the linen away to allow Laralynn to peer inside.

"It's a kitten, mother," Laralynn cooed, as she reached in and picked up the tiny black ball of fur. "Oh mother, it is so soft."

"It is for the rats," Aslev offered. "Of course, it has to get a little bigger before it will be much good, but I can guarantee that it will be a fierce rat hunter."

"Aslev, you should have asked me first," Lara sternly stated.

"I am sorry. It was to be a surprise birthday gift for Laralynn," Aslev said, as she stroked the fur of the kitten. "If I told you, it would not have been a surprise."

"Please? I will take care of it," Laralynn begged.

Lara looked at the kitten and then back at Aslev. Shaking her head, she realized that Aslev had meant no harm by bringing the kitten for her daughter. It might even be nice to see a few less rats around the cottage.

"Yes, you may keep the kitten," Lara announced. Seeing her daughter jump up and down with joy, she began to laugh. "What name will you give the little ball of fur?"

"I shall call him Hunter," Laralynn replied. "He will be the Great Rat Hunter."

"Take Hunter up to your loft. I don't want him wandering around under my feet," Lara ordered. "Remember, it is your responsibility to care for him."

"I will, mother," Laralynn replied, as she rushed to the ladder that led to her loft.

"Would you like some tea, Aslev," Lara asked, as she moved back toward the hearth. "I just put some water on to boil before you arrived."

"I would love some tea," Aslev replied.

She watched Lara pour the steaming water over the bundles of clover into the mugs. Swirling the wooden wand into the honey, she drizzled some of the thick sweetness into each mug. Handing a steaming mug to Aslev, Lara walked over to her chair and sat down.

"Aslev, please sit with me," requested Lara. "I have some things to speak to you about."

Aslev pulled the chair closer to Lara and sat down before she said, "Lara, what is bothering you? I can see the look of worry upon your face."

"I am worried about Laralynn. She has become acquainted with a boy, and she thinks that she has fallen in love," whispered Lara.

"A boy?" gasped Aslev. "Who is this boy?"

"I have not seen him. She has been sneaking off to see him at the pond," Lara softly said. "I fear it could mean trouble. If a boy must sneak to see my daughter, he must have something to hide."

"Have you spoken to Laralynn about this?" Aslev asked.

"I found her crying at the pond after the boy had left," she replied. "She told me she thinks she is in love. I know I am being over protective, but she is too young."

"It may be nothing," Aslev replied. "Do not worry yourself over it. Maybe the new kitten will distract her from the pond."

"Maybe," Lara replied. "There is something else." Lara paused to sip her tea and gain enough courage to tell Aslev her secret. "I have not been feeling well."

"You are unwell?" Aslev asked, as she sat her mug upon the small table between them and reached for Lara's hand.

"If something should happen to me, will you see that Laralynn is taken to her father?" asked Lara. "He is far from here, and I have not seen him for some time. I have written all of my wishes within my journal that is stored in a chest within the cabinet by the hearth. If anything should happen to me, it is to be given to Laralynn."

"I will," Aslev replied, as she gently patted Lara's hand. "You will be fine. You just need rest. You work too hard."

Lara smiled, "You are probably right, but I still worry about what would happen to Laralynn if something happened to me. Aslev, promise me that you will make sure that no harm comes to my daughter."

"I promise," Aslev replied. "I will not allow any harm to come to her. I will protect her." Hearing the strain in Lara's voice, she knew it was time to leave. "I should be going home. You need your rest. I will see myself out."

Aslev walked to the door. As she opened it, she looked up to see Laralynn leaning over the floor of the loft.

"Good night Aslev," she whispered. "Thank you for the kitten. Come back soon."

"You are welcome, my dear," Aslev replied. "I will come back very soon."

Aslev made her way out the door and walked toward the path to the woods. Once she was far enough away from the cottage, she vanished.

Reappearing in her own cottage, she slammed her hand down upon her table. Purple sparks began to fly around the small space, and she quickly swatted at a pot of dried yarrow that had caught the flying sparks and started to burn. Clenching her fists, she turned and spit into the hearth. She watched as it exploded into purple flames.

"You will not have the child," Velsa screamed. "She is not to be touched by your wicked hands or your wicked thoughts of love."

Velsa turned back to her table and emptied a wooden bowl. Placing a bundle of dried herbs into the bowl, she gouged her fingers into a crock of brown salve. Pulling it from the crock, she flicked her wrist causing the salve to plop into the bowl and cover the herbs. Lighting the remains of a black candle, she began to chant.

Protect this child only from him;
He will surely come when the light is dim.
Beware, stand guard and do not sleep;
Her safety, I charge that you must keep.

The herbs began to smolder and a brown mist swirled into the air as Velsa gave the mist directions, "You have your orders. Do not hesitate to strike. Make haste. Be on your way!"

At once the brown mist glided toward the door. Seeping through a crack in the door, it sped through the forest to the door of Lara's cottage. Circling the cottage like a thread coiled around a spool, it tightened itself in place to protect the child.

"That should fix you," Velsa laughed. "A little surprise is waiting for you."

Chapter 26

The rocks continued to crumble under their feet as they made their way up the mountain. Tate had tried leaping with Thomas, but the ground was so unstable that they all decided the safest way to maneuver the mountain was to do it slowly and cautiously.

Fortunately, the dark cloud had disappeared from the sky for most of the morning, but it had returned bringing a light rain and a cold swirling wind. As the wind whipped around them, it stung their faces and their bare hands. Thomas thought he heard the wind whispering for him to beware of the danger. When Tate looked over his shoulder at him, he knew that he had heard the same thing.

As the light rain became a downpour, the men searched for a place to take shelter. Finding a small indentation in the side of the mountain, they all took shelter hoping the rain would soon stop. The sky grew darker, and the men watched as the heavy rain caused several small rivers of water to wash more rocks down the mountain.

Tate suddenly nudged Thomas' arm. Looking over at him, Thomas watched Tate turn his head and nod toward the rain. Deep within the downpour, there appeared to be a dark outline of a figure. The figure raised its arms and complete darkness was upon them. Thomas moved his hand to the hilt of his dagger and waited for what he was sure would be an attack. Waiting for what seemed like forever, the rain instantly stopped, the darkness was slowly replaced with the glow of the setting sun, and the figure was gone.

"Hammer, did you see that dark figure within the rain?" asked Tate, as he stepped from the side of the mountain to face him.

"I saw nothing but the rain," Hammer replied. "If you saw a figure, it may have been the hermit or the old woman. As long as they keep their distance, I am willing to share the mountain with them."

"Whatever it was, it must have stopped the rain just before it disappeared," Tate huffed. "I saw it raise its arms. The rain stopped, and the darkness was replaced with sunlight. It looked like the figure was wielding magic to me."

"If the dark figure wields magic, I will follow Hammer's advice and keep my distance. I don't want to be the one that makes them angry," Thomas muttered.

"Let's take advantage of the light and keep moving," Hammer ordered. "If we hurry, we might be able to reach the first cave before nightfall."

Thomas adjusted his pack and followed closely behind Tate. Feeling like he was being watched, he kept his hand on the hilt of his dagger and frequently turned around to make sure they weren't being followed. They walked for hours before they finally reached the first cave. The last of the sun's light afforded them time to build a fire, dry their clothing, and search the cave for any unwanted inhabitants.

After partaking of the remaining rabbit, they were all ready to sleep. Since the men that were escorting them up the mountain were all humans, Tate felt it was unfair to make them go without sleep. He volunteered to take the first watch. Seeing the men head for the shelter of the cave, Thomas took a dried branch from the branches they had gathered earlier and threw it onto the fire. After moving the branch further into the fire with his dagger, he sat down next to his brother.

"Do you think we made a mistake by climbing this damn mountain?" Thomas asked his brother. "I feel danger in every step we take."

"I think the old woman was trying to help us," Tate countered. "We would have never made it to the cave if it would have kept raining. If she has enough power to stop the rain, she could certainly do us harm. It appears that she chose to help us."

"How did you manage to become such an optimist?" Thomas laughed.

"I don't know. Maybe I got it from mother," Tate sighed. "She looked for the good in everyone and everything."

Off in the darkness, the sound of tumbling rocks drew their attention. They quickly stood and prepared for an attack.

"We hear you. Show yourself," demanded Tate, as he moved to protect his brother.

"Put away your weapons," a raspy voice answered. "I will not harm you."

"Trusting you could be our end," Tate replied.

"I will move slowly toward your fire," the voice replied. "You will see my every move."

Tate could hear the crunching of rocks. As the sound drew closer, he saw a figure covered in a dark cloak stepping toward the fire.

"Remove your hood," Tate ordered. "Show us your face."

They watched as the figure before them slowly raised its hands. Small hands covered in black gloves reached for the edge of the hood. Carefully lifting the hood and tossing it back, the men gasped as they stared into the amber eyes of what appeared to be a woman. Her skin was translucent and cast a light around her face and hair.

"I have been cursed," she offered. Embarrassed, she started to pull the hood back over her face.

"There is no need to hide your face," Tate replied.

She sensed his kind heart and took a step closer.

"Who has cursed you?" asked Thomas. "Who could be so cruel?"

"I dare not mention the name," she whispered, as she stepped closer to the fire. Stretching her gloved hands toward the heat, she closed her eyes and sighed. "I have been cursed to live upon this mountain until I can obtain all items required to break the curse. It has been a lonely existence upon this mountain."

"What items?" asked Tate, fearing she might be wanting to take their eyes.

"I can read your mind," she said, as she lowered her eyes and frowned. "Yes, I took the eyes of a man that climbed this mountain, but he was dead when I found him. I can only retrieve the items without causing harm. If I cause harm in the retrieval of any item, I will be cursed to stay upon this mountain forever."

"Was it you that stopped the rain?" asked Tate.

"Yes, I wanted to help you," she replied.

"Are you a witch?" asked Thomas.

"I was a Seer, a witch with the power of sight. I had all of my powers taken from me," she replied. "I have been slowly regaining my magic with each task I complete. I will be honest with you. I was hoping that you might be able to help me in return for the kindness I showed you."

"How could we possibly help?" asked Thomas.

"Since I was able to determine that you are both mated vampires, I decided to approach you. I am to collect three drops of blood from a mated vampire. You must give it willingly. I cannot take it from you."

"Why would you need our blood?" asked Tate, confused by her request.

"It was purely an unobtainable obstacle preventing me from leaving this mountain until you came along. Even worse, I must also obtain the blood of a wolf shifter," she explained. "I do not know the reason. All the items were just a cruel way to prevent me from returning to my home. You are the first vampires that I have seen upon this mountain. There is nothing upon this mountain that is of interest to vampires or wolves. Therefore, they have no reason to climb this mountain. As you can see, it is a horrid place with nothing but rocks."

"Is anyone else upon this mountain?" asked Thomas.

"Yes," she replied. "The spirit that creates the dark cloud lives upon this mountain. It is a horrible creature. I do my best to keep those that have climbed the mountain away from it. It hides within the caves and frequently comes out during the rain to capture anyone that climbs this mountain."

"Have you seen a woman?" Thomas asked. "We are looking for a woman and a young girl."

"I have not, but I do not always see the creature's wicked behavior," she replied. "It is extremely crafty. It stacks the bones of its victims outside the caves. Sadly, there are piles and piles of bones."

"Can you take us to the caves?" Thomas asked.

"You must not go to the caves. It is not safe for either you or the humans that are with you," she begged. "If the woman and child are held by the spirit, they are beyond help. It devours them slowly. It is a terrible death."

Tate quickly turned when he heard a sound coming toward them from the cave. When he turned back the woman was gone.

"I thought I heard a woman's voice," Hammer said, as he looked about the area. "I must have been dreaming."

Tate saw Thomas look in his direction, and he slowly shook his head.

"Go back to your dreams," Tate ordered. "They will provide more warmth than this dwindling fire. Sunrise will be here before you know it."

Hammer scratched his head and turned back toward the cave. After he was out of sight, Tate looked about for the mysterious woman, but she was gone.

* * *

The next morning the bread and boiled eggs were shared among all the men. It was the last of the food that Thomas had brought from Woods Village. A meager ration for each of the men, but it served its purpose. If they wanted more than dried meat, they would have to focus on securing an animal for the fire pit.

As they continued their climb up the mountain, Thomas began watching the makings of a dense dark cloud that had started forming. It grew larger as they made their way up the mountain and seemed to hover directly over their heads. The darker the cloud, the colder the wind that whistled through the masses of jagged rocks that surrounded them. Just like the day before, the rain began to pummel them. The ground gave way under their boots as they slipped within the soft mud beneath the gravel.

Looking for any sign of shelter, Tate spotted what appeared to be a cave further up the mountain. What looked to be a dark entrance was partially hidden by trees and a mound of rocks. Directing Hammer's attention to the much needed shelter, they safely maneuvered through the mud and rocks to the other side of the wide path until they stood before its entrance. It was indeed a cave; however, the mounds of rocks that stood just outside the entrance were not rocks at all. A meticulously stacked mound of bones that had been broken into small pieces stood just outside the cave's entrance.

"The creature must have done this," Tate quietly whispered, to Thomas. "She told us of the creature."

"This cave belongs to someone," Hammer gasped. "It appears it has been feasting upon humans. Do we keep moving? What say you?"

"Tate and I will enter the cave," Thomas declared, knowing he could not leave without examining the cave. "It is safer if we go first."

"I will be right behind you," Hammer said, as he drew his dagger.

Ray moved away from the cave. His eyes were glazed, and his jaw was clenched in fear. Shaking his head, he turned to look away from the bones. He stumbled to his knees before he scrambled to his feet and ran back down the path that had brought them to the cave. Hammer shouted after him, but Ray kept running.

"Do you want me to go after him?" asked Tate.

"No, let the coward go," groaned Hammer. "He will find worse alone on the mountain. I have no need for a coward among my ranks."

Turning back toward the entrance, Hammer moved just inside the dark opening. Thomas gripped his arm and held him back to step ahead of him. He pulled his dagger and crouched slightly before entering the darkness. The scent of decay was the first thing to greet him. Holding the crook of his elbow over his nose, Thomas moved further into the cave. Light slowly began to fill the entrance, as Tate's outstretched hand began to flame.

"Magic?" asked Hammer.

"One of my gifted powers," Tate smiled. "It is good to use it for something other than causing harm."

With the light, the men could see well into the large cave. Water dripped down the rough walls forming large puddles of mud. Shredded clothing stained with blood littered the ground. Dozens of swords and daggers were lined up at the back of the cave with their tips embedded in the earth. It gave the appearance of headstones honoring the dead. Thomas moved toward the bits of cloth and kicked them with his boot as he looked for anything that might have belonged to Lara. Finding nothing, his shoulders relaxed and he turned to the men.

"Many poor souls brutally lost their lives in this cave," Thomas whispered. "This hermit has made a shrine to remember the dead."

"Or a place to gloat over the trophies he has collected," Hammer offered.

"I count forty-two weapons," Tate said. "I do not see any restraints. If the hermit does not need them, it must be using magic. Best we stay alert."

"It appears to be safe for now. We can wait out the rain," stated Hammer, as he stepped back from the ghastly scene. "As soon as the rain stops, we need to keep moving. There are two more sets of caves. They are near the top of the mountain. At this rate, it will be days before we reach the top of the mountain."

"Where do we go when we reach the top?" asked Tate.

"We will have a choice to make once we reach the last of the caves. We can go down the other side of the mountain which is mainly forest, or go back the way we came. The forest leads to the small villages south of Wintergreen Mountain. It is my understanding that the forest cannot be penetrated by the hermit."

"The forest it is," barked Tate. "No need to risk running into the hermit a second time."

"I will contact Baxter and have him move the horses to Old Mill," said Thomas.

"Hammer, the rain has stopped," the other man shouted, from the entrance.

"Let's get moving before the rain starts again," Hammer said, as he moved through the cave and out into the sunlight. We will have to spend the night out in the open unless we can find a cave along the way."

"Taking one last look at the shrine of swords, Thomas patted Tate on his shoulder, "We will need the help of that woman if we run into the creature that did this."

"Let's hope we see her again before we run into the hermit," Tate replied.

As they exited the cave, Tate released the flame, and they left the cave of death behind.

* * *

Tate watched as Thomas removed the rabbit from the fire pit. The animal had been able to outrun Tate until it found itself cornered behind some rocks. Tate quickly grabbed it by the ears and had carried it back to Hammer's man for skinning.

"You have always been good at catching rabbits," Thomas laughed.

"How do you remember me chasing rabbits," asked Tate.

"I remember we ate rabbit stew more than anything else," replied Thomas. "Since mother didn't send me, she must have sent you to catch them."

"If not for the rabbit, we would be eating dried meat tonight," Hammer said. "I thank you for this fine meal."

The men listened as Hammer told stories of growing up far beyond Alltree Island. Tate enjoyed listening to him talk about the big ship that carried him and his family to Cobb Cove. He had been a young lad at the time, and the only boy in a family of seven sisters. All the talk of his sisters made Tate and Thomas miss their own.

"It is late," Hammer said, as he stood. "Do you want me to keep watch?"

"There is no need," Tate replied. "We will keep watch tonight. You and your men should rest. We'll wake you at any sign of trouble."

Hammer nodded and made his way to the small cave that scarcely allowed enough room for the men to lie down.

Poking the fire with his dagger, Thomas felt the heat of the fire against his face. Letting his mind wander back to Lara, he thought of the first time he had felt the heat race through his body. He smiled and looked back at Tate.

"Were you thinking of her?" asked Tate.

"Yes, I miss her," replied Thomas. "These years without her have been the loneliest of my life."

Before Tate could respond, the same crunching sound drew their attention. Just beyond the fire, the same woman slowly approached.

"Come sit by the fire," Tate said. "The other men are asleep."

The woman released her hood from her face and sat down next to Tate.

"My name is Tate, and this is my brother, Thomas," Tate said, hoping that she would give them her name. "We are from the Evergreen Castle."

"My name is Astra," she replied. "Long ago and too many years to count, I use to live in a cottage in Primrose Pond." Gripping her gloved covered hands in her lap, she looked at Tate and then Thomas. "I see that you continue your journey even though I warned you of the creature. You are either very brave or very foolish. It is not safe for you to be upon this mountain."

"We saw the cave with all the swords," Thomas responded. "It was a sad sight to behold."

"Every cave is filled with the same trophies," she frowned. "Many souls have lost their lives to the creature. As he fills the caves, he moves on to fill another."

"You were explaining the curse to us before we were interrupted," Tate said. "You asked for our blood and the blood of a wolf. How will it help you?"

Astra lifted her hands and carefully removed her gloves. Her hands were glowing a bright red. Seeing the look of horror on both of their faces, she quickly pulled her gloves back in place.

"I cannot touch you with my bare hands," Astra began to cry. "One touch and you would die. The curse took everything from me. It was meant to torture me. It was meant to torture me forever."

"How will our blood help you?" asked Thomas.

"It will get me closer to leaving this mountain," she replied, as she wiped the tears from her face. "I need only your blood, the blood of a wolf, the feather from a white hawk, and the kiss from a vampire's child to break the curse. I fear the last item will never be found. I know of no vampire that has ever been able to conceive."

"What will happen once you succeed in acquiring all of the items?" asked Tate.

"I will return to my true form. My magic will be returned to me, and I will be able to leave this mountain," she replied. "I will return to my long abandoned cottage, if it still exists."

"I believe that we may be able to help you with all of your remaining items," Thomas said, as he watched Astra's eyes glow even brighter. "Tate's mate is a white hawk shifter. I am sure that she would offer a feather for your cause."

"That would be wonderful," Astra gasped, as she brought her glove covered hands to her mouth.

"We know a wolf shifter that lives at Black Thistle Castle. We have exchanged services in the past, and I am sure that Kayleigh would be willing to help you," Tate explained. "If we can find Thomas's mate, we believe that he has a daughter. We just need to find his mate to help you."

"Oh, if that were all true," Astra said, as she stood and moved her hands toward the fire. "If you are able to help me, I would finally be able to leave this dreadful mountain. I would be indebted to you for all time."

Thomas suddenly closed his eyes, and Astra stepped back from the fire and peered into the darkness over her shoulder. Thomas could hear Baxter in his mind.

"I have found nothing at Shepard's Grove," Baxter said.

"Go to Rock Pile and retrieve the horses and take them to Old Mill," Thomas ordered. "We will meet you there. We will be coming down the other side of the mountain."

"When will you be there?" he asked.

"Hopefully, no longer than three or four days," Thomas replied.

"Will do, see you there," Baxter said, before he closed their connection.

"I am sorry if I frightened you; that was Baxter," Thomas said. "I had to tell him to meet us at Old Mill. He found nothing in Shepard's Grove."

Seeing Astra sigh and move back towards the fire, Tate saw what seemed like fear in her eyes. Making eye contact with her, he asked, "What is required to take my blood?"

"Are you willing?" Astra asked. Seeing Tate nod his head, she placed her gloved hands over her heart. "I will be forever in your debt. It is simple really. A prick of your finger or hand and three drops of your blood upon my dagger's blade will be enough."

"Let's do it then," Tate eagerly stood. "Draw your dagger."

"I do not have it with me," Astra gasped. "It is hidden in the cave I have made into my home. I do not carry it for fear that I might lose it."

"Go then and retrieve it," Tate replied. "We will rest until you return."

"I know that you have not slept since you started climbing the mountain," Astra said. "I will keep watch so that you may rest."

"No need," Tate replied. "Hurry, retrieve your dagger."

Astra nodded and watched the men lean back against their blanket. She paced around the fire not wanting to leave the men alone and unprotected.

Could it be that these brave men will help me get off this mountain, she thought.

Suddenly a flash of lightening lit up the sky making shivers run down Astra's spine. She could feel a cool breeze brush the side of her face, and she knew what that meant. Moving toward the men, she knelt down and touched Tate's shoulder and tried to wake him. He didn't wake. Touching the side of his face, he still did not wake. Looking up, she saw the dark figure she feared would find them.

"Astra, they are mine," the creature said. "They are sleeping and will sleep until I decide to wake them. They cannot help you."

"They could have helped me," Astra screamed. "You ruined everything."

"Be gone you foolish girl," he shouted. "I will let them sleep until I am in need of a meal."

Astra stood watching the creature retrieve the two men and vanish into the darkness.

"I tried to protect you," Astra whispered through her tears. "I will find a way to help you. Somehow, I will help you."

Rushing into the dark cave, she brightened its interior and watched the remaining men sit up and shield their eyes. As Hammer stood, she pulled her glove from her hand and cupped her hand in front of her mouth. She blew cool air into her palm and then tossed it at the men.

"Leave this mountain," Astra chanted. "Leave now and do not return."

Closing her fist, the cave returned to darkness, and she could hear the men preparing to leave. Turning, she left the cave and ran to find her dagger.

Chapter 27

It had been eight days and neither Thomas nor Tate had made it down from the mountain. At first, Baxter wasn't worried. He had seen the dark cloud over the mountain and determined they were taking shelter from the weather. It wasn't until after he had tried to reach Thomas and Tate mentally, that he feared something had happened to them. Leaving the horses in the care of the man that ran the mill, Baxter flashed back to Evergreen Castle. Oliver was the first to see Baxter enter the Command Center. Seeing that he was alone made him suspect that something was wrong.

"Where is Lord Thomas?" asked Oliver.

"Both Lord Thomas and Tate were climbing the mountain starting from Rock Pile in search of Lady Lara," Baxter answered. "I last spoke with Lord Thomas eight days ago. They were going to exit the mountain through the forest near Wintergreen Mountain. He gave me instructions to move the horses from Rock Pile to Old Mill. We were to meet there in three or four days. When he didn't arrive, I tried to reach his mind. I have been unable to reach him."

"Who was he with?" asked Oliver.

"Lord Fallon sent Hammer and a few of his men to escort them up the mountain to search the caves," Baxter replied. "They left a young lad to watch the horses, and he was still there minding them when I arrived to retrieve them. I trust them."

"I know Hammer," Oliver replied. "He has scouted for Evergreen many times."

Baxter saw Elda enter the Command Center, and he motioned her over to them.

"Where is Lord Thomas? Did you find Lady Lara?" she asked.

"No, we have not been able to locate her," Baxter replied. "Now, Lord Thomas and Tate are missing."

"What?" Elda gasped.

"They are somewhere on the mountain between the forest near Wintergreen Mountain and Fallon Castle," he answered. "I can't reach either of them with my mind. They are either under someone's control or dead."

"What did you see the last time you spoke with them?" asked Elda. "You do see through his eyes when you speak to him?"

"I saw Tate and a woman that wore a cloak. The moonlight must have been shining on her face; her face was glowing," he answered. Furrowing his brow, he thought back to what he had seen and heard just before Thomas recognized he was waiting to speak to him. "She was telling them that she needed his blood to leave the mountain."

"She must be under a spell," Elda gasped. "Maybe she is holding them prisoner and refusing to let them go until they help her."

"It sounded more like they were willing to help," Baxter replied.

"Have you told Gavenia?" asked Elda.

"Tell me what?" asked Gavenia, as she walked up to the small group. "Where is Tate?"

"Gavenia, he is missing," Baxter quietly said, as he took both of her hands in his and waited for her reaction.

"Tell me where," she demanded. "I can search for him. Just tell me where!"

"They are on the mountain behind Fallon Castle," Baxter repeated.

"The mountain with the hermit?" she gasped, as she began to cry. "The hermit wields magic and eats his prisoners. Oh good heavens, there are rumors about a witch that was banished to the mountain. They say she has to collect a long list of things before she can return to her home. The list is full of impossible things. Does the hermit have Tate?"

"We don't know," Baxter replied. "I saw an image of a woman with them, but she did not seem like she wanted to hurt them. I heard them talking about the list. They spoke about a feather from your hawk, blood from Thomas or Tate, and a kiss from a vampire child."

"If that will allow Tate to return to me, I will gladly give her a feather from my hawk," she exclaimed. "I will go now. Just tell me where to find them."

"Gavenia, we don't know exactly where they are," Oliver said, as he tried to calm her. "You could fly over the mountain, but she may be hiding. Or worse, the hermit may see you and cause you to fall from the sky."

"I don't care. I have to try and find him," she screamed. "I can do no less than he did for me. If your mate was missing, you would do the same."

Oliver and Baxter knew that she was right. They would be unable to stop her from searching.

"We need to try and figure out where they are before you start flying around," Oliver countered. "Baxter, can you try and reach the woman. You saw her. Can you make a connection with someone you don't know?"

"I can try," he replied.

Baxter stepped back and closed his eyes. He focused on the place where he had seen the woman and her image. Retrieving the last glimpse he had of her, he focused on her amber eyes. He pushed with his mind, and he felt a pressure pushing back. Something was blocking him. He tried again, and the same pressure pushed back.

"I am making contact with someone," he said. "If it is the woman, she is pushing back and not allowing me to enter her mind."

"I am going to search for her," Gavenia said, as she ran toward the door leading to the stable. "Maybe I can spot her from the air."

Knowing they couldn't stop her, Oliver and Baxter followed her to the stable and watched her take to the air.

"Go with her," Oliver demanded. "Keep her safe."

Baxter flashed from outside the stable to the roof of the Old Mill. He could easily see the ridge of the mountains from the top of the mill. The dark cloud he had seen hovering over the mountain was gone, and the sky was clear. He stood scanning the sky waiting to see the white hawk. The time passed slowly, but finally, he could see her hawk flying toward the mountains. She made pass after pass over the peaks of the mountains. Each pass she made seemed to be a little lower. When he saw her drop below the peaks of the mountains, he cringed. He was almost ready to flash to the nearest peak when he saw her soar up into the sky. He stood waving his arms trying to get her attention.

Once he saw her heading his way, he jumped down from the roof of the mill to wait for her. Removing his tunic, he wrapped it around his arm. Holding out his arm, he felt her talons gently grip him.

"I am taking you inside the mill. We'll see if we can find you some clothes," Baxter said, as he opened the door and went inside.

Baxter looked around the large room and noticed a woman sweeping the wooden floor. Seeing the hawk, she made her way towards them.

"A fine bird you have there," said the elderly woman.

"Do you have some extra clothes?" asked Baxter. Seeing the elderly woman give him a confused look, he pointed to the hawk. "She is a shifter."

"A shifter?" she replied, looking back and forth between Baxter and the hawk. Finally understanding, she ran to a small closet and pulled out her long cloak. "This is the best I have. Will it do?"

"Yes, we can manage with this," he responded. "Is there somewhere she might change in private?"

"The storage room is behind you," she said, as she pointed to the closed door.

Baxter opened the door to the storage room and hung the cloak over the handle of a broom that leaned against the wall. He knelt down and sat the hawk upon the floor. Backing out of the small space, he closed the door and waited. A few moments later, Gavenia exited the storage room with the cloak pulled tightly around her. She nodded and gave her thanks to the kind woman.

"What did you see?" asked Baxter.

"I saw mainly rocks, but I did see what looked like a small camp outside a cave," Gavenia replied. "I saw bedrolls around a cold fire pit. There was no sign of Tate or Thomas. Can you try again to reach the woman?"

Baxter closed his eyes and focused on the woman's image he had briefly seen. This time, he saw a blurry vision. As it came into focus, he could see small hands covered in gloves. He immediately spoke, "I am a friend of Tate's. I need to speak to you."

"Where are you?" she asked. "Are you on the mountain?"

"I am far from the mountain," he replied. "Gavenia, Tate's mate, was looking for you. She needs your help to find him."

"The creature has the men," she replied. "Sadly, I do not have enough magic to retrieve them for you."

"Is there a place that Gavenia, a white hawk shifter, can bring you one of her feathers?"

"She would do that for me?" she asked, as tears came to her eyes making Baxter's image blurry.

"Yes, she needs to know where to find you," Baxter replied.

"Meet me at the camp where the bedrolls are by the fire," she said. "That was the last place I saw them."

"The hawk was in the sky earlier and saw the camp. She will be on her way shortly. I am sorry that we do not have blood for you. I am not mated and cannot help you," Baxter replied.

"The feather will help me," Astra assured him. "Thank you."

"I will try to contact you later. Keep your mind open for me," asked Baxter. "Keep watch for the hawk. Do not let harm come to her."

"The creature is above the camp," Astra explained. "Tell Gavenia to fly high until she reaches the camp. I will wait for her there."

Baxter told Gavenia what he had heard from the woman, and he watched Gavenia run back into the storage room. Hearing the flap of her wings, he opened the door and knelt down to carry her outside. As she took to the air, Baxter donned his tunic. He took some comfort in knowing that they could help the woman, and she might be able to help Thomas and Tate.

Anxiously waiting for Gavenia's hawk to return, he suddenly felt a push on his mind. He opened it to find the woman was speaking to him.

"She has found me and dropped her feather down to me. She is on her way back to you," she said. "Thank you, this means the world to me. I will contact you again when I find your friends. For now, I need to understand what this item will provide me and if it has added to my magic."

Their connection was ended, and Baxter stood waiting for Gavenia's hawk to return. Seeing her head in the direction of the castle, Baxter flashed back to Evergreen and waited by the stable.

They would all have to wait for word from the woman on the mountain.

* * *

Astra ran from the camp and entered the small cave that she had managed to turn into her private refuge. When she had first made the small cave her home, it lacked all manner of comfort, and it had improved very little since. Over the years, she had been forced to take what was left of the creature's castoffs. She had turned the linen from men's tunics into bedding and their woven blankets covered the ground beneath her feet.

Sitting down upon her bed, she placed the feather next to her and carefully removed her gloves. Picking up the feather, she ran the tip of her fingers over its soft edges.

"I have gained one more item," she whispered, as she closed her eyes. "Give me the magic afforded to me by this wonderful gift. Let me use the magic for good. There are men that need my help. Their friends have helped me gain this valuable item. I must repay them for their kindness."

She could feel her hands begin to tingle. At first, it was a gentle sensation, but the sensation grew to a throbbing ache. Astra began to wildly shake her hands. She watched the heat begin to spread from her fingers to her wrist and up her arms. As the heat increased, she felt a sharp stabbing pain attack her senses, and she fell back against the bed linens. As she screamed, the painful heat consumed her body until she could take no more. Giving into the pain, her amber eyes slowly closed, and she escaped into unconsciousness.

Chapter 28

The first night she transitioned into her wolf was the most terrifying night of her life. It was the most terrifying night and the most wonderful. Lady Kayleigh had helped her understand what would happen to her body, and the white wolf had stayed with her as her body transformed. Alicia had felt all of the pain as her bones snapped and popped during the transition. She had screamed as her back strained, and her head twisted into that of a wolf, but the freedom to run through the forest had overshadowed all of the suffering. Killian's black wolf had run by her side making her feel safe, and her gray wolf longed to run with him again.

Alicia tried to walk slowly through the hallways toward the library. She had to remind herself that she was walking within the castle and certain behavior was expected of her by her mother. Unable to control herself any longer, she lifted the heavy fabric of her long skirt and scurried through the hallways hoping to avoid anyone that would offer a scolding. She was just too excited to walk. It wasn't the library that filled her with excitement, but the young man that stood guard outside its doorway. The sight of him use too make her hands tremble with fear. Now, they trembled with excitement. His thick black fur and his silver tipped ears had been the first thing on her mind upon waking each morning since their first run. She could feel how anxious her wolf was to see him again and hurried to see a glimpse of her handsome friend.

Stopping before she reached the last corner, she straightened her skirt and pushed her curls back in place. Taking a deep breath, she turned the corner and could see him standing against the stone wall with his hand upon the hilt of his dagger. As she approached, he turned to face her and blocked the door to the library. A serious expression covered his face.

"I am here to help Lady Kayleigh," she said, as she did every morning. Looking up into his eyes, she stood hoping to see him smile.

Seeing no hint of a smile, Alicia pursed her lips and sighed. Killian stepped back and allowed her to pass. Disappointed, she stepped into the library and greeted Lady Kayleigh. Turning to look over her shoulder, she watched as Killian took his place against the wall. Taking her seat at the table, she opened the book to the page she had marked the day before and started reading. After reading the same page several times without remembering a thing, she glanced up at Killian. He caught her gaze and offered her a quick smile before his face returned to the serious expression that he always wore. Happy that he had acknowledged her, she returned her attention back to her book and her purpose.

The day had passed slowly for Alicia. Her wolf had been begging all day for a run in the forest. Telling her wolf no had little impact on the anxious pup. Hearing footsteps coming down the hallway toward the library, she looked up to see Lord Gautier standing in the doorway.

"How are my little wolves?" he asked, as he reached for Kayleigh and placed a kiss upon her forehead.

"We are well," Kayleigh replied, glancing down at Alicia and smiling.

"I have come to take you for a walk in the courtyard," he said, as he lifted her chin with his hand and kissed her lips. "You have had enough of books, scrolls and dust for one day. I find that I need the happiness that is afforded me when I look upon your face."

"I would enjoy a walk with you," Kayleigh replied. "Alicia, you may go. Apparently, My Lord feels we have had enough books, scrolls and dust for one day."

"Killian, I will escort Kayleigh. There is no need for you to follow. You may take your leave," Gautier ordered.

As they left for the courtyard, Killian and Alicia looked at each other. Feeling her face blush, Alicia lowered her eyes to the floor.

"Shall I escort you back to your chamber?" asked Killian.

"I would prefer that you walked with me outside in the sun," Alicia bravely said. "It is cool enough for a walk and warm enough to hear the birds sing."

Killian offered his arm, and Alicia slipped her arm through his. As they walked toward the door, Alicia could hear her heart pounding. She paused for a moment and looked up at Killian's face. If she was not mistaken, she could hear four hearts pounding and that made her very happy.

* * *

Jario had been so consumed with finding Lady Lara that he had completely disregarded the training of the vampires he had held in his dungeon. Claudia had seen to keeping them fed, but little else had been done for them over the years. He had hoped when Gusty had come to see him, he would have been able to convince him to take the lead over his army. Since that did not transpire to his liking, he found himself in need of a commander.

With Laralynn's birthday still slightly more than two moons away, he decided to make a journey to Echo Bluff to see what the latest ship had brought to the island. Leaving his chamber, he strode through the hallway heading for the stable.

Making his way down the steps, he could feel the cool night's breeze against his face. With it, the faintest scent of Jasmine drew his attention. Looking about for its source, he noticed Desirae standing in the dark looking up at the stars.

"Do you find something interesting in the sky tonight?" Jario asked, as he moved to stand next to her and looked up searching for something that had drawn her focus.

"I am listening to the wind," she replied. "Something has happened upon the mountain by Fallon Castle. Someone is calling for help. I felt a slight surge of weak magic and then complete quiet."

"The hermit's mountain?" asked Jario.

"The same," she replied. "I fear a witch needs help. To be more specific, a broken witch is in need of help, and I fear that I cannot help her."

"Well, since you aren't busy," Jario smirked. "How would you like to take me to Echo Bluff Harbor? I am in need of a commander. You can help me find one."

Desirae laughed as she looked Jario up and down. She took great delight in teasing the misguided vampire.

"You need more than a commander for that pathetic group you have locked in your dungeon," she sneered. "They are nothing more than animals."

"They just need training," he barked. "A little training and a good dose of compulsion will make all the difference. You will see. They will become fine soldiers. Are you up for an adventure?"

"Do you prefer to travel by horse or by way of Desirae?" she asked.

"Since time is important to me, by way of Desirae will do," Jario said, as he donned a serious expression. "Do not misunderstand my touch for anything other than a need to travel with you."

"Understood," Desirae laughed. "I find I have no need for your personal attention."

She grabbed Jario's hand and squeezed it tightly. Feeling a sudden rush of nausea, he tried to pull away from her. She squeezed his hand tighter, and he winced as he felt her nails pierce his skin.

"I see you like it rough," he grinned, noticing her wicked smile.

"That was nothing, my dear Jario," she smirked. "Do not misunderstand my touch for anything other than a need to travel with you."

He flinched as he heard his own words repeated back at him.

"You no longer find me attractive?" he grinned, as he raised an eyebrow.

"I never did," she smirked, as they disappeared from the castle grounds.

* * *

Velsa sat by the fire studying her book of spells. She had been reading the same spell every evening trying to lock it into her mind. Focusing on one thing had been difficult lately. She had been way too distracted. With the frustrating bombardment of annoying spell fragments and her nerves over Laralynn's coming birthday, she was in need of a relaxing potion.

Suddenly she felt something strange. Her cottage began to shake. Velsa felt a peculiar surge of magic. It lasted for only a moment or two and then it was quiet.

"What the heck was that?" she shouted, holding her hand to her throat.

Listening for any signs of an imminent attack from a spell, she sighed when nothing further disturbed her evening. Trying to relax, she thought again about a relaxing potion.

"Why not?" she laughed, as she looked around her cottage for anything that looked out of place after feeling the peculiar surge of magic. "Every witch needs a little potion, now and then. A little something to take the edge off fluttering nerves."

Standing up she nudged her chair out of the way. Closing her book, she carefully placed it on the table. Calling a clean cup from her cupboard, she lifted one vial after another until she found the one she wanted. Opening the rusted cap of the vial, she let three drops of the green liquid spill into the cup. Selecting a star anise and a dollop of honey for flavor, she flicked her wrist and heated the water in her kettle. Seeing the steam, she lifted the kettle and poured the boiling water into her cup. Green vapor swirled above its rim, and it filled the cottage with a sweet aroma. Scraping her teeth over her bottom lip, she lifted the cup and carried it to her cot.

"This should do it," she laughed. "I haven't done this in years. The last time I did this, I found myself sitting on my roof when I woke."

Downing the hot liquid in one gulp, she stretched out on her cot and started to close her eyes. The room began to spin. As she raised her hands, bright pink butterflies fluttered between her fingers.

"I wish to relax four weeks," she whispered, as she became very drowsy. "Not four . . . I mean for . . . oh my, this is wonderful."

Before she could change her spell, the relaxing potion had taken control of her mind and her body.

* * *

"How long do we wait?" Gavenia screamed. "My mate could be dying. You want me to sit here and do nothing? Just wait until I turn into a hawk. My talon's will scratch your eyes out."

Baxter knew she was frustrated with his demand to wait, but it was for her own safety. He couldn't let her go to the mountain until they heard from the woman. Tate would have his head if he put her in danger. He had to protect Gavenia.

"She will contact us," Baxter replied. "I am sure she will."

"I'm not," she screamed, as she paced the Command Center. "I have to do something. Have you tried to reach Lord Thomas?"

"Yes, Gavenia," he replied. "I have tried over and over. I get nothing. No push back, no acceptance and no vision."

"What about Gautier? Can he help us?" asked Gavenia.

"Preston has sent a messenger to Black Thistle to ask for Gautier's help," he replied. "We are waiting for his response."

"Wait, wait, wait," she shouted. "All we do is wait! What good is waiting? I have to do something!"

"I can hear you all the way outside," Elda said, as she entered the Command Center. "Why are you shouting?"

"Baxter refuses to let me search for Tate," Gavenia growled, through clenched teeth. "I cannot leave him there to die. I have to find him."

"We will find him," Elda said, as she wrapped her arms around Gavenia trying to calm her. "We all want to save them. We need to wait for some word from the woman on the mountain. Your feather may have given her the ability to help them. Try to be patient a little while longer."

"Elda, I love him," Gavenia sobbed, as she tried to take comfort in Elda's touch. "My life is nothing without him. I need to bring him home."

"We will find him," Baxter whispered. "We will find him."

Chapter 29

Baxter stood with his arms stretched out and both hands pressed against the wooden beam above the hearth in the Great Hall. He had come as soon as he had received word that Lord Gautier had information that could help them find Lord Thomas. Lady Kayleigh was the first to greet him, and she assured Baxter that they would do anything they could to help bring Lord Thomas and Tate back home. Seeing Lord Gautier stride into the hall, Baxter tried to read his face. His look was grim, but he couldn't remember ever seeing him smile.

"Baxter, I am glad you could come so quickly," Gautier bellowed. He reached for Baxter's hand with one hand and his shoulder with the other. "With Kayleigh's and Alicia's help, we have discovered some writings about the woman that lives upon the mountain. Her name is Astra, and she has been collecting items to break a curse since before the War of the Witches. There is still a mystery around who sent her there, but I have my suspicions."

"I saw a glimpse of her when I spoke with Lord Thomas," Baxter said. "I also spoke to her and heard of the remaining items she requires to break the curse. We have recently reduced it by one. Gavenia was able to drop a feather from her hawk down to her. Since she received it, we have not heard from her. She still requires vampire blood, wolf blood and a kiss from a vampire's child."

"After finding the writings, Kayleigh has offered to give you her blood," Gautier said, as he pulled a vial from his pocket and handed it to Baxter. "I assume that Gavenia's hawk can carry this to the woman."

"Lady Kayleigh, Evergreen thanks you," Baxter replied, as he took the vial from Gautier. "Gavenia will be glad to carry the vial."

"If Astra can find where the hermit is hiding Lord Thomas and Tate, she should be able to acquire their blood," Gautier added. "That leaves us with the final obstacle. The kiss from a vampire's child. Since you have not been able to find Lady Lara, I assume you have not been able to find the child."

"No, we are still searching the island for her," Baxter replied. "We were searching when Lord Thomas and Tate were taken from us."

"If you can find the child, I believe that I can capture a kiss from her and secure it in a potion for Astra. This should break the curse and allow her to leave the mountain," Gautier explained. "This would keep the child from any danger."

"But, how will Lord Thomas and Tate be able to escape the hermit and leave the mountain?" asked Baxter. "If Astra leaves them, we will have no chance to help with their escape."

"With each item she collects, a piece of Astra's magic returns to her. If she can consume the blood from either Lord Thomas or Tate, she will have enough magic to take them from the hermit and on to the boundary that keeps her confined to the mountain," Gautier clarified. "They will be able to leave the mountain. She will have to stay behind until we can find the child. Once we send her the final item, she will be whole again and able to leave the mountain."

"It sounds simple enough, but it sounds dangerous," replied Baxter. "I hope she will trust us to help her with the final item."

"If she will not trust that you will help her, she may require a blood promise from Lord Thomas," Gautier said.

"A blood promise?" Baxter asked, as he furrowed his brows. "What is a blood promise?"

"A promise sealed with blood from the one that promises. Breaking the promise would bring death," explained Gautier. "A blood promise is final and cannot be altered once made."

"I cannot allow Lord Thomas to make a blood promise. I will make it," Baxter stated. "I will risk death for Lord Thomas."

"We have time before we need to worry about a blood promise," Gautier said, as he gripped Baxter's arm. "Let's try to make contact with Astra and deliver Kayleigh's blood."

"Thank you for your help," Baxter said, as he offered his hand to Lord Gautier. "I will return to Evergreen and try to make contact with Astra. Once we know the vial has been delivered, we will send you a message."

"Hopefully, your message will come soon," Gautier replied.

Baxter bowed slightly and flashed back to Evergreen.

"Gavenia," Baxter shouted. "I have need of your hawk."

* * *

As she opened her eyes, the dark earth above her began to spin. She held the linen bedding tightly with both hands. Closing her eyes, she took a deep breath, waited for a moment, and slowly opened them again. Gradually, the spinning stopped. Sitting up, she looked about her small space and tried to remember what had happened. Bringing her hand to her face to brush her hair from her eyes, she felt something rub against her wrist. Looking down, she saw the white feather, and it all came back to her. She picked it up and brushed her fingertips over its edge. Suddenly, she realized her hands were no longer red.

"It worked," she whispered, before she shouted the words again. "My hands are no longer red. They look like the rest of me. They are glowing, but the horrible *Touch of Death* is gone."

As she started to stand, she felt a throbbing pressure against her mind. Immediately, she knew it as Tate's friend, and she opened her mind to him.

"Astra, it is Baxter. I am Tate's friend. Do you remember me?" he asked, as he gripped Gavenia's hand.

"Yes, it is me," she replied.

"We have been trying to reach you. Has something happened?" Baxter asked, as he tried to focus on their connection.

"The feather took the death from my hands. It was painful, and I must have passed out. How long have you waited?" Astra asked, fearing it had been too long and something may have happened to Tate.

"The moon will be full tonight," Baxter replied.

"Oh dear, it has been a long time," she said. "I just woke. I will try and find your friends."

"We were given a vial of wolf's blood. The white hawk will bring it to you. Can you meet her in the same place as before?" asked Baxter.

"Yes, thank you," she said, as she started to cry. "This makes me very happy. I will gladly wait for the hawk. When will she come?"

"She will leave now," Baxter replied. "Watch for her and keep her safe. Now go!"

Astra broke their connection and ran from her cave as she pulled on her gloves. If the creature should see her, she didn't want him to know that she had gained more magic. The sun was just beginning to set, and she easily found her way to the abandoned camp.

As she stood waiting, she thought about the feather. She knew that she would sleep after each item was retrieved, but the feather had brought horrible pain, and the sleep had lasted much too long. Each item brought her more pain than the last. She feared what the blood would do to her. She paced back and forth as she watched the sky for the hawk. Far off in the distance, she could hear the squawk of the hawk. The closer she came, the more excited Astra felt. Hearing the flap of the hawk's wings, she looked up to see her swoop down and release the vial. Holding up her hands, she snatched it from the air and held it tightly as she ran back to her cave. The pain would come again, but she knew it would be worth it. She would suffer anything to leave the mountain and return to her home.

* * *

The moon was full, and its bright light filled Lara's small cottage. She sat in her chair holding her mug of tea as she watched Laralynn play with Hunter. The little ball of fur was her daughter's constant companion. She had been true to her word and had taken good care of the little kitten.

Glancing out the window at the moon, she felt sadness take over her thoughts. Trying hard not to think of the short time she had left to spend with her daughter, she decided to give her the present she was saving to give her on her birthday. She stood and placed her mug upon the table. Walking to the cupboard, she opened the doors and pulled the wooden chest out onto the floor.

"Laralynn, come here. Sit by me. I have some things to show you," Lara said, as she knelt down and rubbed her hand across the top of the chest.

Laralynn picked up Hunter and sat down next to her mother.

"Mother, did you paint the flowers on the chest?" she asked.

"No, I found it this way," Lara explained, as she lifted the lid and made sure it was securely open. "It is lovely; isn't it?" She lifted her journal, wrapped in a bit of old lace, and placed it in her lap. "This is my journal. It tells the story of our time together. It also has letters to your father."

"Will he ever come to see me?" she asked.

"When he is able; he will come," Lara replied, feeling her heart ache for her daughter. Removing a small bundle, she gently placed it in Laralynn's lap. "This is for you. I decided not to wait until your birthday. It belonged to your grandmother, and I am sure that she would have wanted you to have it."

Laralynn picked up the small bundle and carefully unwrapped it. Lifting the last corner of the linen, a gold chain slipped from her hand. Laralynn gasped as she realized what it was.

"It is grandmother's locket. It is so beautiful," she said. "Oh mother, this is the best present. I will always take good care of it." She lifted the locket by its chain and handed it to her mother. "Please help me put it on."

Lara opened the clasp and placed it around her daughter's neck. As she secured the clasp, she kissed the back of her daughter's neck. Watching her turn around, she saw the happiness in her daughter's eyes.

"Let's see what else is in this chest," Lara said, as she lifted a dress from the chest she had not worn since the day she had found herself in the cottage. She held the dress up to Laralynn. "Would you like to try it on? You have grown so much lately that it will be too short for you, but it will be fun to see it on you."

Laralynn stood and untied the laces of her dress and let it fall around her feet. Taking the dress from her mother, she stepped into it and pulled it up so that she could put her arms through the sleeves that had laces at the shoulders. Lara stood and helped her tie all the laces. Laralynn stepped back and lifted the skirt as she twirled around.

"This was your dress?" she asked her mother, as she continued to wave her skirt from side to side. "Why have you never worn it? It is so beautiful."

"It was much too nice to milk Trouble, or weed the garden," Lara replied, as she laughed. "I was saving it for a special occasion. I will wear it again for your birthday."

"I will wear my favorite dress too," she replied. "Help me take it off. It needs to hang so the wrinkles come out. I want it to look nice for you."

Lara untied the laces and helped Laralynn remove the dress. She draped it over her arm and walked into her bedchamber. Laying it on the bed, tears began to fill her eyes, and she quickly wiped away the few that fell upon her cheeks. She knew that she was looking at her burial gown. She would wear her beautiful dress one last time.

Chapter 30

They had seen the creature the night they were carried to his cave. He stood well over six feet tall and had the body of a man. His feet and hands were slightly webbed with only two appendages on each. They resembled thick fingers with long sharp claws that he used for shredding flesh. His neck was thick and covered with scales. His arms were muscular and built for battle. Two large horns protruded from the top of his forehead, and his pointed ears jutted from the side of his head. His amber eyes rimmed in red made their own eyes burn just to look at them. When he spoke, his voice pierced their mind and caused blood to run from their ears.

The scraping of the creature's feet woke Thomas. He could open and close his eyes, but he was unable to move. The cave had just enough light to allow Thomas to see what was left of his arm. The flesh had stopped regenerating overnight since he had been deprived of blood, and he saw nothing but bones from his elbow down to his fingers. Thomas had been able to withstand the pain from his flesh being ripped from his arm the first night. Since that first night, his screaming was quieted by the creature, but the pain was left for him to endure.

Every time he was allowed to open his eyes, he looked to see that Tate was still sitting across from him. He had saved Tate the pain he had suffered by offering himself to the creature. Sparing Tate from the torture might allow time for him to escape or be rescued.

"You are awake," said the creature. "Your flesh is withering, and it has not regrown. You need blood."

Thomas looked at the ground as the creature spoke. He wanted no part of making eye contact with him. As the creature stepped back away from him, he could see that he was moving toward Tate. Grabbing hold of his brother's' arm, the creature started dragging him across the dirt floor of the cave and threw him on Thomas' outstretched legs. Lifting Tate's arm, he nudged his wrist against Thomas' mouth.

"Drink!" the creature ordered. "If you don't, I will cut off his head. If he is no use to you, he is good for nothing more than a meal to me."

Thomas opened his mouth and his fangs descended. Closing his eyes, he sank his fangs into the flesh of his brother's wrist, and he felt the blood caress his tongue. He continued to pull the thick liquid until his fear of draining Tate rushed through his mind. Pulling his fangs from Tate's wrist, he licked the blood from his lips. Seeming satisfied, the creature grabbed Tate's arm and pulled his limp body away from Thomas.

Watching the creature toss Tate's body back against the wall of the cave, he suddenly realized that he meant for Tate to sustain him. As long as there was flesh upon his body for the creature to consume, Tate might be safe.

What would sustain Tate, he thought. Without blood, Tate will succumb to the madness and eventually die his final death.

The creature looked down at Tate slumped against the wall. He studied him for a few moments. Turning abruptly, he left the cave. Thomas knew that every time he fed from Tate he would be putting his brother at risk. One too many feedings and Tate would be drained of his life's blood. He hoped that the creature had left to find something to sustain his brother, or they were both doomed.

* * *

Astra woke with a start. As she sat up, the room began to spin, and her head began to pound. Closing her eyes and clenching her bed linens did little to stop the spinning sensation. Waiting for what seemed like forever, she finally opened her eyes. She slowly stood and looked about her cave. For a moment, she had forgotten she had consumed the vial of wolf blood. As it all came racing back to her, she remembered the pain that had repeatedly shot through her legs and abdomen until the darkness showed mercy and took her from the pain.

Needing to wash the sweat that lingered on her body, she pulled off her soiled tunic and discarded it in the corner. She longed for the feel of the cool water from the small waterfall that the frequent rain clouds fed. Bending over a pile of clean clothing, she noticed that her feet looked different. She could see her feet. She could no longer see the ground through her toes. Moving toward the opening of the cave, she examined the rest of her body. Her feet, legs, and a portion of her torso were no longer transparent. The blood had partially restored her. She was one step closer to leaving the mountain.

Running back toward the pile of clothing, she dug out some tattered breeches and a tunic. They were both too large, but it didn't matter to her. Everything she had managed to collect over the years were either too big or too small. It was a minor inconvenience compared to what Thomas and Tate were going through. After pulling the tunic over her head, she gathered the fabric and tucked it into the waist of the breeches. Cinching the breeches with a bit of rope to secure them around her waist, she pulled on her boots and gloves. Throwing her cape over her shoulders and flipping the hood up to conceal her head, she made her way toward the opening of her cave.

Remembering Baxter, she took a moment to stand perfectly still as she tried to contact him. She pushed at his mind trying to get his attention.

"Baxter, it is Astra," she said. "I am awake. Do you hear me? The wolf blood has helped me. I am on my way to try and find your friends."

She waited and waited for Baxter's reply. Almost giving up, she heard him finally respond.

"I hear you. Astra, we can do nothing more to help you until we find Thomas' child," Baxter replied. "Be very careful. Know that Tate has gifted powers of burning hands and great leaping that might assist you."

"I fear that the creature has made them sleep," Astra said. "If they are asleep, they will be unable to move. I will do my best to help them. I owe you so much and must repay your kindness. I will contact you when I am able."

"Good Luck," Baxter replied. "We look forward to your next message."

With their connection broken, Astra left her cave and began to climb the mountain toward the caves that belonged to the creature.

* * *

Shouting could be heard as Jario and Seth, his new Army Commander, made their way down the stone steps to the dungeon. Jario had found Seth at the harbor carrying two wooden barrels, one over each shoulder. He was a foot taller than Jario and had huge hands that could easily circle a man's throat. A large tattoo of a mermaid covered one arm and a serpent covered the other. His back bore scares from numerous floggings that had healed badly and remained after his turning. His gravelly voice was deep and strong. Seeing the men jerk at the sound of his voice had immediately drawn Jario's attention to the man. Once he had realized that he was a vampire, he approached him and made him an offer to command his army.

Thirty-two vampires had been secured within the dungeon for over a decade with two dozen added to cells over the years. It had been Claudia's responsibility to make sure that they were all fed and remained secure. For the most part, she had completed the task Jario had given her. Only two had been devoured by the unruly band of mindless vampires. It was time for Seth to mold them into an army that could protect Crimson Claw Castle and eventually bring an end to Evergreen.

Standing before the cell doors, Jario drew their curious gaze. He had seldom entered the dungeon, and they stood anxiously waiting for word of their release.

"If you do not remember me, I am Lord Jario," he smirked. "This is my castle and you are in my dungeon."

The vampires started screaming and banging their fists against the cell walls. Several vampires gripped the bars of the cells and tried to bend the bars to escape.

"Now, now," he muttered. "There is no need for any of that. You have been held for a good cause. Each of you is controlled by the madness. That madness must be driven from you before you will be set free. Your new commander will be teaching you how to control it. You will all have the opportunity to become a member of the Crimson Claw Army. Those that fail in their attempt to overcome the madness will be given their final death. Those that survive will take an oath to me and to Crimson Claw. If you break your oath, you will receive your final death."

Seth stood just beyond the vampires' reach but close enough to inspect them. He scanned their eyes for recognition and examined their bodies for those that were too weak to succeed. Finding two vampires that he felt were good candidates, he pointed to them and directed them to the cell bars. As they came forward and stood before him, Seth looked into their eyes.

"You will follow every command I give you without question," Seth stated, as he used his compulsion against them. "You will not speak unless I ask you to speak. Is this understood?"

The two vampires nodded their heads.

Seth waved his arm, and it pushed the remaining vampires to the back of the cell. They struggled to move as they watched the cell door open and the two vampires walk free. Swinging the door closed, Seth secured the lock and faced the men.

"Follow me," Seth ordered, as he turned toward the steps.

The remaining vampires were released from their hold and charged the locked cell door. Ignoring the uproar, the two vampires followed Seth up the stone steps.

Jario gazed over the snarling vampires' exposed fangs and began to laugh.

"If you only knew how pathetic you look," he continued to laugh, as he headed for the stone steps. "My old friend would have enjoyed entertaining you. Sadly, she is gone."

Jario pursed his lips as he thought of Magna. Shaking his head, he took the steps two at a time and left the dungeon.

Chapter 31

Lara knelt down in her garden and pulled the last of the carrots from the damp earth. She was doing everything she could to keep her mind from thinking about the coming full moon. Hearing the sound of chatter, she looked toward the cottage to see Laralynn, Nollie, and Lettie walking toward her.

"Mother, we are going to walk to the village," Laralynn said. "Shall I take the eggs to Ian and Hazel?"

"Yes dear, the basket is on the barrel by the coup," Lara replied. "Leave a few for our evening meal and don't let Ian cheat you. Make him give you a good price."

Nollie and Lettie followed Laralynn to the coup and watched her carefully inspect each egg as she retrieved them from the nests. Laralynn wanted to be sure to take the best eggs to the market. With her basket full, she stepped from the coup and brushed the feathers from her skirt while Nollie picked a few from her hair. Making their way through the gate, they waved goodbye as they passed the garden and headed for the village. The girls sang as they walked along the dirt road to the village market and occasionally stopped to pick flowers or watch a butterfly dance from flower to flower.

As they approached the market, the girls saw two horses tethered to the rail in front of the market's wooden porch. Laralynn didn't recognize the markings upon the blankets, but knew that they held a royal mark. Stepping through the door, Laralynn could see a man facing Ian and a woman dressed like a man standing beside him.

The man was asking Ian about a missing woman. She heard him say something about wanting to search the village for her. Wanting to hear what they were saying, Laralynn stepped forward to place her basket upon the counter. As she did, Baxter moved to let her pass.

"Let me help you with that," Baxter said, as he lifted the basket from Laralynn's hands and placed it on the counter. As he did, he accidentally brushed her hand with his, and he saw Laralynn flinch. He felt a burst of heat spread up to his elbow. Trying to ignore it, he turned to Laralynn and noticed her blushing. "We will only be a moment more."

She felt something tingling in her hand. Looking at her hand, she reached for her locket and stepped back away from him. She could feel the heat of the flush upon her face, and she quickly looked at the floor.

"That is a beautiful locket," Elda said, as she moved toward Laralynn and the girls to examine it closer.

"It was a gift from her mother for her birthday," Nollie quickly offered. "She will be sixteen on the next full moon."

"It belonged to my grandmother," Laralynn quietly said, as she looked up at Elda and then stole a glance toward Baxter.

"Who are you looking for?" asked Lettie. "I heard the man say he wanted to search the village. Is there a person making trouble."

"No, no," Elda replied. "We are searching for Lady Lara. She has been missing for a long time. We heard rumors that she might be here in Primrose Pond."

"We do not know a Lady," Nollie stated. "We are all simple people."

"If you should see a stranger, please tell Ian," she requested. "He will know how to contact us."

"We will," Laralynn replied.

Laralynn saw the man step away from the counter. Ian waved her toward him as he said, "Miss Thomas, I can help you now."

Baxter stopped after hearing him say Thomas. He stared at the locket that hung around Laralynn's neck. As he started to pass her, he caught the subtle scent of fresh apples.

"Miss Thomas, what is your name?" asked Baxter.

"Her name is Laralynn Thomas," Ian stated, with concern in his voice. "I have known her since she was a baby. I have known her mother too. They have lived here in Primrose Pond for over sixteen years."

"I meant no harm," Baxter said, as he hesitated for a moment and then turned toward the door.

Elda could tell that something was bothering Baxter. Once they were out on the porch she took his arm and made him face her.

"What is it?" she asked.

"Just a moment," he said, as he walked back into the market and approached Ian. "Do you have any apples? I had one the last time I was here. I would love to have another one, if you do."

"No apples today," Ian said. "We have figs."

"I was hoping for an apple. Maybe next time," Baxter said, as he turned and headed toward the door.

Baxter went straight for his horse and quickly mounted him. Nodding his head toward the trees, Elda quickly did the same and followed Baxter until they were well hidden within the cover of the trees.

"Something happened back there," Baxter said. "When I touched that young girl's hand, I felt heat race up my arm. I could tell that she felt it too."

Elda raised an eyebrow and started to laugh.

"I know what you are thinking," he barked. "I know what I felt."

"She is a little young for a mate," Elda said, as she continued to snicker.

"It wasn't just that, that concerns me," Baxter said. "Did you see the locket? It looked just like the locket that Lady Lara wore just before she left Evergreen. The girl's name is Laralynn Thomas. You don't find that strange? Plus, I could smell apples."

"Apples?" Elda snickered. "What does apples have to do with anything?"

"Years back, I came through Primrose Pond looking for Lady Lara," Baxter explained. "There was a woman with a baby standing in the market. It was not long after Lady Lara was discovered missing. She was new to the village. Ian called her Madame Thomas. When I started to leave, I smelled apples. Ian had apples in the market, and I bought one. Today I smelled apples, and he didn't have any. We discovered the scent of apples in the forest near the witch's cottage when we were searching for Lady Lara. I think the scent of apples is coming from the child."

"So she smells like apples," Elda whined. "What do we do?"

"We need to follow Laralynn back to her cottage," Baxter said. "I need to know if Lady Lara is her mother."

Baxter and Elda waited among the trees until they heard the girls leave the market and head down the road. As they started to follow them, Baxter suddenly stopped. He placed his hand to his forehead and closed his eyes.

"Baxter, are you there?" Astra said.

"Yes, I am here," he replied.

"I have found the cave, but the creature is there. I have to wait until he leaves before I can enter," she said. "Stay close. I may need you."

"We will leave Primrose Pond and head for Old Mill and wait for your message," Baxter replied.

"I have started to gain some of my magic. I want to try something," Astra said, as she made two fists. "I am looking at a place just beyond the cave. Can you see it?"

"I see something, but it is blurry," Baxter replied. "Try harder."

Astra focused all her attention on the place she wanted to show Baxter.

"I can see it now. A small clearing with three young pine trees and a hollowed log," Baxter described.

"Yes, I did it," Astra gasped with glee. "Can you flash to that place when I call for you?"

"I believe that I can," Baxter said, but he sounded worried. "I have only flashed to places I have actually seen in person. It might work. Could we try it?"

"You must do it quickly," Astra said. "The creature is near. If he sees you, he will make you fall asleep and then you will be his."

Astra watched the clearing and waited for Baxter to appear. Hiding behind a large boulder, she watched the entrance to the cave. Her hands began to shake, and she tugged at her gloves trying to make them stop. Looking up, she saw a slight blur just before she saw Baxter appear next to the log. She stood and nodded her head and then quickly knelt back down. When she looked back up, Baxter was gone.

"It worked," Astra screamed into Baxter's mind.

"Not so loud. Yes, it worked. If you can get Thomas and Tate out of the cave, I can take them both from the mountain. Let me know if you are able," Baxter replied. "I will be waiting."

Filled with happiness for the first time in a long time, Astra waited for the creature to leave the cave. She would only have one chance. If the creature caught her, he would renege on their agreement. They would become enemies, and he would make her his next meal, piece by piece.

* * *

Waving to Nollie and Lettie at the fork in the dirt road, Laralynn ran the rest of the way to the cottage. Her basket was full of flour, beans, and wax. She made a special effort to be careful not to spill any of the items. As she neared the gate, Laralynn saw her mother standing in the open doorway waiting for her.

"Did Ian give you any trouble?" her mother asked.

"No trouble," she replied, as she began to giggle. "Hazel kept an eye on him. She never lets him cheat me."

Lara laughed and hugged her daughter before they entered the cottage.

"I saw two horses with royal markings today," Laralynn said, as she placed the basket on the table. "There was a man and a woman in the market asking Ian questions."

"What kind of questions?" Lara asked, as she glanced out the window to see if Laralynn had been followed.

"They were looking for Lady Lara. She has been missing," Laralynn said. "The man asked me my name, and the woman thought my locket was beautiful. Nollie was a talker, as usual, and told her it was a gift for my birthday."

"Did you tell them your name?" Lara asked.

"No, Ian told him," Laralynn replied. "Was that bad?"

"No sweetheart," Lara said, as she moved to wrap her arms around Laralynn. "We must not speak to strangers. It isn't safe."

"They were very nice. The man helped me with my basket," Laralynn said, as she hesitated for a moment. "The man accidently touched my hand, and I felt a very funny tingle."

"What did the man look like?" Lara asked.

"He was tall with very light hair that touched his shoulders. His beard looked funny," she replied.

Lara knew immediately who she was describing. It was Baxter. The woman with him must have been Elda. They were always sent out on patrol together. If Baxter saw the locket, he would know that it belonged to Lady Lara. They were close to finding her. There was nothing they could do to stop the bargain that she had made with Velsa, but they would be close enough to collect Laralynn and keep her safe. Feeling a strange sense of relief after hearing her daughter's news, she kissed Laralynn's forehead and picked up the sack of flour from the basket.

"He was probably from the castle. We shouldn't worry. The army works hard to protect the people of this island. You probably felt a tingle in your hand because you were afraid or nervous. It is nothing to worry about. Let's get ready for our meal," Lara said, as she turned and headed for the large pot that hung in the hearth.

"She has found her mate," Lara softly said. "Baxter will take good care of my daughter."

Chapter 32

The creature's usual dark stormy clouds were absent from the sky bringing a much needed warmth to the mountain. Astra pulled the hood of her cape down over her forehead to help shield her eyes from the bright sunlight. She had stayed huddled behind a cluster of boulders long after seeing Baxter disappear. Safely out of the way, she could clearly see the entrance to the creature's cave and patiently waited for him to leave. Astra knew she wouldn't have very much time once he left. He seldom strayed too far from the entrance unless he knew there were hunters or trackers on the mountain.

The slight echoing of shuffling feet drew Astra's attention. Holding her breath, she carefully raised up to see the creature exiting the cave. As he unfolded his large frame from the small entrance, she could see his horns curl around his ears and his eyes brighten from amber to a deep reddish-orange. She knew what that meant. He was searching the area. Not knowing if she had enough magic to hide herself from view, Astra closed her eyes and whispered a chant she had learned as a child.

The shuffling of feet grew louder and suddenly the creature was standing before her. He began to sniff the air and appeared to be looking directly at her. Afraid to move, she watched as he moved the tall grass beside her feet that grew up from between the rocks. Reaching his hand in between two small rocks, she heard a small squeal before she saw him pull his hand back wrapped around a wiggling rat. Dangling the rat by the tail, the creature swallowed it whole and then backed away from the boulders making his way down the rocky path away from the cave. Astra waited until she could hold her breath no longer. Gasping for air as quietly as she could, she slowly stood to make sure the creature was gone.

Still listening for the sound of the creature's return, she bent over at the waist and crept into the cave. Surrounded by darkness, she pulled the glove from her hand and snapped her fingers. A small flame appeared on the palm of her hand and gave her just enough light to maneuver the small space. There in the darkness sitting opposite from each other, Thomas and Tate sat perfectly still leaning against the wall. Their eyes were closed and appeared to be sleeping. Astra cringed as she looked down to see Thomas' arm stripped of its flesh and blood smeared across his chin. She was sure he had fed recently. With no signs of an animal carcass, she surmised that he must have fed on Tate. Astra touched the side of Thomas' face and saw his eyes flutter for a moment before he was able to open them.

"I am going to try and save you from the creature," she whispered to Thomas. "Can you speak?"

Thomas blinked his eyes in response.

"Can you move your arms?" she asked, as she looked down at what was left of his ravaged arm.

Thomas blinked his eyes again.

"This makes it more difficult," she said, as she patted Thomas' leg for reassurance. "I will do my best to get you out of this place."

She crawled over to Tate and stroked the side of his face. Hearing a soft moan, she took hold of his hand and felt him lightly squeeze her fingers. Gasping with relief, Astra continued to whisper to Tate until he finally opened his eyes. She felt Tate's body shiver and saw a timid attempt to grab her with his other hand before it dropped to his lap.

Leaning forward and placing her mouth close to Tate's ear, she whispered, "Tate, I have come to help you. I have been in contact with your friend, Baxter, and he knows that I will help you if I can. If I can get you out of the cave, he can retrieve you."

Tate realized what she was saying, and he tried to give her his full attention.

"I need one thing from you before you can leave," she said, as she brushed the matted hair from his face. "I am sorry to ask this of you, but I need your blood. I need you to place your hand upon the point of my dagger. Can you do this?"

Tate looked at her and lowered his eyes to the dagger. He tried to lift his hand, but he could only manage a small movement.

"I will help you," she said. "I will place the dagger in your lap next to your hand. Try to move your hand against the point as hard as you can."

Astra moved to the other side of Tate and placed the dagger on his lap. She lifted his hand and rested it upon the hilt of the dagger to keep it from falling. Lifting his other hand, she carefully placed it next to the point of the dagger. Pulling her hands away from Tate, she nodded that she was ready for him to try. Tate moved the wrong hand and the dagger fell from his lap.

"Tate, not to worry," Astra said. "We will try it again."

Placing the dagger and his hands back in place, she nodded for Tate to try again. Again, Tate knocked the dagger from his lap. Seeing the frustration in Tate's eyes, she smiled and shrugged her shoulders.

"We will try again," she whispered, as she felt her stomach nervously churn.

This time she turned the dagger the other way and placed the stronger hand near the dagger's point. Taking a deep breath, she nodded at Tate that she was ready. He lifted the same hand and grazed the blade. She could see the blood dripping from the dagger onto his breeches. Picking up the dagger, she carefully moved the blade over her mouth and let three drops of Tate's blood drip onto her tongue. She had completed the task and knew that she wouldn't have much time before the pain would take her. The pain always took her into the darkness.

"Baxter! Oh my stars, Baxter can you hear me?" she yelled into Baxter's mind, as she dropped the dagger. "Please! Please hear me. Baxter, can you hear me?"

"I am here Astra, I am here," Baxter replied.

"Come quickly to the place that I showed you," she said, as her words began to slur. "I have taken Tate's blood, and I fear that I will succumb to the pain before you can get here. The cave where Thomas and Tate are hidden is very close to where you appeared."

Baxter started to flash as he responded, "I am on my way."

Standing by the hollowed out log, he could see the small entrance to the cave. He ran to its entrance and knelt down to crawl forward into the dim light. He could see Astra sitting on the ground leaning against Tate as she held a small flame in the palm of her hand.

"Astra," Baxter said, as he rushed to Tate's side.

"Take them . . . quickly," she slurred, as her eyes began to close. "The creature . . . may return . . . at any moment."

Baxter pulled Tate away from the wall of the cave and began to drag him over next to Thomas. Holding Tate in his arms, he could hear the sound of someone approaching the entrance of the cave.

"Astra, he is coming," Baxter whispered.

Looking over at Astra, he saw her open her eyes and try to stand. Unable to stand, she could only kneel without falling. She stretched her arms out in front of her and made tight fists. She nodded to Baxter to keep going. Baxter sat down next to Thomas and pulled Tate into his lap. With one arm around Tate's waist and the other around Thomas' neck, Baxter looked up at Astra and silently mouthed his thanks. Right before her eyes, they vanished.

Loud snarling drew Astra's attention away from the spot she had last seen Baxter. She could see the creature standing outside the entrance to the cave. Astra could feel the air cool around her. She began to shiver as the creature bent to enter the cave.

"You have betrayed me, and you will soon be dead," screamed the creature, as he made his way into the cave. Standing before her, he raised his arm and extended his claws. "You will never leave this mountain alive."

As she opened her fists, jagged shards of blazing light flew from her hands and into the body of the creature. One shard after another penetrated his chest and abdomen causing the creature to scream. He raised his hands to fight back, but Astra was too strong. Years of pent up magic had finally been released directly into his body. The creature fell to his knees and swayed back and forth. His amber eyes slowly dimmed to black. Feeling the strain of exhaustion, Astra shrieked as one final shard raced from her hand and severed the creature's head. Hearing it fall to the ground, her hands dropped to her side. She felt only a moment's peace before a sudden sting of scorching pain race from her feet to her head. Holding her head she collapsed to the ground. Her screams were the last thing she heard before the darkness took her.

* * *

Seeing Baxter, Tate, and Thomas sprawled on the floor of the Command Center, Will and Oliver rushed to offer help. Without uttering a word, Oliver lifted Thomas' limp body into his arms and headed straight for the Healing Room. Before Baxter could stand, he saw Will lift Tate and race after Oliver.

Oliver laid Thomas down on the cot and carefully placed his ravaged arm across his abdomen. The sight of his arm without flesh made anger swell up so fast in him that he had to leave the room for fear he would demolish the walls of the Healing Room. Will looked over at Thomas and cringed as he placed Tate on the cot next to his brother. He could hear Tate moaning, and he began to speak incoherently calling out for his brother.

As Flora entered the room, she glanced down at Thomas and quickly knelt by his side. Will watched as Flora placed her hands directly upon the bones of Thomas' arm. Glowing heat radiated from her hands as his arm slowly began to mend itself. With only muscle covering the bones, Flora let go of his arm and stood swaying by his cot. Will quickly reached for her arm to steady her.

"I have given him all that I can," Flora said. "He should be able to heal himself the rest of the way; however, he needs blood."

Will stood alongside Thomas' cot and knelt down beside him. Pulling his dagger from its sheath, he drew the blade across his wrist and placed his wrist over Thomas's open lips. He let the blood drain into Thomas' mouth until he saw his own wound heal. Will repeated the process three more times before Flora insisted he had done enough.

"He needs rest," Flora said, as she inspected his healing arm.

"He will be out for days," Will said. "He has difficulty flashing, and the pain he has endured will cause him to sleep until he is healed."

"Until he wakes, I will care for him and Tate," Flora replied. "Run and retrieve Gavenia for me. She will surely want to wait by Tate's side."

Heading for the door, he turned and looked over his shoulder at the men that lay helpless upon the healing cots. He hated to leave them.

"Will, ask Meadow to come to the Healing Room. I need her to determine if there are any lingering spells that might keep them from waking," requested Flora, as she began to cut the soiled clothing from Tate's body. "Now leave me to my work."

With those words, Will was gone.

Chapter 33

Torches burned around the small arena behind the Crimson Claw Castle. Seth, the new commander, stood watching several of the vampires retrieved from Jario's dungeon hurling large heavy stones to one another. Since receiving the command of the army, Seth had chosen the strongest of the lot to begin their training. He had given one his final death for disobeying a direct order and none since. The example had reinforced his authority over the men and instilled a certain amount of fear. He wasn't looking for their respect. Respect would come much later. For now, he demanded total obedience.

Seeing Seth observing the training session, Jario approached his commander and stood quietly with his hands clasped behind his back. He stared at the men as they groaned from the weight of the stones. Curious as to why they were throwing stones, Jario looked over at his commander.

"Does this make them a stronger soldier?" asked Jario.

"In a way it makes them stronger, My Lord," Seth replied. "It teaches them obedience."

"Obedience?" asked Jario. "Why obedience?"

"They are to do as I command," Seth explained. "They are to throw stones, lift logs, sleep, or whatever I command them to do without hesitation. Those that cannot comply are given their final death."

"I understand," Jario replied. "An obedient soldier is a stronger soldier."

"Yes, My Lord," Seth chuckled. "When repeated over and over, the order used with compulsion becomes second nature. No thought is needed. Their immediate reaction becomes the required response."

"And how long will it take for you to complete their training and achieve an immediate reaction?" asked Jario.

"I cannot say at this time," Seth said, as he turned to look directly at Jario. "An army proficient with a variety of weapons, strategy of war, and devotion to their master takes time. If this is what you require, I will complete the task. I can promise you that when I say your army is ready, they will be ready for any challenge set before them."

"I cannot wait forever," Jario sneered. "I have desires that I wish to be filled."

"If you want this done in a very short period of time, you will end up with a band of useless vampires that might follow orders or might attack you if the right price is offered," Seth said. "If this is what you want, I suggest you go back to the dock and search for a new commander. If I am to be the commander of this army, it will be done my way."

Jario could feel his temper rising. He had never let anyone speak to him the way Seth had done. Looking away from Seth and out into the arena at the men throwing stones, he realized that he needed Seth. He could not let his arrogance get in the way of his goal. Rushing had caused him to fail before, and he couldn't take another failure.

"We will do it your way," Jario huffed. "I require regular updates on their progress. If I feel no progress is being made, I will make a change which will relieve you of your duty."

"Yes My Lord," Seth replied, as he turned back toward the men in the arena.

Jario quickly left before his anger made him do something he would regret. As he made his way toward the stable, he noticed Desirae standing in the dark looking up into the darkness.

"Again, I find you looking up at the stars," Jario laughed.

"I have told you before; I am listening to the messages on the wind," snapped Desirae. "There is trouble on the wind. A witch is in agony. I have felt her pain."

"Is it Velsa?" he asked. "She could use a little pain."

"No, this witch is being held against her will," Desirae said, as she lowered her eyes from the sky and wiped tears from her face. "She desperately needs help."

"You're a witch, help her," Jario smirked.

"She is blocked by an old spell," Desirae snapped. "I am unable to help her."

Stomping her foot in frustration, Desirae turned and stormed from Jario's presence.

He looked up at the sky and tried to listen to the wind. Shaking his head, he started to laugh at the idea of messages being sent upon the wind. He knew he needed to find a diversion that would take his mind off things. Heading for the stable, he opened its door and made his way to Ash's stall.

"Ash, we are going to the village tavern for some fun," Jario smirked, as he readied his stallion for the night's ride. "I feel the need for a strong ale and a woman's blood upon my tongue."

Mounting Ash, Jario raced from the stable. It wasn't long before Desirae heard his laughter floating on the wind.

* * *

Astra opened her eyes to the darkness of the cave. Her whole body ached and her ears were ringing. Lifting her head, she tried to focus on the small opening that would allow her to leave the creature's cave. Seeing the light was gone, she knew that the night had come. She wondered how many nights had come and gone. Slowly she sat up and rubbed the dirt from her hair and the side of her face. Remembering what had happened, she wanted to get out of the cave and back in her bed.

The air was cool, and a slight breeze blew in from the cave's entrance carrying the scent of stale blood. Slowly and cautiously, she forced herself to crawl toward the cave's exit. Placing one hand in front of the other and feeling her knees scrape against the dirt floor, she made her way closer to the outside. Feeling her hands slide against a thick slick surface, she knew it was the blood of the creature, and she hoped for her sake that he was still dead. Finally reaching the outside, Astra stood and took a deep breath trying to rid herself of the stench of the creature's death. Needing to wash the blood from her body, she ran from the cave toward her waterfall.

It will wash away the death and pain from my body, she thought, as she stumbled in the dark.

Standing in front of the waterfall, Astra stripped the clothes from her body and threw them as far as she could. Stepping under the cool water, she rubbed her hands over her arms and legs trying to remove the last of the blood from her skin. She stood under the flow of the water and let it rinse her hair clean. Finally feeling her skin begin to shrivel, she dashed from the waterfall to her cave. Her bed was a welcome sight, and she snuggled down into the pile of rags. Before she closed her eyes to sleep, she thought of Tate and Thomas.

"Baxter, are you there?" whispered Astra. Feeling exhausted, she tried again. "Baxter are you there?"

"Yes," Baxter replied. "I was so worried about you. It has been days since we left you. Did the creature harm you?"

"No, the creature is dead," she sighed. "He is finally dead. Are they well? Are Tate and Thomas well?"

"Thomas still sleeps, but Tate is well," he answered.

"Good," Astra sighed, once more. "You will still come for me?"

"I promise we will come for you when we find Thomas' child," Baxter said. "You have my word."

"I will be waiting," Astra replied. "I must sleep. Goodnight Baxter."

"Goodnight Astra," Baxter replied. "Thank you."

Breaking their connection, Astra drifted off to sleep. For the first time since she was bound to the mountain, the nightmares that plagued her sleep vanished. She dreamt of spring, green grass, flowers and butterflies. She dreamt of her cottage, and the fire she would make to keep her warm.

✳ ✳ ✳

Gavenia and Tate walked hand and hand through the hallway toward the Command Center. She leaned against his shoulder happy to have Tate back by her side. With the help of Oliver's blood, he had easily healed the symbolic marks the creature had left upon his back and chest. Meadow had searched his body to find the remains of a *Sleeping Spell* that had kept Tate slipping in and out of consciousness. Locating the spell hidden within his ribs, she was able to remove it without causing Tate any additional pain. Fully recovered, he was ready to continue the search for Lady Lara, and anxious to help retrieve Astra from the mountain.

As they entered the Command Center, Preston greeted the couple, "It is nice to have you back among us, Tate. We were all worried that we would not be able to bring you home."

"It is good to be back," Tate replied. "My brother took the brunt of the creature's torture and still sleeps under Flora's watchful care. Now that I am able, I want to help in the search of Lady Lara."

"Baxter and Elda have gone once again to Primrose Pond in search of our Lady," Preston replied. "I need you and Gavenia for another assignment."

"What is more important than finding Lady Lara?" barked Tate, as he clenched his fists and sternly glared at Preston.

"I need help from Gavenia's hawk. We have heard rumors of a new army at Crimson Claw Castle," he explained, as he looked over at Tate's irritated expression. "Word has spread that Jario has a new commander. He is said to be a fierce vampire that has sailed the sea attacking ships for their treasures and kidnapping their women. I would like your hawk to make a flight over Jario's castle to confirm or deny the rumors. We cannot afford to be surprised with an attack upon Evergreen with our Lady missing and Lord Thomas recovering in the Healing Room."

"Gladly," Gavenia responded, without hesitation. "When do you want me to go?"

"Now," Preston stated. "The sooner we know, the better."

"How will I know him?" asked Gavenia.

"He is a large bulky vampire with a tattoo of a mermaid on one arm and a serpent on the other," Preston said, as he ran his hand from his shoulder to his wrist. "Rumors say his powers are many and strong. Be very careful."

"I will have Tate with me," Gavenia sighed, as she looked up at Tate's face. "He will protect me."

"Let's get what we need for the journey and head out," Tate encouraged Gavenia by turning her toward the hallway. "The sooner we leave, the sooner we will be back to help search for Lady Lara."

Looking up at Tate, Gavenia softly whispered, "There is enough light for us to make it to Hunter's Point. We can spend the night there and search the castle grounds by morning light."

Tate saw the warm flush upon her face and smiled.

"You liked Hunter's Point did you?" Tate chuckled, seeing Gavenia nod her head.

Chapter 34

Lara sat in her chair next to the warm fire as she stitched the pouch that Meadow had given her into the hem of her blue burial dress for safekeeping. She had kept the small worn pouch in her apron pocket every day since waking in Primrose Pond. Her daughter had often seen her pull it from her pocket and rub it between her hands calling it her smelly good luck charm. On Meadows demand, Lara had kept it with her at all times. She didn't know if it was Meadow's pouch or Velsa's spell that had kept them safe throughout the many years at Primrose Pond, but they had safely reached the coming of Laralynn's sixteenth year.

In preparation for her death, everything else had been prepared to Lara's liking. She had shown Laralynn her journal full of letter's to her father, given her the gold locket, asked Aslev to watch over her daughter, and bundled the items she had taken to remember Thomas for Laralynn to find. Finishing the last stitch to secure the pouch, Lara carried the dress to her bedchamber and hung it on the wooden peg by the doorway.

I am ready, she thought. I have done all I could do to raise our daughter. I trust that you, my love, will find her and keep her safe from Jario. My coming death will be worth the bargain made to have protected her all these years from the darkness.

Hearing the chatter of Laralynn and her friends as they entered the cottage, Lara made her way to greet them. The smell of bread pudding lingered in the air.

"Do you smell that?" Lettie asked, as she licked her bottom lip. "Bread pudding."

"I thought you deserved a treat," Lara said, as she hugged each one of the girls. "You have all been such good helpers today. Wash your hands, and I will pull the pot from the fire."

A loud knock startled Lara. Before Lara could stop her, Nollie opened the door to find Baxter standing before them.

"Excuse me, Madame," Baxter said, as he glanced around the room not recognizing the young girl that answered the door. "We are searching for a missing woman. She is known as Lady Lara. She has been missing for just over sixteen years. We are asking everyone in Primrose Pond if they have seen her. Her people are in need of her return." Seeing Laralynn, he noticed the locket and knew he had found Lady Lara. Even though she did not resemble her, he was sure that some spell had been cast upon her to protect her image from recognition. "She is fair of skin with strawberry blonde hair. Her smile would light up a room, and she is full of kindness for everyone."

Lara's eyes began to water, and she quickly turned toward the pot hanging over the fire to hide the tears than began to run from her eyes. As she lifted the pot and carried it to the table, she shook her head.

"No sir, we have not seen this woman that you speak of," Lara replied. "Would you care to join us? We were about to have some bread pudding. I learned how to make it from a very sweet friend. Everyone said that her bread pudding was wonderful."

Baxter looked at the pot and remembered the story told by Tate of eating bread pudding the night that Lady Lara woke in the Healing Room. He was sure that she was confirming that he had found his missing woman, but she was not free to acknowledge it to him.

"We would love to join you, but we have many other cottage doors to visit before we can return back to Evergreen Castle," Baxter replied. "Our Lord has fallen ill, and we must not stay longer than necessary."

Baxter could see the sudden look of fear cross her face and a single tear run down her cheek. Silently, he nodded to her that he knew she was Lady Lara.

She now knew that Baxter had found her.

"I hope your Lord recovers fully," Lara replied, as her hands began to shake. "I will keep him in my thoughts."

"We must bid you good evening, Madame," Baxter said, as he brought his hand to his chest and bowed slightly. "We will offer your good wishes to our Lord."

Baxter turned from the open door and walked toward Twiggs that was tethered by the gate. Elda smiled and offered her the same royal salute. As they rode away, Lara felt her body sway and she quickly sat down on the bench next to the table.

"Mother, are you unwell," Laralynn asked, as she knelt before her mother and took hold of both of her hands.

"Lettie, get Madame Thomas some water," Nollie ordered, as she jabbed her sister in the arm. "I'll get her shawl."

The girls tended to Lara with words of loving comfort. Helping her to her chair by the fire, Laralynn directed Nollie and Lettie to serve the bread pudding. Laralynn was sure her mother was just hungry, and a warm serving of bread pudding would make everything better.

"I am fine," Lara insisted. "I was just surprised by the visit and saddened to hear of the Lord's illness."

"I hope they find her soon," Laralynn said, as she took the small bowl from Lettie and handed it to her mother.

"I do too," Lara whispered. "I do too."

✳ ✳ ✳

Elda followed Baxter deep into the forest. When Baxter halted and dismounted, Elda did the same.

"What happened back there?" Elda asked. "It sounded like you were both speaking in riddles."

"Did you see her reaction?" asked Baxter. "As sure as I am a vampire, that woman is Lady Lara. I know it doesn't look like her, but I am sure it's her."

"What?" Elda gasped. "How can you be sure?"

"As sure as I can be," he replied. "First of all, the locket that Laralynn wore belonged to Lady Lara. I saw her wear it after Lord Thomas gave it to her in their private courtyard after their return from Black Thistle Castle. Next, she spoke of bread pudding."

"What does bread pudding have to do with anything," Elda smirked. "How does a sweet dessert prove it was Lady Lara?"

"Lord Thomas, Tate, and Lady Lara ate Charlotte's bread pudding in the Healing Room when she woke from Magna's attack. I heard Tate joke about it."

"So, she likes bread pudding," Elda sneered. "It doesn't prove that she is Lady Lara."

"Did you see her eyes fill with tears when I described Lady Lara?" asked Baxter. "She was humbled. I had seen that look on Lady Lara's face before. But, the one thing that proved it to me was her reaction to hearing of Lord Thomas being ill. Elda, fear crossed her face. Her hands began to shake. Why would someone that had never met Lord Thomas react that way? It was her. I know it was her. What I don't understand is if she was free to acknowledge it to me, why she did not come forward."

"If a spell has kept her hidden, the spell must be keeping her silent," offered Elda.

"That can be the only reason," Baxter replied. "Elda, go back to the castle. I will stay here and watch over her. When Lord Thomas wakes, bring him here. The spell must have a loophole. Maybe if she sees Lord Thomas it will break the spell."

Elda mounted her stallion and raced for Evergreen Castle while Baxter made his way through the forest to find a good place to keep watch over Lady Lara and her daughter. Finding the perfect location, he dismounted and stood watching the reflection of the candlelight flicker in the cottage window.

"I owe you my life, Lady Lara," Baxter whispered. "You saved me from the madness, and I can do no less for you. I will stand guard until your mate can retrieve you and bring you home to Evergreen."

Chapter 35

Sitting on a swaying branch in the moonlight and holding on to a thin branch above her, Velsa woke from her *Relaxing Spell*. The last thing she remembered were the bright pink butterflies that fluttered between her fingers. They were beautiful butterflies, and she had carried them outside through the forest. Looking at her hands, she saw that the pink butterflies were gone and so were her clothes.

"For the love of stars, where are my clothes?" she shrieked.

Velsa disappeared from the swaying branch back into her cottage. A fit of uncontrollable giggles filled the cluttered space as she yanked her favorite robe from the wooden peg. As if someone was watching her, she quickly donned her silky robe and collapsed into her rocking chair. Covering her face with her hands, she took a deep breath and tried to calm herself.

"How long have I been dangling from the treetops?" she choked, as she tried to control her laughter. "No more of that special tea for me."

Closing her eyes and pressing her bare toes to the floor, she began to slowly rock back and forth. Her mind was full of scrambled thoughts and memories. She knew she had important things to do, but she couldn't remember what was important and what was useless. There was something extremely important that she should be doing. One by one, she dug through her mind for that one very important thing. Startled, she opened her eyes and stood clutching her robe tightly around her body.

"What day is it?" she shouted. "What day is it?" Dashing outside, she looked up at the nearly full moon and sighed with relief. "Thank the stars. It isn't full yet. I haven't missed it."

Stepping into her cottage feeling her face flush, Velsa leaned against the closed door and calmed her breathing. She hadn't missed the full moon. It was three days away. She needed a clear mind and steady hands to complete the spell that would provide her Lara's heartbeat.

Gathering her book of spells and magic orb from the cupboard, she lovingly placed them on her table. Opening the large worn book, she carefully turned page after page until she found the perfect spell. Pointing her hard yellowed fingernail at the first word of the page, she began to read the list of ingredients. Smiling, she realized she had everything including the strands of hair she had taken from Lady Lara while she slept.

Snatching a wooden bowl from a stack next to her table, she began to fill it with each and every precious ingredient. Dropping the strands of Lady Lara's hair into the bowl. A strong scented red vapor that smelled of cherries began to swirl up into the air. Carefully holding a vial upside down over the vapor, she watched as the vapor made its way into the vial. When it was full, Velsa carefully secured the lid into place. Clasping the vial tightly within her hand, she began to laugh.

"The time is near, my sweet Lara," she whispered. "A bargain made is a bargain kept."

Velsa opened a small wooden chest and laid the vial upon its soft lining. As she closed the lid, her thoughts wandered to Laralynn and sadness began to fill her heart. She knew the child would be heartbroken, but she would see that her father would find her. That was the least that she could do for the child after the wonderful prize that Lady Lara had promised her.

"She will always remember the love of her mother," Velsa sniffled, as tears ran from her eyes.

Finding her rocking chair, she began to rock back and forth. Wiping her nose with the sleeve of her robe, Velsa's back stiffened.

"Foolish witch," she uttered, for no one but herself to hear. "Have you forgotten? You are a powerful witch. A witch that won the War of the Witches. You have no need of tears. Tears bring weakness. Keep yourself focused on your desires. Keep yourself focused on revenge and pain. After all, it is only a justified payment for what has been done to you."

Velsa spit into the empty hearth and watched purple sparks turn to a roaring fire. Satisfied with herself, she kept rocking in her favorite chair.

With her eyes closed and a smile upon her face, she whispered, "I am not the good witch. Do you hear me? I am not the good witch."

* * *

Flora wiped a cool damp cloth across Thomas' forehead. Beads of perspiration covered his face and neither Flora nor Meadow could find the cause. The creature had hidden the *Sleeping Spell* within Thomas' ribs, and like Tate, she had easily been able to remove it. His body had been covered with large symbolic marks. One by one, Meadow worked to remove them until his body was free of them all. It was after the final mark was removed that the illness appeared.

"Is he any better?" asked Oliver.

"Nothing we do seems to help him," Flora replied. "The spell and marks are gone, but a new illness has taken over his body. I cannot find the source."

"Does he need more blood?" asked Oliver, as he moved toward the cot and drew his dagger from his boot. "I will willingly give him all that I have to save him."

"Both Frances and Will have fed him this evening," she said, as she applied another cool cloth to his forehead.

Oliver knelt down beside his friend and took hold of his hand. As Flora brushed the damp hair from Thomas' forehead, Oliver noticed a strange bruise above his ear.

"What is this?" asked Oliver. "Have you seen this bruise?"

Flora moved around the cot to stand next to Oliver. Bending over, she moved the hair away from Thomas' ear. She could see the small purple bruise and what looked like a tiny blister.

"Give me your blade," requested Flora.

Oliver handed his dagger to Flora and watched her hold its blade over the flame of a candle. Knowing what she intended to do, Oliver held Thomas' head with one hand and pulled his hair away from the blister with the other. Flora carefully scraped the hot blade across the blister, and they watched as blood and pus ran from the small wound. Oliver felt Thomas' body tremble, but he made no sound. Flora leaned closer to inspect the fresh wound. She could see movement under the skin.

"Something has bored its way under his skin," she said, as she pointed the tip of the dagger at the pulsing skin above Thomas' ear. "Hold his head tightly. I am going to try and dig it out."

Oliver strengthened his hold on Thomas and watched Flora carefully pierce the skin and twist the dagger's point. Lifting the blade, blood dripped from its edge and revealed a tiny red spider with one claw. Quickly running the blade through the flame of the candle, the spider's life was ended.

"What was that?" Oliver asked, as he pressed a cloth to Thomas' bleeding wound.

"A Poison Crawler," she replied. "It produces a slow and deadly poison by feeding on its host. They are often found in dark caves. He probably carried it back with him."

"Hopefully, this will allow Lord Thomas to wake," Oliver said, as he noticed that the wound was starting to heal. "Flora, he needs a clean tunic. Let me help you."

Oliver removed Thomas' sleeping tunic, and he helped Flora bathe his friend. Lifting him from the cot, Flora replaced the soiled linens with clean. Dressing Thomas in a clean sleeping tunic, Oliver draped a fresh linen to cover his friend. Kneeling down next to Thomas, he placed his hand over his chest and closed his eyes. He silently asked the stars in the heavens to bring his friend safely back to him.

Chapter 36

Jario woke to the sound of a hawk's squawk far off in the distance. He pushed the bed linens back exposing a naked woman draped over his torso. Carefully extracting her body from his, he left his bed and headed for the balcony. Reaching through the heavy drapes, he unlatched the glass doors. Covering his hand and arm with the heavy fabric, he pushed the door open. Stepping back away from the light, he pulled the drapes back careful to stand in the shadows. He continued to listen to the squawk as he yanked his breeches and tunic from the back of a chair. Quickly donning them, he stood waiting for what he thought was his beloved hawk.

Hearing the flap of its wings, he patiently waited for the hawk to enter his bedchamber. It wasn't long before the hawk flew through the door and perched high upon the bedpost. He stood in awe as it spread its wings wide and then proudly folded them back against its body.

"You are as beautiful as ever," Jario whispered, trying not to wake the sleeping woman in his bed. "I thought you had forgotten me. It is truly a good sign that you have arrived today. I leave tonight for my journey to Primrose Pond. For in three days, I will be collecting my new bride. She is a pretty young thing, pure and innocent to man and vampire. I have always wanted a mate, and she will be a perfect mate once I have turned her.

Gavenia's hawk ruffled her feathers at his comment. Turning her head to look at the woman tangled in the bed linens beneath her and then at Jario, she saw him smirk.

"You are not pleased with me," Jario gave the hawk a wicked smile. "I have not been with a woman for some time. I needed the practice."

Flustered with his attitude and fearing Jario's new focus, she lifted from the bedpost and flew through the open door and up into the sky.

"Are you Jealous?" Jario laughed, as he stared at the open door.

The woman sat up in bed and whisked her long black hair from her face. Tapping the bed linens beside her and pouting her swollen lips, she waited for Jario to join her.

"Now, where were we?" Jario smirked, as he removed his tunic and breeches, leaving them on the floor.

* * *

Gavenia couldn't wait to get out of Jario's bedchamber. To see a woman in his bed made her sick. To hear of his plans to wed a young human girl from Primrose Pond made her shutter. Jario needed to be stopped.

She flew over the castle's three turrets and searched for any sign of the vampire with the tattoos. She had forgotten that most vampires did not come out during the daylight hours. She would have to wait until the sun set and fly in the moonlight. That would require her waiting until Jario left the castle before she could search further.

Just as she was ready to fly back to Tate and wait for the darkness, she heard the slam of a heavy door. Off in the distance, she could see someone dragging someone behind him. Flying toward the trees next to the low building, she watched a large man throw a man half his size to the ground in full sun. The man began to scream, and she watched in horror as he burst into flames. The large man brushed his hands together as if he was removing dirt from his hand. As he turned to return to the building, Gavenia saw the tattoo of a serpent upon his arm. She had what she needed and lifted from the tree branch.

As she flew across the open space behind the castle, she heard the sound of something coming toward her. Quickly banking her wings, she avoided the object. Looking down at the man, she saw a dagger falling from the air and then pierce the ground. He had thrown a dagger at her.

"Who has sent a shifter to spy on me?" he yelled.

Fear filled her mind, and she raced back toward the safety of Tate and his loving embrace. She was done with Crimson Claw Castle. She never wanted to see it again.

* * *

Baxter watched as Nollie and Lettie opened the gate and walked toward the door of Lady Lara's cottage. He had seen the girls come to her cottage often. Laralynn and the girls spent a great deal of time together, and he was glad that she had made friends.

He could hear a horse off in the distance. As it came into view, he saw a woman that he had never seen before. She was not young but not old either. Her hair was the color of flax and her gown was simple. Sitting astride a large palomino, she slowly dismounted and made her way to the cottage. The girls ran from the open door to greet her, and she took the time to hug and kiss the heads of each of them. As they all made their way into the cottage, Baxter leaned back against a tree. Letting his mind wander, his thoughts went to Astra.

"Astra, are you there? It is Baxter," he said, a little too loudly.

"I am here," she replied, sounding sleepy. "Are you coming for me?"

"No, Astra," sighed Baxter. "I am sorry. I wanted to make sure you are well."

"Can you come visit me?" she asked, hoping for a visitor.

"I am on guard duty," he replied, starting to feel badly for getting her hopes up.

"Another time," she said.

"As soon as I can," he answered her.

He felt her abruptly cut the connection and drew his focus back to the cottage. It wasn't long before he tried to reach someone at the Command Center. He wanted to know if Lord Thomas had recovered.

"Will," Baxter said. "Will, can you hear me?"

"Yes," he replied, holding his head. "I am not very good at this. It causes pain in my head."

"Has Lord Thomas recovered yet?" he asked.

"The spells have been removed, but he still sleeps," Will answered.

"Let me know when he wakes," ordered Baxter.

"I will," replied Will, letting the connection end.

"Why won't he wake?" whispered Baxter. "He needs to wake."

As the sun began to set, Baxter looked for the moon. He knew that tonight there would be a full moon, and he would have to be careful not to allow anyone to see him. He sat down on the hollowed log that he had used every night since he arrived and watched the light flicker in the window.

* * *

"Look who is here, mother," Laralynn said, as she pulled Aslev into the cottage.

"We brought a cake for Laralynn's birthday," Nollie said, as she pointed to the cake on the table.

"It looks delicious," Aslev said. "Laralynn, I have brought you something for your birthday."

She took the cloth from her basket and pulled a bundle wrapped in linen and tied with a colored ribbon.

"Open it," shouted Lettie. "Hurry, open it."

Laralynn took the bundle and carried it to the table. She carefully, untied the ribbon and unfolded the linen.

"A journal," she cried. "A beautiful journal. I have a journal just like yours, mother. Thank you, Aslev."

"It was my pleasure. You can write down all your secrets and desires," Aslev whispered. "Write down all your memories. That way, you will not forget them."

Looking up at Lara, she noticed the blue dress that she was wearing. She hadn't seen it since the night she had come to her cottage asking to make a bargain. She knew she was prepared and waiting for Velsa.

"Sit down everyone. We have cake to enjoy," Lara softly said.

The night was full of singing and dancing. Everyone spoke of the people that they loved and places they wanted to go. It gladdened Lara's heart to see her daughter full of so much happiness.

Not being able to wait any longer, Aslev reached into her pocket and clasped the vial into the palm of her hand. She slowly moved toward Lara and stood by her side watching the girls play with Laralynn's kitten. Moving her hands behind her back, she removed the cap from the vial. As the vapor escaped, she whispered under her breath the spell she had practiced.

The moon is full, and the time is near.
Calmly and quietly, you will show no fear.
There is no pain or worry, my dear.
You feel it beginning as your heartbeat decreases.
You need only rest while your heartbeat releases.
Payment is paid as your life with us ceases.

Lara swayed and Aslev caught her arm to keep her from falling. Looking up, Laralynn saw her mother stumble and fall into Aslev's arms.

"Mother," Laralynn shouted, as she rushed to her mother's side. "What is wrong?"

"I need to rest. I am so tired," Lara answered her daughter. "Take me to my bed."

Aslev and Laralynn helped her to her bed. As Laralynn knelt down beside her mother, Aslev covered her with the blanket that had been folded at the foot of her bed. Lara knew what was happening. She was surprised that she had not seen Velsa. She looked over at her daughter and tried to smile. She saw tears in Laralynn's eyes.

"I am just tired. I will be fine once I rest for a while," Lara said.

Looking up to see Aslev standing behind Laralynn, her blurry vision caused her to blink her eyes to focus. There before her stood Velsa in Aslev's place. She suddenly realized that it had been Velsa all along. She saw Velsa tilt her head and give her a smile in return.

"May I be alone with my daughter?" asked Lara.

"Of course," everyone responded, as they left the bedchamber.

"Laralynn, I fear my time has come to say good-bye," she weakly whispered to her daughter. "I have known for some time that I would have to leave you. I made a poor bargain with a witch for your safety. In return she demanded my heartbeat on your sixteenth year."

"No, mother," Laralynn sobbed. "You can't leave me. I need you."

"Aslev will see that your father comes for you. He will love you and take care of you," she gasped and coughed trying to breathe.

"Rest mother, you will get better," Laralynn said, as she kissed her mother's face. "I won't let you die."

"There is nothing you can do, child," she replied. "I have loved you from the moment I knew that you grew within my body. I will watch over you from the heavens. Find the brightest star in the sky and you will know that I see you."

"Mother, when you see a shooting star in the sky, you will know that I am sending my love to you," Laralynn said, through her tears.

"Laralynn, please bury me in the flower garden. I have worn my very best dress for the occasion," she tried to laugh.

Not able to keep her eyes open any longer, she felt her daughter wrap her arms around her. The last thing she felt was the warmth of her daughter's face against her own.

Feeling her mother's limp body, Laralynn released her mother and wiped the tears from her eyes. She stood and slowly walked from the bedchamber.

Holding her head high, she softly said, "My mother is gone. She has gone to shine brightly among the night's sky."

"I will go get mother," Nollie shouted, as she flung the door open and ran from the cottage.

Baxter noticed her sudden departure and quickly stood. Before he had a chance to move forward, he noticed a young man stop Nollie outside the gate. What he heard shocked him to his core.

"What has happened?" Jario asked, as he stood before her in the image of Laralynn's friend Jack.

"Madame Thomas has died," she said, as tears streamed down her face. "I must go get my mother to help Laralynn."

Shocked, Jario watched the young girl turn and run. Making his way through the gate, he approached the door and lifted his hand to knock. He felt something strange surrounding the cottage. It kept him from touching the door, and he knew exactly who was behind this. The hag was protecting Laralynn. He would bide his time and wait for a more appropriate time to visit her. After all, she had just lost her mother. Jario turned and left the cottage. Feeling someone watching him, he kept walking down the dirt road until he was far enough away to bolt into the forest. Finding Ash, he mounted his stallion and headed back toward Crimson Claw Castle.

* * *

Elda sat on the rim of the fountain looking up at the light in the tower. Tossing a coin over her shoulder into the fountain, she closed her eyes and made a plea for Thomas' recovery. He needed to wake. He needed to wake and ride to Primrose Pond to collect Lady Lara. Since his arrival back at Evergreen, he had slept unknowing that she was within reach.

Having made sure that the tower's light burned, she decided to visit Flora and offer her help in caring for Thomas. He needed blood, and it was her turn to help. Stopping to take one last glimpse at the tower, she noticed the tower's light start to flicker. The air was still, and she was sure that the lantern was well protected. Worried, she stared at the light as it flickered again and then dimmed for a moment before it brightened. Taking a step back to get a better view, she watched as the tower suddenly went dark. Elda waited to see if the light would reappear. She waited and waited for the light, but nothing happened. The tower stayed dark. Running from the courtyard, Elda rushed through the hallways afraid of what it meant. Entering the Command Center, she yelled for everyone's attention. One by one, they all looked in her direction.

"The light has gone out in the tower," Elda shouted. "The light has gone out."

Chapter 37

He had been walking for miles searching for Lara. The heat of the sun beat down upon his head, and he felt perspiration run from his forehead into his eyes. Wiping his eyes, he tried to focus on the light that was before him. The closer he got to it, the bigger and brighter it appeared. With his arm outstretched he tried to touch the glowing object that was before him.

"Thomas, go back," a soft voice lingered on the air. "It is not your time. You are needed by others."

Thomas stood still looking at the beautiful light. He could feel it pull him forward. The closer he got, the more he could feel his pain drifting away and the more comfort he felt. The light seemed to embrace him.

"Please, Thomas," the soft voice begged. "Turn back before it is too late."

Ignoring the voice, he let the light draw him even closer until he seemed to recognize something familiar in the voice that had been calling to him. He stopped and turned around. He could see the image of a woman floating slightly above the ground. He strained his eyes to see her face.

"Mother?" asked Thomas. "Is that you?"

"Yes, my son," the woman whispered. "You must not follow the light. Your loved ones need you. They are in terrible danger."

"Who is in danger," he asked, as he moved closer to the image of his mother.

"My son, Lara is in need of your help," she whispered, as she stroked the side of his face. "You must hurry. If you wait too long, she will be lost forever."

"Lara? I have already lost her," he said, as he lowered his head not wanting to show his mother the tears in his eyes.

"She has been hidden from you, and your friends have found her. You must hurry to her side," she said, as she lifted his face.

Placing a kiss upon his forehead. He watched as her image slowly began to fade.

"Don't go. Where is she?" asked Thomas. Not hearing an answer, he screamed again. "Where is she? Where is Lara?"

Bolting into a sitting position, he felt someone clasp his hand and utter words that he could not clearly understand. As his eyes focused, he saw Flora sitting on the edge of his cot.

"Where am I?" he asked.

"Evergreen, My Lord," Flora said, trying to reassure him. "You are in the Healing Room. Baxter brought you back from the mountain. You have been asleep and dreaming."

"Where are my clothes?" he demanded, quickly standing beside the cot. "I need to see Tate."

Before Flora could stand to obey Thomas, Elda and Oliver burst into the room. Finding Thomas awake brought only a moment of relief before they realized they must tell him of the sudden darkness in the tower. Seeing him scramble to dress himself, Flora and Elda stepped out into the hallway. Elda leaned her head against the stone wall and waited.

Hearing Baxter's voice, she looked down the hallway for him. It was then that she realized he had entered her mind, and she froze.

"Elda, do you hear me?" he gasped. "Something dreadful has happened."

"I know, Baxter. The light in the tower has gone out," she replied.

"Send Tate, he is Laralynn's uncle," he ordered. "He will protect her."

"Baxter, Thomas is awake," she said. "Oliver is going to tell him the sad news. I am sure we will be heading that way very soon."

"Finally," he replied. "I will be waiting for him. I am standing watch outside the cottage. A woman I have never seen before is with

Laralynn. A young boy came to visit but left. It was very strange. Hurry, things don't feel right."

"We will get there as soon as we can," she said, as she felt the connection end.

A sudden painful howl could be heard coming from Thomas. Flora grabbed Elda's hand, and the two women listened to Thomas' painful sobs. Footsteps could be heard as they echoed through the hallway. Elda looked up to see Tate racing toward them.

Without saying a word, Tate entered the room to find his brother kneeling on the floor and his shoulders heaving.

"She is gone," he sobbed. "They have told me that she is gone."

"Brother, I have heard from Baxter. He has found your daughter," Tate said, as he took Thomas' arm to help him stand. "Baxter is standing watch outside her cottage. We must ride."

Without hesitation, Thomas followed his brother out into the hallway.

"To the horses," Thomas yelled. "Tate and Elda, come with me. Oliver, my friend, I leave you to lead Evergreen in my absence. I fear that this may be a trap of some kind devised by our enemy, Jario, to draw us from Evergreen."

"My Lord, I am at your service," Oliver said, as he raised his fist over his chest. "Now go and find your daughter."

Thomas placed his hand upon Oliver's shoulder and said, "I have never doubted it."

Seeing Tate and Elda start to run, he followed behind them.

Mother, thank you for the visit, he thought as he ran toward the stable. *Thank you for waking me.*

Following Elda from the stable riding his black stallion, Thomas' yelled, "Take the shortest path. I fear danger surrounds my daughter."

* * *

Jario suddenly pulled up on the reins of his stallion and stopped him in the middle of the meadow. He was having second thoughts about leaving Primrose Pond. She would need his support. What better way to show her that he cared for her than to stand by her side as she mourns the loss of her mother. He had told her he would return on her sixteenth birthday. If he didn't, she would think that he had lied again.

"What was I thinking?" he shouted. "Laralynn is all alone. She will need someone to care for her. I can easily take her now."

Looking up at the sky and dreading the coming sunlight, Jario headed for the abandoned cottage. He would spend the daylight hours there until it was dark enough for him to make his way to Primrose Pond. There he would collect his new mate and carry her to Crimson Claw Castle. Delighted with his plan, he kicked Ash with his heels, and they sped off to the abandoned cottage.

Chapter 38

Laralynn stood looking down at the empty grave lined with sweet grass that Ian and Kenneth had dug in the flower garden. She still couldn't believe that her mother was gone, and she would be burying her at sunset. Her mother loved to watch the sunset and the night sky fill with stars. It would be her final gift to her mother.

It was clear that her mother had made many friends in the village. She had often helped care for a sick child or cleaned a cottage for a bedridden woman. Everyone loved her. Out of respect for her kindness, people from the village came to the cottage to offer their condolences and bring Laralynn a gift of food. She had gone through the motions of thanking each visitor and graciously accepting the food that they had lovingly prepared.

Feeling Aslev's arm wrap around her, she laid her head upon her shoulder. She wanted to cry, but she had cried until there were no tears left.

"Come inside, child," Aslev said. "You need to eat something."

"I'm not hungry," Laralynn replied.

"Well then, come in out of the cool air," she said. "It will be sunset soon."

Agreeing, she softly said, "I need to visit my mother." Wrapping her arm around Aslev's waist, she snuggled in to hug her. "I don't know what I would have done if you had not been with me."

"Hush," she replied. "Let's go now. Say goodbye, and we will prepare your mother for burial."

Laralynn took Aslev's hand and walked back to the cottage. Mollie and Kenneth McCash along with their daughters, Nollie and Lettie, were quietly talking by the hearth. Ian was helping his wife organize the food that covered the table. As they saw her come through the door, they all stopped and offered her a sympatric smile. Making her way to her mother's chamber, she saw her mother dressed in her beautiful blue dress. Hazel had braided her hair and placed flowers in her hands. To Laralynn, she looked as if she were sleeping and wanted to wake her.

Kneeling down, she kissed her mother's cheek and whispered, "I love you, mother. I will never forget you."

She turned and nodded for Aslev to help her with her mother's shroud. Carefully, they folded the clean linen over her body making sure it was secure.

"Ian, I am ready," Laralynn called and stood back waiting for him.

Laralynn watched him lift her mother's body and carry her from the chamber. She slowly followed him to the flower garden. Ian carefully placed Lara's body in Kenneth's arms and then jumped down into the grave. Kenneth knelt down and gave her body over to Ian, while everyone watched Ian place Lara gently upon the sweet grass. Ian took Kenneth's hand and climbed up to stand next to Hazel. They were all quiet waiting for Laralynn to speak.

Off in the distance, Laralynn could hear a thundering sound. She looked up at the sky but realized the sound was coming from the dirt road. The thunderous pounding grew louder, and Ian moved to the gate to see what was causing the disturbance.

"There are horses coming this way," Ian said.

Laralynn hurried to stand beside Ian and saw three riders come to a halt before her. She saw the royal markings and immediately recognized the woman from the market. From across the road, she watched as the man she had met at Ian's market make his way from the trees toward the others.

"I must protest this intrusion. This young lady has lost her mother, and we were about to bury her," Ian grumbled. "Please respect the dead. Please give us privacy."

"I beg your pardon," Thomas said, as he looked at Laralynn. "I find I am unsure of what to say at this moment." He couldn't pull his eyes from her. Her likeness to Lara was undeniable.

"Tell her," encouraged Tate. "Tell her who you are."

"Yes, who are you?" Ian complained. "This is uncalled for."

"My name is Thomas," he said, as he moved closer to the gate and Laralynn.

Laralynn furrowed her brows and tilted her head. Hesitating for a moment, she quietly asked, "Are you the Thomas in my mother's journal? Are you my father?"

"I believe that I am," he smiled and reached for her hand.

"How do we know you speak the truth?" Ian asked, pulling Laralynn back away from the gate. "Can you prove it?"

Unsure of what to say, Thomas looked at Ian and then back at his brother.

"The locket, Thomas. Tell her about the locket," whispered Baxter.

Looking at Laralynn, he said, "I gave my Lara, your mother, a locket just before she vanished. It had a tree engraved on the outside. It belonged to my mother."

"This man saw her wearing it at the market. He could have told you," smirked Ian, pointing to Baxter. "What other proof do you have?"

"Since I have not seen a certain item for a long time, I assume that she took it with her when she left. I gave her a gold ring encrusted with blue and green gemstones when I asked her to be my mate," he said, hoping that she had seen the ring.

Laralynn gasped bringing her hand to her mouth, and tears began to fall from her eyes. She had seen the ring bound in a piece of linen tied with a blue cord. Her mother had nestled it in the bottom of the wooden chest.

"The ring was in the flowered chest. My mother never showed me the ring. I saw it when I removed her journal last evening," Laralynn said, as she pushed past Ian and rushed toward Thomas. "Father!"

Thomas felt her arms wrap around his neck and his own tears upon his face. He held her not wanting to let her go, but his thoughts of Lara made him gently push her back so he could look into her eyes.

"May I see your mother's face?" he asked. "It has been a very long time since I have looked upon her beautiful face."

Laralynn took his hand and helped him through the gate. She slowly led him to the flower garden. Looking down, he could see the body of Lara wrapped in linen. He patted Laralynn's hand and carefully lowered his body down into the grave. Pulling the linen away, he looked upon the woman's face that hid Lara's. She had saved him, loved him, and given him a daughter. He lifted her body and kissed her lips one last time. Pulling her into a loving embrace, he thought of the last time he had held her in his arms. Laralynn was the only one standing above him, and she quietly waited as he said his goodbye.

"Thomas?" a woman's voice softly said. "Thomas?"

He thought that he was imagining hearing her voice when Laralynn suddenly shouted at him. He looked up to see Tate and Elda standing over him. Looking down at Lara's face, he saw that her eyes were open, and her body had started trembling.

"Tate, take her," Thomas said, as he lifted Lara up to his brother.

Tate laid Lara carefully upon the ground while Elda pulled the linen from her body. Jumping from the grave, he reached for Laralynn and held her until Tate helped Lara stand.

"Mother," Laralynn screamed, rushing into her open arms.

The onlookers stood in shock. They had never seen anyone wake from the dead. Stepping closer to see if his eyes had been fooled, Ian boldly touched Lara's arm. She was still cold to the touch, and her appearance had changed.

"Ian, I am well. Do not be afraid," she smiled and hugged her daughter tighter.

Aslev stood alone clenching her teeth. She looked up at the sky and pressed her tongue against her front teeth until she could taste blood. A cold breeze began to blow causing the branches of the trees to sway. Leaves began to flutter through the air. Smirking, she headed for the cottage door.

Damn loopholes, she thought. If I have lost that heartbeat, I will make their lives miserable.

"Let's get inside before it starts to rain," Hazel shouted, over the sudden whistling of the wind.

Tate patted Baxter on the back as they entered the cottage behind Elda.

"We have our Lady back," Tate said, looking over his shoulder at his brother.

Catching his brother's eyes, he saw Thomas silently offer his thanks before he returned his attention back to the women wrapped in his arms.

Everyone else scurried into the cottage leaving Thomas, Lara, and Laralynn standing together with their arms wrapped around one another.

Afraid to let go, Thomas kissed Laralynn's forehead as he gently released Lara and his daughter.

"Laralynn, may I have a moment alone with your mother?" he softly asked. "It has been so long since I have held her in my arms under the stars. We won't be long."

"Of course, father," Laralynn replied. Feeling a few drops of rain, Laralynn hurried to the door of the cottage. She took one last look at her mother and father as they embraced before she stepped inside to celebrate with her friends and family.

"I have no words to describe my feelings at this moment," whispered Lara.

"There are no need for words," he replied. "You are here with me and that is all that matters."

As Thomas looked down upon her face, he noticed a hint of red within her eyes.

"Lara, you are in need of blood," he said, as he held his wrist toward her mouth. "Take all that you need. No one is watching."

He could feel her fangs pierce his wrist as she drew from him, and he held her tightly against his body.

"We will have to explain a few things to our daughter before we return to Evergreen," Thomas said. "I will need your help. I have no idea what has happened and where to start."

"I will explain everything," Lara replied, as she took his hand and led him toward the cottage. "I will explain everything to everyone."

Chapter 39

Safely hidden within the shadows of the trees, the sight of the tethered horses and the royal markings made Jario furious. The Evergreen Army had found Lady Lara's cottage. He could see the flicker of candlelight against the window and wondered why he saw no one outside. Dismounting Ash, he crept toward the cottage. Leaping over the gate, he could see the grave was still open which meant Lady Lara had not been buried yet. Making his way to the side of the cottage, he peered through the window. He saw Velsa, two men and two women that were unfamiliar to him, and two young girls sitting on the floor with Laralynn. Smiles were upon everyone's faces.

Is this how young Laralynn mourns the loss of her mother, he thought?

Hearing someone laugh, he leaned to the other corner of the window to get a wider view of the room. He could now see Elda badgering Baxter, and Tate was moving toward the table of food. What he saw next made him freeze. In the flickering candlelight sat Lady Lara on the lap of Thomas. Shock and then rage swelled within his mind and body. His plans had been ruined. He forced himself to keep his fists from smashing through the window. He wanted to kill them all.

Jario stormed from the cottage window ripping the gate from its hinges. He had let Lady Lara and Laralynn slip right through his fingers. Nothing but rage and hatred filled his mind making his fangs descend and pierce his bottom lip. Feeling the blood run from his lips, he raked the back of his hand across his mouth. Seeing his blood smeared across his knuckles and the sleeve of his tunic made him envision his fangs deep in Laralynn's throat and longed for the taste of her blood.

Mounting his stallion, he pulled tightly on the reins and forcefully jabbed him with the heels of his boots turning Ash's head away from the cottage. They raced through the forest dodging trees and jumping over logs. Moving deeper into the darkness of the forest, a thick layer of fog stretched out over the ground before them. Fearing another one of Velsa's spells, he clenched his jaw and waited for an attack as he quickly guided Ash through the damp fog that encircled the stallion's legs. The force of his hooves caused the fog to swirl up into the air around them like tendrils of smoke aggressively reaching for him. He swatted at the imaginary fingers that brushed against his face, and he shouted for Ash to run faster until they were clear of it.

He rode for miles until he found himself facing familiar black stone walls. Slowing down and then stopping, he took in the sight of the castle that once belonged to him. He had rebuilt it from ruins, but nothing good had come from it. His army had been destroyed, Gautier had banished him from the castle, and Magna had received her final death.

As he stood staring at the balcony that was once his, he thought of the white hawk that had visited him. She had been the only thing that had helped him through the pain and darkness. He needed to return to Crimson Claw Castle. He needed to look upon his hawk and to apologize for his recent behavior. Before he could return to his castle, he needed to make good on a debt. Feeling a slithering shiver run down his spine, he grinned as he thought of grasping the white wolf's tail and hearing her howl from the pain as he sliced it from her body.

Making his way along the edge of the forest hidden from view, he searched the castle walls for an open gate. Finding none, he tethered his horse and pulled his haze. Approaching the gate near the barracks, he pounded his fist against the thick wood and waited. He could hear the boots of someone approaching and then the sound of the large wooden gate moan as it slowly opened. He saw Gusty look about for the source of the pounding. Seeing nothing, he stepped out from behind the gate allowing it to open wide. Jario took advantage of the open gate and slipped in undetected. He heard the gate close as he made his way to the back entrance of the castle.

I will deal with you later, my disloyal friend. You too will feel my wrath.

Jario crept along the quiet hallways listening at each door he passed for the sound of Kayleigh's voice. As he approached the stone steps that led to the dungeon, he felt a strong sense of grief grip his chest. The thought of Magna sitting at her dressing table pulling the pearl covered pins from her long red hair kept him from moving away. Something was drawing him down the stone steps, and before he realized what he was doing, Jario was standing in the middle of the dungeon. The door to Magna's bedchamber was gone, and the metal hinges that had held it were mangled. Stepping toward the doorway, the sight of her empty bed made him pause. Closing his eyes, he could remember the feel of Magna's claws dragging against his chest and could hear her moans of twisted delight. The scent of smoldering coals filled his senses, and his nostrils flared. He could feel the tips of her fangs scrape against his neck and a gentle pressure just before they pierced his skin. The sensation was pleasure and pain rolled into one. Startled, he opened his eyes and pressed the palm of his hand to his neck. It had felt real. Jario looked about the dark dungeon expecting to see her, but he was alone. Or, was he? Confused, he looked at the palm of his hand but saw nothing.

Refocusing on his plan, Jario climbed the steps trying to shake the uneasy feeling of being followed. He continued down the hallway looking for any sign of Kayleigh. Realizing the late hour had probably long sent everyone to their bedchambers, he started looking for a place to hide and rest. Morning would come very soon. It would bring everyone to their posts and his opportunity to retrieve the tail that Velsa demanded for payment.

* * *

Jario woke to the sounds of early morning chatter and the scurry of footsteps upon the stone hallways. He had securely slept in a hallway alcove near the library by pulling his haze. He sat and stretched his arms over his head as he carefully listened to the voices. He heard the cooks and the servers preparing and delivering trays of foods. He could hear the bed linens being removed from the beds and carried outside to be washed. He was surprised by the sounds of children playing in the courtyard. None of it interested him, and he patiently waited for what he was longing to see.

It wasn't long before he heard the sound of her voice followed by the sound of heavy boots. He knew that sound. She was being escorted. Gautier had cleverly given her a private guard. The sound of her delicate footsteps grew louder, and he watched as she turned down the hallway that led to the library. She would have to pass right by him. He could easily grab her, but he needed her to shift into her wolf. He watched as she walked past him followed by her guard. She entered the library, and her guard stood right outside the door.

Standing, he was only able to take one step before he heard more footsteps coming toward him. A young woman with dark hair smiled as she walked past him and then hurried toward the library doorway. Jario noticed the guard turn and prevent her from going any further. Smiling, the guard finally let her pass as Jario noticed that he brushed her hand with his own. Disinterested in their obvious affection for one another, he approached the library and silently entered the room to find Kayleigh standing at the end of the table with a leather bound book in her hands.

"Killian," Kayleigh called.

Stepping back away from the doorway, Jario allowed enough room for Killian to enter and stand waiting for Kayleigh's instructions.

"Will you please ask Gautier to come to the library? I have found another passage about the woman on the mountain that might be of help," Kayleigh requested.

"Yes, My Lady," Killian replied and exited the library.

Jario could hear him running through the hallway and smirked at his good fortune. He moved closer to Kayleigh and dropped his haze. He wanted to see the fear in her eyes when she saw him standing before him. Kayleigh's expression turned quickly from fear to anger. Seeing the danger, she quickly shifted into her wolf baring her teeth in warning. He pulled his dagger from his boot and forced her back into the corner. He could see the young woman pressed against the wall, but he knew she didn't have a weapon and refocused his attention to the white wolf. Moving toward the door, the young woman quickly exited the library, leaving them alone. He smiled as he realized there was no one left to protect her.

"I have come for your tail, and I won't leave without it," Jario shouted, as he lunged toward her.

Kayleigh's wolf anticipated his attack and moved putting the table between them. Saliva dripped from her fangs, and she growled eager to ripe Jario's head from his body.

"Gautier, I need your help. It is Jario," Kayleigh screamed into Gautier's mind.

Killian heard the growling and Lady Kayleigh's warning to Gautier in his mind. His clothes shredded instantly as he shifted into his wolf and charged down the hallway toward the library. Bolting through the open doorway, he lunged at Jario with his jaws open and his fangs bared. Jario turned dropping his dagger and grabbed the black wolf's neck with both hands. He strained to keep the wolf's jaws from his arm as he pulled his gift. Jario could hear the sound of whimpering as the black wolf slowly turned to stone. Releasing the wolf, he watched as the heavy stone fell to the floor.

Searching for his weapon, he heard the sound of running. Pulling his haze, he looked down desperate to find his dagger. Before he could grasp it, he heard the door slam and saw Gautier standing before him.

"He is still in the room. He has made himself invisible," Kayleigh said into Gautier's mind.

Gautier raised his hands and began to chant words in a language that Jario had never heard. He felt his body pulse and begin to burn.

Slowly his haze dropped, and he stood paralyzed in full view of Gautier. He could see the movement of his lips, but he couldn't hear a sound. He watched as his dagger twitched on the floor beside him and flew up onto the table. The room started to blur. He could feel his body shrinking. With a blast of light, Jario was gone.

Gautier quickly moved toward Kayleigh and bent down to place his face against her soft fur. He rubbed behind her ears and felt her tongue lick the side of his face.

"Did he hurt you?" he asked.

"No," replied Kayleigh, as she began to shift back into her human form. Gautier removed his tunic and pulled it over her head to cover her nakedness. He felt her body tremble as she placed her arms around his waist. Taking comfort in the fact that she was unharmed and Jario could no longer hurt her, he sighed as he let his lips brush against her neck.

"See after Killian," she said. "I am well enough."

Gautier stood and looked at the stone wolf that had fallen to the floor. He raised his hands and began to whisper as he walked toward Killian's wolf. His foreign phrases were repeated over and over, but nothing changed. Killian was trapped in stone until they could find someone strong enough to release him. Seeing Alicia swaying in the doorway looking down at the stone wolf, Gautier quickly pulled her toward him and held her as she began to cry.

"Help him, please," she sobbed through muffled tears. "Please help him."

"I am sorry, Alicia," he whispered and lightly kissed the top of her head. "I am not powerful enough to change him back."

Alicia gasped and fell limp in Gautier's arms.

"I will carry her to her room," he said. "Come with me."

"Wait, where is Jario?" asked Kayleigh.

"He is bound in his dagger where he will stay," barked Gautier, as he looked back toward the dagger resting upon the table. "It will be put somewhere that no one will accidently set him free. He is out of our lives forever."

Lifting Alicia up into his arms, Gautier stepped through the doorway followed by Kayleigh. They would care for Alicia and never stop searching for a way to release Killian from the stone that held his wolf. He would be remembered by all at Black Thistle Castle for offering his life to protect Lady Kayleigh. He would be given the honor of "The Great Guardian" for his sacrifice.

Chapter 40

Tolin looked up from grooming Arrow to see Baxter and Elda riding toward the stable. A short distance behind them, he could see Tate and Lord Thomas with women nestled behind them. Dropping the brush to the ground, he moved in front of Arrow to get a better view of the female riders. He thought his eyes had betrayed him until he saw her unmistakable smile.

"I have brought our Lady home, Tolin," Thomas exclaimed, as he halted Midnight letting Tolin take the reins. Thomas quickly dismounted and lifted Lara safely from his horse's back to stand next to him.

As everyone else dismounted, Tolin removed his cap and knelt on one knee bowing his head before Lady Lara. Placing his hand over his heart, his voice caught as he said, "My Lady, you were truly missed."

"It is good to be home," Lara softly said, as she approached Tolin and reached for his arm to allow him to stand. "I see that my colt has been well taken care of during my absence. He has grown into a fine stallion." Softly touching Arrow's nose, she ran her hand up and down the familiar white blaze. "Do you remember me, sweet Arrow?" He nudged her cheek and then lowered his head toward her pocket. "It appears you remember the carrots that I brought you." Laughing, she looked back at Thomas and then at her daughter.

Turning and taking Laralynn's hand from Tate, Thomas led his daughter to stand before Tolin.

"Laralynn, I would like you to meet Tolin. He is the Horse Master of Evergreen Castle," Thomas said, as he lovingly looked at his daughter. "Tolin, this is my daughter, Laralynn."

Tolin looked surprised and then bowed his head slightly. "I am honored to meet you," Tolin said. "I am at your service."

"It is a pleasure to meet you," Laralynn replied.

Looking up at her father she asked, "Are there more horses in the stable?"

"Yes my dear, there are several," Thomas laughed. "Once you are settled, I am sure that Tolin would be happy to show you the horses and let you choose one for your own."

Feeling exhausted from their long journey from Primrose Pond, Lara fondly brushed the stray hairs from her daughter's face. She could tell that she was tired and a little nervous.

"Laralynn, let's get you inside and settled," Lara said, as she took Thomas' arm. "It has been a very long ride, and you need your rest. We all need our rest."

Thomas patted Lara's arm and led her toward the castle. Tate offered his arm to Laralynn and they followed closely behind them. She had become quite fond of her new uncle, and she was anxious to meet Gavenia to hear all about her hawk. It seemed impossible that a woman could shift into a hawk, but she was anxious to see her soar through the air.

Elda watched Baxter hang his head after seeing Laralynn take Tate's arm. She gave him a jab with her elbow and tried to distract him. Baxter had been glum the whole trip back to Evergreen. Nothing Elda said or did seemed to lighten his mood. She knew what was causing his dejected appearance. He had stood in the background and watched Laralynn lovingly lead her father to her mother's grave. He had seen the sadness in her eyes as she spoke of her mother's death and was unable to comfort her. He was seen gripping his chest as he watched Elda wipe the tears from her cheeks when she heard her mother's voice.

"Baxter!" Elda taunted him. "Race you to the Command Center."

I know what I felt, thought Baxter. Nothing Elda can say will convince me that she isn't my intended mate. I felt the warmth race up my arm and fill my chest, more than once. I know that Laralynn felt it too; however, I know she is too young to understand what it means. I will have to wait as long as it takes for her to realize the bond we share.

"Where were you?" Elda asked, as she jerked him by the arms and began to shake him. "Everyone has gone inside."

Baxter gave her a sneer. Feeling some comfort from his thoughts, he turned and raced toward the Command Center leaving Elda behind.

"You cheated, Baxter," Elda shouted. "You always cheat."

* * *

"Laralynn, this will be your bedchamber," her mother explained. "Our chamber is at the end of the hallway. You need not worry; we aren't far from you."

Lara heard her daughter's gasp as she entered the chamber and moved toward the canopied bed covered in pale blue linens.

"Laralynn, this is Caprice, and she is here to help you with your bath and ready you for bed."

Nervously, Laralynn watched as Caprice made a small curtsey and smiled.

"Caprice, please ready my daughter for bed," requested Lady Lara. "The ride was long, and we will all feel much better tomorrow evening after we have rested. Do not worry, my dear. I will be back to kiss you before you sleep. I know you are curious about the castle, but it will have to wait until tomorrow."

Lady Lara gave Caprice a nod and stepped into the hallway closing the door behind her.

"My Lady," Caprice said, as she stepped toward the bath chamber. "Let's get you bathed. Flora was kind enough to heat the water for you. So, let's get you in the tub before it cools."

Laralynn followed Caprice to the bath chamber to find a large copper tub full of water. She watched Caprice pour something from a decanter into the water that smelled of warm sugar.

"How long have you known my mother?" Laralynn asked, as she untied her cloak and let it fall to the floor.

"Almost a decade before Lady Lara left Evergreen," Caprice replied, as she knelt down to untie the laces of Laralynn's boots. "She is loved by everyone, and we are all glad that she has returned."

"And my father?" she cautiously asked.

"For more than two decades. He is fair and good, Laralynn," Caprice said, as she stood to face her. "He is kind and loves your mother very much. Now, let's get you undressed and into the water."

Anxious to feel the heat of the water on her skin, she stood quietly as Caprice removed her clothing. Stepping into the tub and lowering herself down into the lovely scented water, she leaned her head back and closed her eyes.

"Caprice, we had a tub at the cottage, but it was very small," Laralynn whispered. "It rarely had warm water. This is heavenly."

Feeling her body relax, she closed her eyes.

"Caprice, my parents are vampires. Are you afraid of them?" she asked.

"My Lady, of course not," Caprice replied.

"It seems so hard to believe. I still have trouble understanding everything my mother told me," she said.

"Speak to your mother," whispered Caprice. "She will have all the answers to your questions."

* * *

After closing the door to their bedchamber, Thomas turned to see Lara gazing back at him. He could see tears beginning to form in her eyes. Taking her in his arms, he held her as she began to cry. The warmth he had longed for had finally been returned, and he had her back in his arms. Placing his hand under her chin and lifting her face so that he could see her beautiful blue eyes, he wiped the tears from her cheeks with his thumbs.

"There is no need to cry, my sweet," whispered Thomas. "You are home. You are safe, and you are with people that love you and will protect you."

"Thomas, I am sorry for the pain I caused you," Lara said. "I meant only to protect our daughter from Jario. Not a day passed that I did not think of you."

Thomas gently took Lara's hand and kissed each finger until he saw her smile.

"It is I that must apologize to you," replied Thomas, as his words began to catch in his throat. "I gave up on you, on us. I let myself slip dangerously close to the madness, and I did not care if it took me. I abandoned our people and left others to stand in my station when it was my sole responsibility to protect them. Your absence left my mind broken, and I came to believe that you did not want to be found. I was weak. I began to think you no longer wanted me. At one point, if I had found that you had received your final death, I was prepared to enter the Canyon of Obscurity and let the sun take me. I lost all hope. Lara, I lost the need to live. So you see, I am the one that is sorry. I failed you while you were strong and sacrificed everything to protect our daughter. Can you forgive me?"

"Gladly, my love! Will you ever forgive me?" she asked.

"You need not ask. If you must hear the words, I will say them. All is forgiven and forgotten," Thomas replied. "Now let me take you to bed. I find I need to show you how much I have missed you."

"There is one thing more we must do before you take me to bed," she said, as she smiled at his confused expression. "Our daughter is waiting for us to kiss her before she sleeps."

"Let's not keep her waiting," he replied. "I still can't believe it. I have a daughter. You have given me a daughter."

Taking his hand, Lara led Thomas back to Laralynn's bedchamber. They found her sitting among the pillows and linen covers. Her hair had been braided, and she wore a white sleeping gown adorned with tiny satin flowers.

"You look like an angel," Thomas said, as he sat upon the side of the bed.

"My sleeping gown is very pretty," she said, as she ran her fingers over the tiny flowers on the sleeve. "Everything is pretty."

"Including you, my sweet daughter," Lara smiled and kissed her daughter's forehead. "It is time for sleep. Have sweet dreams and tomorrow we will explore the castle. I will take you to meet Meadow."

"And the horses?" asked Laralynn.

"Yes, the horses too," she replied.

Thomas took hold of his daughter's hand and kissed her palm.

"I am so very glad that we found you, Laralynn," he said, as he tried to clear the catch in his throat. "I have never been a father, and I will rely on you to help me. Can you do that?" he asked.

"I will, father," she replied. "I am glad that you found me too. I am glad that you found my mother. She missed you very much. She didn't know it, but I use to hear her cry at night and whisper your name."

Lara gasped and looked surprised.

Thomas reached for Lara's hand and said, "I use to cry at night too. I missed her more than I can say."

"It is time to sleep," Lara said, as she helped Laralynn settle into the pillows. "Tomorrow will start a new page in your journal. I hope you have many wonderful things to write about."

Lara and Thomas kissed their daughter and made their way to the door. As Thomas opened the door, he turned back to gaze upon his beautiful daughter. She lovingly blew him a kiss and silently whispered *I love you father* before she closed her eyes to sleep.

Chapter 41

News of Lady Lara's return spread throughout the castle and the surrounding villages. Even more of a surprise to everyone was the announcement that Lady Lara returned home with a sixteen year old daughter. A celebration had been planned in their honor, and the people of the castle buzzed with excitement.

Laralynn had asked that invitations be sent to her friends in Primrose Pond, and they had all accepted except one. The messenger had not been able to find Aslev's cottage to deliver her invitation. Laralynn was broken hearted, but promised herself that she would make a special trip to visit her and tell her everything about the castle.

Thomas had sent a messenger to Black Thistle Castle to invite Lord Gautier and Lady Kayleigh to the celebration. He also wanted to ask for Gautier's help in assisting with the final item to release Astra from the mountain. When word came that they were on their way, Laralynn stood on her balcony to watch them approach. Once she spotted their carriage flying colorful flags, she ran from her bedchamber and through the hallways. Finally reaching the Grand Hall, she slowly made her way to stand beside her mother and father and await for their arrival.

Seeing the couple enter the Grand Hall, Thomas walked forward and reached for Gautier's hand. Grasping it firmly, he offered his appreciation for their visit. As he did, Lara greeted Kayleigh with a kiss to her cheek. Gautier and Kayleigh both smiled upon seeing Laralynn for the first time.

"Lara, it is good to see you again," Gautier said, as he leaned over to lightly kiss her cheek.

"And you, Gautier," she replied. "I hope to see more of you and Kayleigh."

Reaching for Laralynn's hand, her father watched as she gracefully curtsied before their guests.

"Gautier, Kayleigh, I would like to introduce you to our daughter, Laralynn," announced Thomas.

"It is lovely to meet you," Kayleigh softly said, as she kissed Laralynn's cheek.

"It is a pleasure to meet you, Lady Kayleigh, Lord Gautier," Laralynn replied.

"And you," Gautier replied. "We have waited a long time to meet you."

"I hope to see more of you," she shyly replied.

"Is now a good time to retrieve your daughter's kiss for Astra?" Gautier asked.

"I know that Astra is anxiously awaiting news that we have retrieved it for her," replied Thomas. "Gavenia is prepared to carry it to her as soon as it is available."

Gautier pulled a small vial from his pocket. He looked at Laralynn and saw her worried look.

"This will not hurt in any way, my child," he said. "You will feel only a tickle upon your lips. Are you ready?"

"Yes, Lord Gautier," she replied.

"Stand very still and close your eyes," he requested, as he watched Laralynn follow his instructions. "Now, I will hold the vial under your bottom lip next to your chin. You will hear me whisper a few words, and when I stop, kiss the air. I will capture your kiss and seal it in the vial."

Laralynn felt the vial press against her chin just under her bottom lip. She wanted to laugh at the strange sounding words he said, but she stood very still. When his words stopped, she kissed the air. She heard a tiny sizzle, the tickle upon her lips, and heard the cap snapped into place.

"You may open your eyes," Gautier said. "I am finished. I have your kiss. Would you like to see it?"

Laralynn eagerly nodded and looked at the clear vial held in Gautier's hand. It shimmered a soft rose color and a little flashing light dashed from side to side.

"It looks like tiny fireflies," she laughed.

"It does, doesn't it," he laughed, as well. "Now where is Gavenia?"

Hearing her name, Gavenia entered the Grand Hall and made a small curtsy.

"Gavenia, here is the vial that contains Laralynn's kiss. There is enough daylight left for you to take this directly to Astra," Thomas said.

"I will be honored," Gavenia said, as Gautier handed the small vial to her. "If you will excuse me."

Gavenia left the Grand Hall headed for the Command Center to find Baxter. She found him sparring with Tate and ran toward them holding the vial up for them to see.

"Baxter, send word to Astra that I am coming with the vial," she said. "Tell her to stand where I saw her before. I will leave you now to head to the stable."

She tilted her head toward the door, and Tate ran after her toward the stable. Tate waited until she was safely in the air before he returned to the Command Center.

"Astra! Astra, are you there?" Baxter said, trying to contain his excitement. "Astra?"

"Yes, I am here. Do you have news for me?" she asked.

"I do have great news. Gavenia is on her way with your last item," he shouted a little too loud.

"I can't believe it. This is wonderful," Astra said, as she started to cry. "I will finally be able to leave the mountain."

"Let me know when you receive it. I will be waiting to hear from you," he directed. "Tate will want to know that Gavenia made it safely to you."

"I will. I am running to the location now," she screamed. "I hope to see you soon."

"Good luck," replied Baxter and let the connection drop.

* * *

Laralynn sat on a stool as Caprice curled and braided her hair. Tonight she would be presented to the members of Evergreen Castle, and she wanted to look perfect. A beautiful rose colored satin dress had been hanging on the armoire door, and she could hardly wait to put it on. Hearing the door open, she saw her mother dressed in a dark burgundy gown that complimented the color of her own dress. She had never seen her mother look so beautiful.

"Mother, I am so excited," Laralynn said, as she tapped her toes on the stone floor and clasped her hands in her lap. "Do you think they will like me?"

"They will love you. Just be yourself. Smile and be polite to everyone. I have known many of our people for a very long time," she replied. "They are all loyal to Evergreen."

"All except Jario," Laralynn cringed.

"What do you know of Jario?" her mother asked.

"I heard two men's gossip today. They said that Jario was bound to a dagger by Lord Gautier. Is that true?" she asked.

"It is true, but we don't need to worry about Jario anymore," Lara quietly replied, as she reached for Laralynn's gown. "Now let's get you dressed. There are many that wait to meet you."

* * *

Thomas stood behind the closed doors to the Grand Hall waiting anxiously for Lara and Laralynn. Tate, Gavenia and Baxter stood by his side. Baxter was nervous. He had been asked by Lady Lara to be Laralynn's escort for the evening. He was feeling the pressure of his assignment as he fidgeted with his sleeves and flicked his hair from the collar of his tunic. He wondered if Lady Lara knew what he had discovered about Laralynn.

Hearing the rustle of satin, everyone looked up to see Lady Lara and Laralynn coming toward them. Standing before her father, she smiled as he leaned down to kiss her forehead. He caught the scent of fresh apples that lingered upon her skin, and it quickly brought back memories. He had first noticed the scent of fresh apples upon Lara the night of Tate and Gavenia's ceremony. He now knew what had caused it. She had been carrying his daughter and her daughter's scent.

"You look lovely," he whispered to Laralynn. "And you, as well, my dear Lara."

Lara greeted Thomas with a smile and a kiss upon his chin.

"Are you all ready?" asked Omar.

Everyone nodded and got ready to enter the Grand Hall. Omar walked to the heavy doors and pushed them open. He walked forward and stepped to the side as everyone in the hall stood waiting in silence.

"It is my honor and privilege to introduce Lord Thomas and Lady Lara," he shouted loud enough for everyone to hear.

Thomas and Lara entered the Grand Hall as everyone knelt and then stood to receive them with exuberant applauds.

As the room quieted, Omar's voice bellowed another introduction, "It is my honor to present the Lord's Chancellor, Tate Harrington, and Gavenia Harrington."

The hall filled with more applauds as they walked toward Lord Thomas and Lady Lara. Standing beside them, they all waited for Laralynn's introduction.

Omar waited for the hall to quiet and then cleared his throat before he shouted, "It is my greatest honor and utmost privilege to introduce to you the daughter of Lord Thomas and Lady Lara. She is escorted by Lt. Baxter Marsh of the Evergreen Army." He paused as the room stilled. "I give you the Lady Laralynn."

As Baxter escorted Laralynn into the Grand Hall, everyone in the hall, including her parents, knelt before her. Overwhelmed, Laralynn tightly gripped Baxter's arm to keep herself from fainting. They had all welcomed her to her new home and to her new life.

Feeling a sudden warmth surrounding her, she remembered what her mother had told her about finding love.

You will know when it is love, my dear. It will warm your soul. You will feel his love race through your body as it mingles with your own.

Looking up at Baxter, she softly said, "Thank you Baxter for finding me."

Epilogue

With her feet propped up on her wooden stool, Velsa peered into the small black box that sat on her lap. It held her most precious possession, and she had sat with it in her lap every evening since bringing it back to her cottage. She had waited sixteen years to retrieve the little treasure and couldn't stop looking at it. The brilliant violet color was fascinating, and it shimmered with each and every beautiful pulse. It was her very first heartbeat, and she wondered why she had never taken one before now.

Hearing the swirl of the wind outside her cottage, she closed her eyes and listened for the messages that it often carried. The spirits were whispering something about Black Thistle Castle. Tilting her head slightly so that her ear faced the window, she hoped to hear of the white wolf's anguish over losing her tail or a spell that had gone wrong that might have ended Gautier for good. To her surprise, the wind was whispering about Jario.

"What kind of trouble has that vampire gotten himself into now?" she sneered.

The wind spoke of an attack at Black Thistle Castle. Jario had surprised Lady Kayleigh and tried to attack her wolf. Her private guard had come to her rescue.

"Must he fail at everything?" she sighed, as she shook her head. "Poor Jario, it appears that he cannot accomplish anything without the help of a woman or a witch. He has become a helpless vampire."

As the chattering in the wind continued, she heard that the guard had fought to keep Jario from the white wolf. The guard had shifted into his wolf, and Jario had turned him to stone as he had begun to leap toward him.

"That must have been fun!" she said, as she clapped her hands. "I wish I could have seen that fight."

Suddenly, Velsa became very quiet. She wasn't sure she had heard the words correctly. She repeated what she had heard over and over again as if she were making sure the words were true.

"Oh my stars, Gautier blasted Jario with a *Binding Spell* and bound him to his dagger?" she mumbled, for the fifth time.

Stunned, she stood and placed her precious box on the table and closed its lid. Wringing her hands, she wondered if Gautier knew that she had demanded the wolf's tail for a favor. If he did, he would be coming for her. She would be next to receive Gautier' wrath. Scurrying about to light a candle and retrieve her book of spells, she prepared to put up barriers to protect the cottage against the likes of Gautier.

"Wait, I have handled his spells before," she barked, as if someone was listening to her. "Why do I need to worry? After all, I won the War of the Witches and bound him to Black Thistle Castle. My powers were stronger than his or anyone else's. I am sure they are still stronger. I have nothing to worry about."

Taking a deep breath, Velsa tried to calm her thoughts and think of the fun she would have creating her new spell. Turning to reach again for the black box, a rap at the door startled her.

"Who is there?" Velsa shouted.

Hearing no response, she wondered if it could be Gautier and nervously took a step towards the door. Someone had managed to find her cottage without her knowing. Trying to mentally search the area, she discovered they had blocked her from seeing their image. She could hear the strange call of a blackbird off in the distance, and she knew she had heard that bird's call before. Her thoughts immediately went to Desirae. She expected her to visit and try to avenge her sister's death. She had put an end to her sister, and she could do the same to Desirae.

Releasing a nervous laugh, she whispered under her breath, "That witch doesn't frighten me."

Angry over the intrusion, she strode to the door and yanked it open with her hand full of sparks ready to strike. What she saw made her lift her hand to her throat. Her hands began to tremble, and her ability to take a breath seemed to vanish at the sight before her. A hooded figure stood on her doorstep. She watched as the woman lifted her gloved hands to remove her hood and reveal her face. Seeing the hood fall back against her shoulders, Velsa gasped when she realized who stood before her.

"It cannot be," Velsa shrieked. "Magna?"

A NOTE FROM THE AUTHOR

Thank you for reading Protected from Obscurity. I hope you enjoyed reading more about Thomas and Lara. Now that Thomas has brought Lara and his daughter back to Evergreen, how will he handle Laralynn's adventurous ways? Will Baxter be able to capture Laralynn's heart? What new trouble will the return of Magna cause? Has Gautier put a plan in place to deal with Velsa? Find the answers to these questions and more in the final book of the Evergreen Series, Shattering Obscurity.

If you enjoyed this book, please take a moment to write a review on Amazon and Goodreads. Your comments are greatly appreciated.

I would love to hear from my readers. You may contact me by email or by leaving a comment on Facebook. I hope to hear from you soon!

info@authorjoannherley.com

https://www.facebook.com/authorjhbooks

Join my mailing list and I will send you an email when my next book is released. Also, anyone that joins my mailing list will receive early notification of giveaways and become eligible for private mailing list giveaways.

www.authorjoannherley.com

OTHER BOOKS BY THE AUTHOR

EVERGREEN SERIES

www.ingramcontent.com/pod-product-compliance
Lightning Source LLC
Chambersburg PA
CBHW071134170626
46809CB00002B/618